THE
MAFIA KING'S
SISTER

BY P. RAYNE

THE MAFIA ACADEMY SERIES

Vow of Revenge

Corrupting the Innocent

The Mafia King's Sister

Craving My Rival

THE MIDNIGHT MANOR SERIES

Moonlit Thorns

Shattered Vows

Midnight Whispers

Twisted Truths

STANDALONES

Beautifully Scarred

THE MAFIA KING'S SISTER

THE MAFIA ACADEMY

PREVIOUSLY PUBLISHED AS *COVETING THE MAFIA KING'S SISTER*

P. RAYNE

AVON

An Imprint of HarperCollins Publishers

THE MAFIA KING'S SISTER. Copyright © 2023 by Piper Rayne. Bonus epilogue copyright © 2023 by Piper Rayne. All rights reserved. Printed in the United States of America. No part of this book may be used or reproduced in any manner whatsoever without written permission except in the case of brief quotations embodied in critical articles and reviews. For information, address HarperCollins Publishers, 195 Broadway, New York, NY 10007.

HarperCollins books may be purchased for educational, business, or sales promotional use. For information, please email the Special Markets Department at SPsales@harpercollins.com.

Originally published as *Coveting the Mafia King's Sister* in the United States in 2023 by Piper Rayne Incorporated. Bonus epilogue originally published online in 2023.

Avon, Avon & logo, and Avon Books & logo are registered trademarks of HarperCollins Publishers in the United States of America and other countries.

FIRST AVON PAPERBACK PUBLISHED 2025.

Interior text design by Diahann Sturge-Campbell

Interior art © Oleksandr/Stock.Adobe.com

Library of Congress Cataloging-in-Publication Data has been applied for.

ISBN 978-0-06-341248-4

24 25 26 27 28 LBC 5 4 3 2 1

To all the women with a thirst for adventure

AUTHOR'S NOTE

This book contains references to content that may be upsetting to some readers. Trigger warnings include alcohol, attempted murder, murder, profanity, sexually explicit scenes, stalking, physical violence, and gun violence. Reader discretion is advised.

PLAYLIST

Here's a list of songs that inspired us while we were writing *The Mafia King's Sister.*

What Was I Made For? – Billie Eilish
Help I'm Alive – Metric
Free – Florence + The Machine
The Motto – Tiësto, Ava Max
Bad Idea Right? – Olivia Rodrigo
I Feel Like I'm Drowning – Two Feet
Way Down We Go – Kaleo
The Hills – The Weeknd
Play with Fire – Sam Tinnesz (feat. Yacht Money)
Apocalypse – Cigarettes After Sex
We Fell in Love in October – girl in red
Running with the Wolves – Aurora
Bullet with Butterfly Wings – The Smashing Pumpkins
Vampire – Olivia Rodrigo
Don't Look Back in Anger – Oasis
Yet – Switchfoot
Cosmic Love – Florence + The Machine

SICURO ACADEMY – ITALIAN CRIME FAMILIES

Northeast Territory

Specializes in running weapons
Marcelo Costa
(head of the Costa crime family)

Southeast Territory

Specializes in counterfeit rings and embezzlement schemes
Antonio La Rosa
(next in line to run the La Rosa crime family)

Southwest Territory

Specializes in drug trafficking and money laundering
Dante Accardi
(next in line to run the Accardi crime family)

Northwest Territory

Specializes in securities fraud and cyber warfare
Gabriele Vitale
(next in line to run the Vitale crime family)

THE
MAFIA KING'S
SISTER

CHAPTER ONE
ARIA

Gabriele Vitale has barely spared me a glance the entire evening.

I've looked at him a hundred times between the ceremony at the church, the cocktail hour, and now dinner. Every single time, he hasn't been looking back at me. Not once. As if I'm invisible to him.

Months ago, during my orientation at the Sicuro Academy, Gabriele was my adviser. I didn't know much about him—no one does—except for the fact that he's the son of Angelo and Mia Vitale. Angelo Vitale is the head of the crime family that runs the northwest portion of the country, and obviously Gabriele is next in line.

The only rumors I'd heard about Gabriele are that he's a master with computers and keeps to himself. So when I heard I was paired with him for the weekend, I expected to be counting the minutes until I could be unleashed from his side. I wasn't prepared for the instant attraction I felt when he towered over me and introduced himself. It was as if his cognac eyes could see into my soul, and I instantly wanted to kiss the man. To feel his short facial hair rub my cheek.

Gabriele was clear right from the start that he wasn't interested. In fact, he treated me like an annoying kid sister—even worse than my brother. But I caught a glimpse of desire in his eyes. Still, when I attempted to kiss him that weekend, he pushed me away, much to my mortification.

Ever since that fateful day, he's been on my mind, and today, at the wedding of Antonio La Rosa and his new wife, Sofia, is the first time I've seen him since.

I slide the fish off my fork, chew, and swallow, trying to get a view of Gabriele's table. The room is overcrowded with all the different Italian crime families, and I can't get a good look at him.

Antonio and Sofia's wedding is a big deal since Antonio will run things in the southeast section of the country one day. As such, there are representatives here from each of the major families: the Vitales, who run the northwest; the Accardis, who run the southwest; my family—the Costas—who are in charge of the northeast; and of course Antonio's family, the La Rosas.

There's relative peace at the moment between all the powerful families, but that hasn't always been the case. So I can't be the only one who feels an undercurrent of wariness from being in a room with so many made men.

I look up from my plate, and my older brother, Marcelo, and his fiancée, Mirabella La Rosa, Antonio's sister, are headed in my direction. From what I can tell as an outsider, they're majorly in love with each other.

"Mother." Marcelo gives our mom a kiss on the cheek where she sits beside me, then straightens and nods at me. "Aria. Staying out of trouble?"

It's all I can do not to roll my eyes. I want to, so badly, but I would never show my brother such blatant disrespect in front of the other families. Alone? Hell yes. But not in front of others in such a public setting. After all, he runs our family, as he has since our father was murdered.

"Of course I am." I lift my water glass to my lips and sip. I attempted to fill my wineglass when dinner began, but my mother took the wine bottle from my hand.

Mira smiles. "Are you having fun?" She's a breath of fresh air after my overprotective brother.

I don't know Mira all that well because she's a La Rosa, but for the past year, she's attended the private college for Mafia children along with my brother. Every time I'm around Mira, I'd be lying if I said I didn't rejoice at the way she puts my brother in his place. I honestly never thought I'd see the day.

"I'd be having more fun if I was allowed to have a glass of wine," I say with an annoyed smile.

Mira giggles, and my brother narrows his eyes.

"You have a few years yet," my mom says beside me.

Don't I know it. I'm counting the days until I'm on campus at the Sicuro Academy. Maybe then I'll be able to be a regular college kid and discover what life has to offer outside the confines of my house. In my eighteen years, I've played the role of an innocent, virginal, sheltered girl who watches everyone else have fun.

Things were worse when my dad was still alive. The only attention he ever paid me was to make sure I wasn't doing anything to shame him or the family. Which is why he had my bodyguards sit outside my room. I was merely a hidden pawn to be played to further his power at some point. If he needed to, he could marry me off for his own gain. But with him dying and Marcelo living away from me all year, I've felt a little more freedom.

And the little fun I found only makes me anxious for more.

"How did the pictures go?" my mom asks.

"Long," Marcelo says with a sigh.

They're both in the wedding party since the bride and groom are Mira's best friend and brother. Marcelo, since he's engaged to Mira, is now a part of their family.

"Painfully long," Mira says. "Let's not let my mom talk us into that many when we get married next year."

Marcelo slides one arm around Mira's waist and places his finger and thumb around her chin, tilting her face to look up at him. There's so much adoration there, my chest squeezes. Will anyone ever look at me as though I'm their everything?

"I'll stand and pose with you for hours," he says.

She laughs and grabs a hold of his tie, pulling him closer. "I highly doubt that. You'd be trying to sneak us away after the first snap of a picture."

His smirk says they both know she's right.

I laugh and my mom smiles at them while they kiss tenderly but briefly. Their nauseating affection causes me to take a quick glance at Gabriele's table. I suck in a breath watching him stand. I'll never get over his height. He's getting up from the table to speak with Sofia and Antonio. She and Antonio must be making the rounds, thanking their guests and pocketing the cash envelopes. This is my time, the one I've been waiting for since I arrived at the ceremony.

"Excuse me, I have to use the restroom." I slide my chair back and stand with a small smile, leaving before any of them can answer.

I force myself not to bolt across the room. Gabriele leans in and kisses each of Sofia's cheeks. Before I reach them, Antonio finishes his conversation with Gabriele's dad, Angelo Vitale, and joins them. The closer I get, the more my stomach feels as if a million ballerinas are pirouetting through it. Despite my nerves, I raise my chin and step up to them. I've received enough compliments tonight to know I look good. Now I just need Gabriele to notice.

"Hey, guys." I close the last few feet of distance, and they all turn in my direction.

Antonio and Sofia smile, but Gabriele's jaw sets as if he's sculpted out of stone. Is he annoyed that I'm here?

"Hi, Aria. Are you enjoying yourself?" Sofia asks, hugging me.

"I am. My mom and brother are so involved making sure they

talk with everyone that I'm almost able to do my own thing." Which was true until dinnertime.

"I'm starting to understand why you and Mira get along so well. You're very similar," Antonio says.

The four of us laugh, knowing Mira and I don't like authority and tend to disobey.

"Your brother is going to have his hands full at Sicuro," Sofia adds with a smile.

I feel my cheeks heat, and I sneak a look through my eyelashes at Gabriele. His face is void of emotion.

As soon as our eyes meet, Gabriele says, "I'm going to get back to my *date*." Asshole. "Congratulations again, you two." He turns and walks the short distance back to his table, where he slings his arm around the back of the blonde's chair.

All the air leaves my lungs. How did I miss that he brought someone? Where was she at the church? Now I feel like a silly little girl for chasing after him . . . again.

"I'm going to go see if I can sneak some wine off a table," I say, turning and pushing my way into the crowd before Sofia or Antonio can respond.

I refuse to let the tears that flood my eyes fall. I drown in embarrassment, dodging people left and right in search of somewhere to hide. Gabriele has done everything in his power to let me know he's not interested in me. It's time I listen.

CHAPTER TWO
GABRIELE

Jesus Christ. Why does she have to look so damn sexy?

I've been avoiding Aria all day. I have no choice. She's nothing but trouble. She's made it clear she wants me to pursue her, and I admit I'm intrigued. But she's off-limits. Not only is she Marcelo Costa's little sister, but she's way too young. She's way too innocent. She's way too inexperienced for someone like me. The last thing I need is to start a war with the Costas because I corrupted Marcelo's baby sister.

No pussy is worth the wrath of Marcelo Costa.

But she's hard to resist. Every time my gaze has fallen on her today, I forced myself to look away. That proved impossible to do once she joined my conversation with Antonio and Sofia, though, so I was stuck being near her. Smelling her perfume and soaking her in.

She's wearing a deep red silk dress, and her long, shiny hair is set in waves hanging down her bare back. The gold locket she's rarely without hangs down her neck, nestled between her cleavage. Add her big, dark doe eyes staring up at me with expectations, and who could expect me to ignore her?

Which is exactly why I had to remove myself from the situation with the excuse of my date. Why couldn't Aria Costa be anyone else? Because anyone else would have been in my bed already.

The blonde beside me isn't my date. I lied. And I'd be an even bigger liar if I pretended the hurt that flashed in Aria's eyes didn't flay me moments ago. Stephanie is the daughter of one of my dad's associates who happened to be seated beside me for the evening. But none of that matters. I chat with Stephanie as if I have interest for only Aria's benefit if she's spying on me.

When Stephanie excuses herself to go to the restroom, my father leans in to me. "You know with Antonio married now, and Marcelo well on his way, perhaps it's time we find you a bride."

My veins grow hot. This bullshit again. I suppress an eye roll and force myself not to react.

"They're shoring up their alliances, and we're being left out."

"I've already told you that I have no interest in finding a bride. I have years before you need to worry about adding to the family line."

"Perhaps, but while you're sitting there in front of your *computers*, our competitors are making inroads with each other. I just heard that Marcelo is regularly supplying the La Rosas with weapons now for them to sell in their territory."

My father has always believed that the man with the most muscle is the most powerful, but I disagree. The man with the most information holds the power to bend others to his will. Not to mention, he should be happy he raised me to have respect, or I'd tell him how many times I saved his ass with my computers.

"You act as though we have nothing," I say.

"There's always more to be had, Gabriele. Someday you'll realize this."

I take a large mouthful of my drink. My dad has always wished I'd be just like him. He doesn't outright say that I'm a disappointment, but I feel it with his judgment. The same as I feel this damn tie choking me.

It's not that I've never cut a man's throat to further the cause of my family, but too often, the men in our world let their base instincts control them, rather than using their heads to determine the best course of action.

"Don't even think about arranging a marriage behind my back."

"I can't promise that, but I can promise it won't be Aria Costa. Whoever Marcelo convinces to marry her is only giving him more power than he already has—if it's outside of their family."

"Good."

Last year when I was assigned Aria as my orientation student, Marcelo warned me off his sister, and I wasn't lying when I told him I have no interest in a child—and that's exactly what Aria is to me. A sweet, innocent, inexperienced child. As tempting as she's become to me, I need to remember she could never handle me. Not the real me. Which is why I prefer older, more experienced women.

"It doesn't matter. He's made it clear that she'll finish her time at the Sicuro Academy before he'll consider a match for her."

I don't understand why my chest loosens with the knowledge that Aria won't be sold off to the highest bidder anytime soon.

"Now the Accardis' daughter—"

"Is a literal child. She's fourteen." I toss back the remainder of my drink.

"She won't be fourteen forever."

The veins in my neck bulge. But before I can say anything, Stephanie sits in her seat. At least I don't have to worry about my father trying to arrange a marriage with her. Her family isn't powerful enough for her to be an option.

This conversation makes it clear that sooner or later, my father is going to force me to wed someone in the name of loyalty to do what's best for the family. It's not something I can put off forever, no matter how much I want to.

* * *

THE NEXT EVENING, as I make my way back to the hotel lobby, I spot Aria immediately. It's like my subconscious is tuned to her presence, and my inner radar knows when she's around.

My father and I are spending the next few days in Miami to conduct some meetings with the heads of the other three families. They thought that since we'd all be here for Antonio and Sofia's wedding, it was a good time to work out some minor issues that are brewing.

I'm alone in the lobby since my father hung back to have some drinks and shoot the shit with the other dons. I bailed.

Now, curiosity grips me in its clutches because Aria's dressed seductively in a short, black bodycon dress, but she's obviously trying not to draw attention to herself. She walks along the far wall of the lobby, head down, her long hair hanging in front of her face. In her hand is a small purse and an oversized black envelope.

What's inside it?

She slips through the lobby doors, none the wiser that I have eyes on her, and slides into the back seat of a small white sedan with an Uber sticker. Where is her security? One tap from another vehicle and that car would crush like a tin can.

Unease settles in my chest, but I shake my head and turn around, continuing toward the elevators. She's none of my business, even if the fact that she's slipping away unnoticed and unprotected probably means she's seeking trouble.

I head to my room, unbuttoning the top two buttons of my black dress shirt, and pour myself a drink. I swallow the amber liquid while trying to push down all thoughts of Aria, but the image of her slipping out of the lobby bubbles back up. I push a hand through my hair and flop down on the couch in my suite, drink still in hand.

Why should I care where the hell she's going? What difference does it make to me?

But a few minutes later, I'm still imagining a million scenarios in which someone as sweet and innocent as her gets taken advantage of, or even worse—hurt.

"Fuck." I stand and set my drink on the end table, heading to the safe in the room.

Once I enter the code, I retrieve my laptop and bring it over to the dining table, swiping my black-rimmed blue light glasses off the edge. I log into my computer with my fingerprint and get through the extra two lines of security I installed to pull up my tracking app.

I internally reprimand myself again because I shouldn't have a tracking app on Aria's phone. But I do.

I don't even know why I bothered to install it the weekend she visited campus. Something in my gut told me to install it, knowing I shouldn't. I've resisted the urge to check what she's up to until this point, but tonight, it'll come in handy.

The Costa family and the Vitales aren't exactly enemies, but if anyone ever found out I added the app to her phone, there would be a major blowback. Perhaps the kind that ends in a bullet to the temple. Mine.

But no one is ever going to find out because I know more than anyone in either family about computers.

I find her tracker in the list of ones I've installed and watch for a few minutes as it moves down the freeway. I don't know the Miami area well, but I know enough to know that she's not headed to the best part of town.

What the hell is she up to?

Eventually the blinking icon pulls off the freeway and takes a few streets until it comes to a stop in front of a building.

Pulling my phone from my pants pocket, I thumb in the address where the vehicle stopped. It sounds vaguely familiar to me. Is it the home of someone from the La Rosa family? Is she visiting one of Mira and Antonio's relatives?

But when the maps feature shows me the exterior of the building, the blood drains from my face for a few seconds before it rushes back in anger.

What the fuck does she think she's doing?

CHAPTER THREE
ARIA

The invitation came in a conspicuous black envelope left in my hotel room last night when I returned from the wedding. Thank God I'm not sharing a room with my mom. She would have had a heart attack if she'd seen what was written in cursive on the thick, expensive paper inside.

Ready to explore your darker side?
Present the card inside this envelope at
the front door to gain entrance.
Leave your inhibitions behind.

I have no idea who left the envelope or what the black card with only a gold CW in the middle signifies, but I'm going to find out.

Which is why as soon as I finished my dinner with Mom, I feigned a headache and told her I was going to bed early. I rushed up to my room and changed into a short, black bodycon dress I ordered online without my mom noticing. Then I head outside the hotel and meet my Uber. I relax back into the seat once the vehicle pulls away, and I successfully escape undetected.

This is probably the stupidest thing I've done. I'm alone and headed God knows where to be met by God knows who. I may live a sheltered life, but my family has plenty of enemies. I could be walking right into a trap.

But somehow, I don't think I'm being lured to my death. Whoever left me the envelope left it in my hotel room. Which means they had access to me. If they wanted to hurt me, they would've done so.

In only weeks, I'll be on the Sicuro Academy campus, stuck under my brother's watchful gaze. Living on campus will be a step up from how I live now, but it's still not the total freedom I crave. This, whatever it is, feels like it promises to be the last adventure I'll find.

Twenty minutes later, the vehicle pulls up in front of a nondescript building. It's contemporary in design with no signage and very few windows, all of which are tinted so dark it's impossible to see if there's a light on inside, let alone tell if there's anyone in there.

"You sure you want me to leave you here?" the driver asks.

I look down the street of mostly businesses in large buildings that don't appear to be open. The street is deserted. A ripple of fear reverberates up my spine. Maybe I don't trust myself tonight.

I should have this guy turn around and return to the hotel. I'm about to ask him to do so when a memory of Gabriele's arm around the back of the chair of his date at the wedding flashes in my mind. It's not as though he owes me anything, but I was looking forward to being on campus and seeing if I could make something happen between the two of us. Once again, Gabriele made it perfectly clear that he has no interest in me.

I deserve a little fun, don't I? Even if I don't know exactly what kind of fun tonight will entail.

I push open the back door. "I'm good, thanks."

Envelope in hand, I slide out of the back seat, climb the stairs and walk toward the black door at the front of the building. Once I stand there, I'm not sure what to do. There's no handle to open it from the outside. Do I knock?

But before I have time to decide, the door opens and a man the size of a water buffalo fills the doorway, causing me to startle back, my neck craned to look at him. His penetrating gaze is intimidating as all hell, and I struggle to pull the card from the envelope.

"I . . . I have this." I hold it out to him, willing my hand not to shake and to be the confident woman I'm pretending to be. Adrenaline pumps through my veins. Though I enjoy the feeling of the rush, I'm equally on edge.

He gives me the once-over and steps aside. "Head on in."

I do as he says and step into a dimly lit foyer that still gives no indication as to what this place is all about.

"I need to frisk you before you go in the main room," the behemoth's deep voice says behind me. Without waiting for me to answer, he gives me a thorough frisking, and he asks to see my purse. I hand it to him, and he removes my phone. "Can't go in with this."

My forehead wrinkles. "What am I supposed to do with it?"

"Choose one of the storage compartments and take a key." He points at the wall to my left where there's a series of small lockers. Some of them are open and empty, keys still in the locks, and others are closed with the key missing.

After I've set my phone in one and slipped the key into my purse, I turn to him.

"You can go in now." He motions to a door in front of me. I didn't see it at first, but now that my eyes have adjusted to how dark it is in here, I can just make out its outline.

I nod and lift my chin, feigning confidence I don't feel as I step forward and push open the door. I'm not sure what I expect, but it isn't what I find.

A sensual beat thrums at the perfect volume, loud enough so you can feel the bass in your chest but still low enough that you could hear someone talking.

Or moaning.

A long backlit bar runs along one wall. On the stools in front of it sit men and women in various states of undress. Some of the men are wearing full suits, the women dresses like me, while other women are scantily clad in lingerie, men wearing just black briefs.

The room is split in two, but the other half is a full story below. Two sets of stairs are surrounded by a glass railing so I can look down at the expansive space. There are large couches set up along the outer walls, several padded leather platforms in the middle of the room, and even a small stage on the farthest wall. And people are . . . fucking. Giving and receiving oral sex. Participating in group sex. You name it, and it's happening.

There are a few doors along the wall, and with a hard swallow, I take in the large words above each.

Private Rooms.

Viewing Rooms.

Devil's Dungeon.

Below each one of the descriptors, it says: Consent is key.

The urge to race out of here roars to life, but I quickly dampen the flame. I'm curious what goes on here. I probably won't participate in anything, but there's no harm in watching, right?

I wonder who invited me here? Is it someone who wants to sleep with me? Are they watching me? Someone I know or perhaps someone I met at the wedding? The larger question remains—am I even into this stuff?

I make my way over to the bar, confident I won't be asked for ID. It wasn't as if the guy verified my age before I stepped in here.

"Gin and tonic, please," I say to the bartender dressed in all black.

He smiles and pulls a glass to prepare my drink. I've never had a gin and tonic, but I heard a bunch of the women at the wedding order them last night, so I figure I'll give it a try.

He slides the drink over the bar and heads down to help someone else. My face almost puckers at the first sip, but I school my features, not wanting to appear like a child who doesn't belong. I probably don't, but some part of me deep inside feels as if I'm exactly where I'm meant to be.

I quickly finish my first drink, then order another. When the bartender passes it to me, I go stand at the edge of the railing and look down. Men and women moan in rapture both from giving and receiving pleasure. I'm forced to squeeze my thighs together in an effort to ease the throbbing. Of course I've watched porn before, but watching sex live and in person is completely different.

I've had sex twice in my entire life, both with the same guy. My nonno always told me I was like a cat and that my curiosity would lead me to trouble. Which is how I ended up losing my virginity to Bruno Albis in the janitor's closet of the high school. I was curious about sex and what it felt like. Two times with Bruno was enough to know I wasn't missing much—at least with him. Sex with him was awkward and disappointing, and I knew something was missing.

And watching the intensity on some of these people's faces tells me my assumption was right.

Do I want to go down there?

I bite my lower lip for a minute while I consider it. The space between my legs is thrumming now, wanting relief. I can either go back to the hotel room and satisfy myself or . . . go down there and have someone satisfy me.

As I take in the various scenes, my mind is already made up. If I leave, I'll always wonder what it might have been like, so I finish my drink, leave the empty glass at a nearby table, and descend the stairs. With each step, my stomach bubbles a little more in excitement and worry. But I set aside the worry. I don't have to do anything I'm not comfortable with. If I change my mind, I'll leave.

It's hard not to feel as though every person I pass is checking me out as I walk the length of the room. I'm not really sure how this even works. Do I approach someone? Do they approach me?

But I don't have to wait long because a woman dressed in black see-through lingerie meets my gaze and motions for me to come over. Her dark brown hair is pulled back into a severe-looking ponytail, and she sits beside an attractive man with sandy-colored hair. His eyes appraise me as I get closer.

"I don't think I've seen you here before. What's your name?" she asks.

Now that I'm closer, she looks as though she's a few years older than me. Twenty-five maybe. And she's beautiful. Her body is long and lithe like a model's.

"Hi, this is my first time," I say, proud of how my voice doesn't shake and give away my nerves.

"Fresh meat," the man beside her says with a salacious look.

She rolls her eyes at him. "I'm Mika, and this is Alex."

"Nice to meet you. I'm . . ." I pause, not sure whether I should use my real name. I opt not to. "Starla." God, why did I pick that name? It sounds like a stripper name.

But if she realizes it's a fake name, Mika doesn't say anything. She just smiles. "Why don't you have a seat, Starla?"

Alex moves to his right without having to be told, leaving a space between the two of them.

My breath grows shallow. Am I really going to do this?

Yes.

I'm young and will have very few opportunities to let loose before I'm plucked to marry someone I don't love. I'm not naïve enough to think I'll escape an arranged marriage set up by my brother.

So with a smile, I step forward and sit between them.

It's not that I thought they'd pounce on me the moment I sat down, but I'm surprised when rather than making any type of advance, they engage me in conversation for ten minutes. Turns out Mika is a model, and Alex works as a photographer, which is how they met.

"So, it's your first time?" Mika asks.

"Yeah." A nervous chuckle leaves my lips.

Mika's finger travels over my shoulder, and I suppress a shiver.

"You keep looking around. It's always a dead giveaway," Alex says.

I make a mental note to stop being so obvious. If you're here enough, you must become desensitized to what's going on around you.

"Would you be interested in fooling around?" she asks, her gaze floating over my body.

My nipples pebble in response, and she must notice because I hear a low moan leave her lips.

It's now or never.

Am I really going to do this?

Of course I am. I'd hate myself if I left now and didn't see where this might go. "I think I'd like that."

She gives me a satisfied smile.

Alex leans in and nuzzles my neck. "For now, don't worry about giving, just receive." His hand lands on my knee, and I inhale a deep breath.

Mika leans in on the other side and moves my hair behind my shoulder, trailing her tongue up my neck. My eyes drift closed, and I stifle a moan.

It's all so consuming. Alex runs his nose through my hair and squeezes my knee. A moment later, Mika's hand is on my chin, turning my face toward hers. She leans in and kisses me. Slowly at first, her tongue sliding between my lips to meet mine.

I've never kissed a woman—hell, I've never done anything with a woman—and I don't know what I expected, but it's really not any different than kissing a guy. A little softer, gentler.

While we're kissing, Alex slides one spaghetti strap off over my shoulder, then slides his hand across my collarbone to my shoulder closest to Mika. She pulls away as if they have a rehearsed dance, and he slides the other strap down. They both glide the top of my dress down to pool at my waist, revealing my bare breasts.

I should feel exposed or embarrassed, but I don't. The space between my thighs aches with anticipation.

Mika's lips trail down my neck and over my collarbone. I'm transfixed, watching as her tongue darts out and flicks across my nipple, which hardens in response. She pulls it between her lips, and I suck in a breath, unable to look away, even when Alex's weight lifts off the couch beside me.

All the noise surrounding us—the music, the other people talking, moaning—sounds like a dull fabrication of what it was minutes ago, as if someone stuffed cotton balls in my ears.

She tugs on my nipple with her teeth, and my fingers weave through Mika's hair. She moans in response, her breath coasting over my breast. She pulls back and looks down toward my legs, and that's when I notice Alex sitting on his knees, watching and patiently waiting. They share a smile, and Mika turns her attention back to me.

"Can he eat you out?" She smooths her hand up my stomach and cups my breast.

I nod, not giving it a lot of thought. All I know is that I need some relief from the pressing need between my legs.

She gives me a salacious grin. "He gives the best tongue, sweetie. You're in for a treat."

I'm engrossed watching Alex's hands as they slowly coast up my legs. But for some reason, as excited as I am for this to happen, something about his hands on me feels wrong.

Mika goes back to playing with my nipple with her tongue while Alex's hands slide under the hem of my dress. I lift a bit so that he can push the fabric up and slide my panties down my legs. It's not that I'm not into it, but as he pushes my legs apart and settles himself, I can't help but shake the feeling that this is all wrong. *Him* being there is wrong.

My eyes drift closed as Mika pinches my other nipple between her thumb and forefinger.

Gabriele flashes through my mind.

Is that why it feels off with Alex? Because it's not Gabriele?

No. I will not let Gabriele ruin this. He's made it clear he doesn't want me.

Maybe watching Alex work me will help to dissolve all thoughts of Gabriele, but I open my eyes and startle at who's standing in front of me. Shit, Gabriele isn't just in my head, he's standing here, off to the side of Alex, taking in the scene. He must have seen me leave and followed me here.

But what's most shocking isn't that he's here. It's that he's staring at Alex as though he's about to kill him with his bare hands.

CHAPTER FOUR
GABRIELE

What. The. Fuck.

When I raced down here to attempt to save Aria from herself, I expected to find her wide-eyed and dumbstruck, nursing a drink. I never expected to find her half naked with some asshole between her legs, tasting her.

Rage hits me like a hot poker in the chest, and it takes every ounce of my self-control not to slice this guy's throat open and watch him bleed out. I typically solve my issues with logic and a well-formulated plan, but right now, violence seems like the only option.

How dare this piece of shit get to taste her when I don't even know how sweet she is?

Aria's eyes open, and like a heat-seeking missile, instead of paying attention to the guy between her spread legs, she finds me.

"What the fuck do you think you're doing?" I say loudly enough for the three of them to hear, but not to cause alarm with anyone else around.

I can't afford to draw any unnecessary attention to us. At the first sign of conflict in these places, security will step in, and my goal is to get Aria out of here unnoticed. So as much as I'd like to pummel this piece of shit ten feet into the ground, I can't.

"Gabriele. What are you doing here?" Aria scrambles to close her legs and fix her dress.

The guy on his knees moves back and gets off the floor. He puffs his chest out and sizes me up. "Who the hell are you?"

Idiot. I could have this guy in a choke hold in two seconds flat.

"Doesn't matter. We're leaving." I grab Aria's hand and pull her up off the couch.

The woman beside her gawks at me.

Aria frantically pulls her dress straps back up her arms to cover her bare chest.

"Don't get modest on me now. You've flashed this whole place with your tits." My molars grind together, hating the fact that everyone here saw her half naked. "Let's go."

"Maybe she doesn't want to go with you." This prick really doesn't know what's good for him.

I stop as if I've run into an invisible wall, then slowly turn.

Aria tugs on my arm. "Gabriele, let's just leave. Come on."

It takes me another few seconds for the haze of rage to leave my vision and realize she's right. I can't beat this idiot. Not here, not now anyway.

Without another word, I drag Aria up the stairs, through the bar, and into the foyer.

"I need to get my phone," she says in a small voice.

I drop her hand and nod toward the boxes on the wall. I left mine in my rental car. Something I didn't want to do, but I knew I wouldn't be able to go inside with it because tonight isn't my first time in a sex club.

"There a problem here?" the guy guarding the door asks.

"No problem." I watch as Aria retrieves her phone and slides it into her purse.

"That true?" He raises an eyebrow at Aria.

She hesitates and looks over her shoulder at me. "No, no problem." Her tone is less than believable, and the guard picks up on it, stepping toward me. "Do you want me to remove him from the premises?" he asks her.

"Just fucking try it. I'm not going anywhere without her," I seethe.

He reaches back behind him and pulls out a gun.

I internally sigh. *This guy has no idea who he's fucking with.* "Get that thing out of my fucking face."

The idiot takes another step forward. "You need to leave."

"It's not a problem. He's just picking me up."

I spare a quick glance at Aria because of the note of fear in her voice. Sure enough, she's staring at us wide-eyed with a trembling lip. With a brother like Marcelo, how has she never seen or been part of a confrontation in our world?

This asshole is scaring her.

With a lightning-fast movement, I free the gun from him and pin him to the floor with the gun pointing at his temple. Aria yelps, but I don't spare her a glance.

"I told you not to point that fucking thing at me. Be happy I didn't do worse." I straighten with the gun in my hand and smooth my hand down my shirt. "Let's go." I nod to Aria to move toward the door while I remove the magazine from the gun and the bullet in the chamber, then toss it all onto his chest. "Be smart and stay down there."

Because I'm not an idiot, I walk backward toward the door, keeping my eye on him. A lot of men would do something stupid to try to save face. Let's hope he's not one of those guys.

Once we're outside, I hurry Aria to my car, open the passenger door, and get her inside.

My ass isn't in the seat for more than two seconds before Aria questions me. "How did you do that?"

"Do what?" I put the car into gear and race away from the building before the guy grabs his friends and tries to get me.

A quick glance in the rearview tells me I was right to worry, because the idiot flies out along with some of his bouncer friends.

"Get the gun from that guy like that. It was in his hand one second, then in yours."

"Krav Maga." I shouldn't answer her. The less she knows about me, the better. Plus, I prefer to keep to myself that I'm well-versed in martial arts. It's always more fun to take your opponent by surprise.

"You take Krav Maga?"

"Among other martial arts." When we stop at an intersection, I type the name of the hotel into the GPS. The light changes, and the vehicle surges forward, trying to get Aria back to the hotel where she'll be safe and not get into any trouble.

"I didn't know that about you," she says.

"Why would you? We don't know each other."

She knows nothing about me except who my family is and maybe that I'm good with computers.

When she's silent for a beat, I glance over and see her lips turned down. Oh well. The sooner she figures out we're not going to be besties or bed buddies, the better.

"Are you going to tell my brother?"

It'd be for her own good if I told Marcelo. He needs to get her ass in line. That club is no place for her. She's too damn young.

"I haven't decided. What the hell were you doing there anyway?"

She doesn't say anything, and I take a quick look at her before merging onto the freeway. Whatever it is, she clearly doesn't want to tell me.

"Say it. Otherwise I'll definitely tell your brother."

She shifts in her seat. "There was an invitation left in my hotel room. I found it last night after the wedding."

My hands grip the steering wheel so hard I'm surprised it doesn't bend. "You went on an anonymous invitation? Do you have any idea how fucking stupid that is?"

"It could have been from you," she mumbles.

Without warning, I crank the steering wheel to the side and slam on the brakes, so the vehicle comes to an abrupt stop on the shoulder of the road. Vehicles whiz past us as my chest rises and falls, and I work to get a hold of my anger.

Once I've taken a few breaths, I turn to look at her. "I've told you over and over again that nothing is ever going to happen between us. You're a naïve little girl, and this shit you pulled tonight only proves it. How did you grow up in our world and not think anything bad ever happens? Do you have any real idea of the life you're a part of? You're the sister of the don. Do you know how many enemies of his would love to cut you up into little pieces and send you back to your brother that way?"

Her face pales, and her head presses back against the passenger window. But I don't care. Aria needs to hear the truth. She needs to realize what can happen to her if she continues to pull shit like she did tonight.

To hammer the point home, I continue my rant. "Nothing is ever going to happen between us. The last thing I need is to be a fucking babysitter."

A spear lodges in my chest from the flash of hurt in her eyes. Whatever. It's for her own good.

I turn away, put the car in gear, and merge back into traffic.

The sooner Aria realizes the truth of everything I've said, the better. I'm doing her a favor. I don't care if I've hurt her feelings. It's a hell of a lot less than the Costas' enemies would do to her.

CHAPTER FIVE
ARIA

A few weeks later . . .

I finger the locket hanging around my neck while standing in front of the closed door to my room. It's a nervous habit I picked up ever since my dad gifted it to me before he was murdered.

I'm not sure why I'm nervous. I was so excited to start my life at the Sicuro Academy, but now that I'm here, and it's the first day of class, my stomach is queasy, my heart racing. It doesn't help that I have no one to walk to breakfast with. My brother made sure of that.

He somehow managed to segregate me in a room by myself. No roommate. I think he thought he was doing me a favor, but I would have liked to have roomed with another girl in the hopes of having a built-in friend.

I've spent my life isolated and not knowing where I belong. Sure, I've always had my identity as it relates to other people—the don's daughter, the don's sister—but who am I without those labels? Sometimes I wonder if that's why I'm always chasing adventure . . . to figure out who I am and what feels right.

Having someone to share space with every day, to get to know and do fun girly stuff with would have been a nice change of pace. But since that's not going to happen, I raise my chin, open my door, and step into the hallway wearing the Sicuro Academy's standard-issue uniform—a white button-down shirt and a tartan skirt. Since I'm from one of the Italian families, the pattern on my skirt is white, red, and green.

The Sicuro Academy is a private college created by the four Italian crime families that run the United States. Three decades ago, after a series of fights over territory that resulted in a bloodbath, killing a lot of young men on the rise to prominent positions, they built the academy. The word Sicuro in Italian means safe.

They can all send their children to the academy after high school without having to worry that we'll kill each other since there's a zero-violence policy—and no weapons allowed except for weaponry class.

Eventually, the board let in other mob families, like the Irish and the Russians, even cartel members, and finally, the politicians' kids because it made financial sense. Everyone's astronomical tuition pads the pockets of the four founding families—as well as giving the Italians knowledge about who's up-and-coming in their ranks.

I make my way down the path outside toward the dining hall. When I was here for my orientation this past spring, Gabriele showed me around, but my future sister-in-law, Mira, was nice enough to take me around again when I arrived two days ago. The campus is huge, and I don't have it all committed to memory yet, but I'll get there.

Being around people from different nationalities than my own still feels weird, but Mira assured me I'll get used to it. Never did I think that Russians, Irish, and cartel members would be my classmates.

When I reach the dining hall, I look in the direction of the tables where Mira told me I'd find her. Apparently, she sits at either the Costa table with my brother or the La Rosa table with her brother and best friend. I find her at the Costa table with my brother, and he's got his hands all over her, no surprise there. My cousin, Giovanni, and my brother's two good friends, Nicolo and Andrea, are sitting with them.

Before I head over, I take in the large space with soaring ceilings. Now that it's full of my schoolmates, I can get a better idea of the lay of the land and who sits where. My gaze reaches the tables directly opposite the Costas, and all the air whooshes from my lungs.

Gabriele is staring at me, sitting with a bunch of other people from the Vitale family. He looks extra good in his school uniform.

I haven't seen him since he dropped me off at the hotel in Miami. After he hurled all that bullshit at me, cracking the fragile walls of my ego where he's concerned, I bolted out of the car and up to my room without a word.

Why is he even looking at me? He made it pretty clear he wants nothing to do with me.

Forcing myself to drag my gaze away from his, I start over to the Costa table—where I belong, according to him.

Mira spots me and raises her hand with a big smile. "You ready for your first day?" she asks once I sit across from her.

All the guys at the table grunt out a hello to me and go back to whatever they were talking about. Typical.

"Ready. A little nervous, though, if I'm honest."

"You'll be fine." She squeezes my hand. "A few days in and you'll know this place like the back of your hand."

"Just stay out of trouble," my brother says from beside her. I thought he was paying attention to whatever story Nicolo is telling, but I suppose he probably always has one ear open for what's going on around him.

I narrow my eyes. "Why would I do that when it's so fun to watch you act like a crotchety old man about everything I say and do? Not sure when you turned into my dad."

Marcelo's jaw clenches, and he's about to say something, but

Mira slides her hand from her lap over to his thigh. Instead, he returns his attention to the story Nicolo's telling.

Mira winks. She told me that she's going to try to keep my brother from acting like an overbearing parent while I'm here, but we'll see how successful she is. I'm not holding my breath.

I don't bother eating anything—my stomach is too unsettled. It takes a huge effort to resist the urge to look at Gabriele. Which pisses me off after the way he spoke to me the last time I saw him. I should hate him, loathe him, want him dead. He made it especially clear how he felt about me in Miami, but still, I feel his burnished copper gaze on my back. He's probably more annoyed than anything that I'm in his presence.

"I'm going to go find my first class. I'll see you guys later." I stand from the table.

"Have the best day," Mira says.

All the guys give me a half-ass goodbye before turning back to their conversation.

I wave to Sofia and Antonio at the La Rosa table and head toward the exit.

I don't know why, but I can't help glancing over my shoulder at the Vitale table. My breath freezes when once again I meet Gabriele's gaze. His expression is blank, void of any emotion. There's nothing there that indicates interest or desire. But I can't help but wonder, as I push through the doors, if he doesn't want anything to do with me, why is he always staring at me?

* * *

I'M LEAVING MY computer science class when a girl calls out to me.

"Hold up!"

I turn and wait. She has light brown hair just past her shoulders, blue eyes, and though I'm not sure what family she's from, the colors on her skirt tell me she's Italian.

"You're Marcelo Costa's sister, right?" she says.

I can't help but frown. Is this what I'll be known for here?

"Sorry, sorry." She waves her hand in front of her. "I just don't know your name. I'm Bianca."

"Aria. Nice to meet you. What family are you from?"

"The Accardis. I'm Dante's cousin."

Dante Accardi is in his last year here at Sicuro Academy and is next in line to run the southwest quadrant of the country. I don't know Dante, but I know *of* him. Everyone does. I'm not sure how I missed crossing paths with him at Antonio and Sofia's wedding, other than the fact there were five hundred guests.

"This your first year here?" I ask.

She nods. "Yeah. I know people from our family, but they're not really into the same things I am. I wanted to see if you wanted to hang out sometime. Rumor is you know how to have fun."

I freeze for a beat. Does she know about Miami? But I force myself to relax almost as fast. No one knows about Miami. Well, except for one. If Miami was common knowledge, my brother would already have me under house arrest.

I paste on a smile. "I do enjoy fun from time to time. Freedom is hard to come by in our position."

Bianca rolls her eyes. "Tell me about it. Thank God I only have sisters, but still, Dante can whore himself around, but God forbid me or my sisters even talk to a guy."

"Exactly!"

We walk together, and the conversation comes easily and isn't forced.

It's not unheard of or strictly forbidden to be friendly with people from the other Italian families—not in the way it is with the Irish, the Russians, or the cartels—but it's an unspoken rule that you can't get *too* close. Trust with the other Italian families only goes so far. Which is to say, not really that far at all.

Still, I like Bianca. She seems fun and a lot like me.

I love Mira and Sofia, and there are some other girls here I know from my family, but part of being here for me is figuring out who I am outside of my family. I crave having my own friends, my own identity.

It's very likely that at some point, my brother will pair me off with someone from our world, and if I don't know who I am by that point, how will I ever figure it out? I'll be thrust into a role of Marcelo's choosing and just sort of meld into the mold.

We reach a fork in the pathway, and Bianca motions toward the right. "I'm going to head over to Café Ambrosia before the Roma House. Want to come with?"

I shake my head. "I'm going to head back. I want to get my homework done before dinner so I can do what I want tonight."

"All right. Sounds good. You want to hang tonight?"

"Sure. That sounds fun." I pull my school-issued phone from my bag. The same phone that has no contact with the outside world and is only good for texting other students and administration on campus. "Here, add yourself in here."

She takes the phone, enters her information, then texts herself. "There. Now I have you, too. I'll text you after dinner."

"Okay, sounds good."

We go our separate ways, but the rest of the walk back to Roma House, I have a light feeling in my chest. Sure, Bianca and I will never be besties since we're not part of the same family, but we can be friends. This is exactly what I wanted when I arrived here—a place to carve out my own life, discover my identity.

CHAPTER SIX
GABRIELE

I step into the elevator at Roma House to head up to my room on the fourth floor only to find Dante Accardi already in there.

"Vitale," he says.

"Dante." I give him a nod of acknowledgment but otherwise stay silent, moving to the back corner. I don't like the guy. He's too flashy. Too "look at me." Too obnoxious.

And I'm not stupid enough to let him stand at my back in an enclosed space. Even if there is a zero-violence policy on campus.

"Well, well. What do we have here?" he mumbles to himself. The elevator doors start to close, but he punches the button to swing them back open. "Hello, gorgeous. I don't think we've officially met."

I can't see who he's talking to from where I am standing until the girl steps inside the elevator. My jaw clenches when Aria's gaze meets mine, but she turns around, giving me her back and standing beside Dante.

"We haven't, but I definitely know who you are." She looks up at him with those doe eyes of hers.

Fuck me. She's so sweet and innocent. Dante would eat her alive with his man-whoring ways and make her just one in a long line of women he's discarded.

"Dante Accardi." He holds out his hand as though he's some sort of gentleman.

What a joke.

"Aria Costa, but you seem to already know that." She takes his hand, and he holds on for a beat too long when she tries to pull it away. "I just met your cousin, Bianca. She's great."

He chuckles and pushes his hand through his light brown wavy hair. "Watch out for that one. She can be trouble." He steps closer to her. "Of course, so can I. Maybe you like trouble?"

"Watch it." The words fly out of my mouth before I can stop them.

Dante looks at me over his shoulder. "Why's it any of your concern?" He arches an eyebrow.

He's right, it's not. Aria is not my concern, and I need to remember that. My father made it clear before I even arrived at school that he didn't want me anywhere near her.

"We had enough bullshit on campus last year. I'm tired of cleaning up everyone's messes." The elevator dings, and the doors swing open on the fourth floor. "I can only collect so many favors."

It's a lame excuse, and my only hope is he doesn't call me out on it.

I push between them to exit on my floor. Dante is on the sixth floor and Aria is on the fifth, which means they'll be alone in the elevator together. I hate the way I want to drag Dante out by his golden boy hair just to prevent him being close to her.

My shoulder brushes Aria's arm as I pass, and she sucks in a breath. My dick twitches in my dress pants. Will this fucking want ever go away?

My already sour mood plummets further when Alessandro is waiting at my door. Not because I don't like my cousin, but because I didn't know he was there.

Every year, I smuggle in everything I need to keep tabs on my room and the comings and goings of the entire Roma House. At the end of the year, I have to remove everything from my dorm room. Now I'm in the process of smuggling in all my shit again.

We're not even allowed to have our own laptops here, so you can imagine how many strikes the chancellor would hammer down on me if he saw the amount of technology I normally keep in my room. We're completely cut off from the outside world except for our Sunday phone call, where we're allowed to make an outgoing call on a secure line.

I get it. They don't want what's happening in the outside world to trickle into campus life. There would be fistfights all over the cobblestone paths. But it's a pain in the ass, and it takes me weeks to get everything I need in here. Thank fuck this is my last year.

"Hey, man." I nod at Sandro and unlock my door.

When I enter, he follows, and I do my usual routine, glancing around to see if anything was disturbed. Maybe I'm paranoid, but since I don't have my security system set up yet, I trust no one.

"How was your day?" he asks, flopping down on my bed. "It's so weird in here without all your geeky shit."

I roll my eyes. He, along with a lot of other guys in our crew, is always riding me about my obsession with computers. I don't let it bother me. One day they'll see that I'm right and that this is the future of our business. I'm working on something I haven't shared with anyone yet, and if it works, maybe it will shut them all up for good.

"It was fine. Same shit as last year."

"Yeah, except there's a new crop of first-year girls now." He laughs when I shake my head. "Have you seen Costa's little sister? That girl is already on the top of every guy's list."

Jesus. I'm not surprised she ended up on everyone's radar today.

"You'll stay away from her if you know what's good for you." Hopefully that didn't sound protective.

"Yeah, yeah, I know. Your dad had a chat with me before I came here."

All the families know that at some point Marcelo will marry Aria off, if she doesn't find someone for herself that he'll approve of. She's still young and has a few years, though it's not uncommon that she could be paired anytime. Not only is she fucking gorgeous, her family is powerful.

Some might think that everyone would be clamoring for their son to be arranged with her, and probably some are. But my father made it clear to me, along with the rest of the guys at the top of the Vitale family food chain, that any of us marrying Aria would give Marcelo too much power, what with him about to marry someone from the La Rosa family. It would mean he had a foothold in three quadrants out of the four.

Dad hasn't said it, but I think he has his eye on finding someone from the Accardi family for me to marry. That would give us the western half of the country while Marcelo had the eastern half.

I can't swallow the idea of being tied to Dante in any way. He's too impulsive, too much of a loose cannon ready to react at a moment's notice.

"Too bad, though. I think Aria Costa and I could have some fun together."

I turn away from Sandro, so he doesn't see how tight my jaw is. I don't know why the hell it bothers me so much to think of Aria with someone else. It's not like we've ever been in a relationship or anything. Hell, we've never even kissed. But I am attracted to her, and I can't deny that.

"My dad's right when he says that any of us being with Aria would give her brother too much power." I walk over to my fridge. "Marcelo already has enough of it." I reach into my fridge and pull out an energy drink, then turn and hold it up. "Want one?"

Sandro waves me off. "It's no wonder you can't sleep for shit, drinking that stuff."

If I hadn't struggled with sleep my whole life, I'd agree with him. Unfortunately, laying off the energy drinks doesn't have an impact on my insomnia.

It's the whole reason I got into computers in the first place. I'd be up all night, and I quickly got sick of the usual distractions—TV, music, and masturbation. That's when I stumbled upon a website about hacking. The deeper I dove, the more I realized the kind of power in holding information. How you could wield it how you wanted, use it to sway people's opinions, judgments. Release just enough of it at the exact right time, and people are malleable, and you can make them do what you want.

"So what's going on?" I ask before sipping my drink.

"Heard there's gonna be a forest party this weekend. Figured I'd come by and try to force you into going." He stares at me in a way that makes me think he's not going to take no for an answer.

"Not really my scene." Most people wouldn't exactly call me social.

Sandro sits up. "I get it. But this is our senior year. Thought maybe you could make an exception for some fun this year."

I chuckle and sit on the couch. "You ever stop to consider that maybe you and everyone else here is too preoccupied with the idea of fun?" When he doesn't answer, I arch an eyebrow.

"I'm not in your position, but I get it. You're going to take over the entire operation one day. I can't imagine what that feels like. But soon we'll be out of this place and in a world where we don't get much say over our lives. Even you." He gestures to me. "You might be in charge someday, but there's still established rules and conventions you're going to have to follow. This is as much freedom as we'll get. Why not have fun with it?"

I blow out a breath. "I'll think about it." That's mostly a lie, but it gets him off my back for now.

My cousin smiles and stands from the bed. "I figured you'd give me the damn runaround. I'll take it."

He leaves, and I change to go work out before dinner, after which I'll start on my efforts to get my computer equipment smuggled onto campus. That will distract me enough that I absolutely won't think about Aria.

The lie tastes bitter on my tongue.

CHAPTER SEVEN
ARIA

I wasn't sure what to expect when I arrived at Bianca's room before the forest party, but what I was not expecting was what I found.

Since she's part of the Accardi family, I figured that's who I'd find there. I wasn't sure I'd be entirely comfortable being the only member of the Costa family included. But instead, it's a hodge-podge of students from various Italian families.

There's Dom, Dante Accardi's younger brother and Bianca's cousin, as well as Vincenzo and Beatrice, who I remember seeing at the wedding this summer. They're children of some of the under-bosses in the La Rosa family. And there's Elisa, whose father works for Gabriele's father in the Vitale crime family. Doing what I'm not sure, and I didn't want to come off as though it mattered and ask.

I was the only one from the Costa family, but it didn't matter. Everyone was nice and welcoming—as welcoming as we can be while not ever fully letting our guard down around each other. Someone had smuggled in some booze, so we drank before heading off to the party.

Excitement, and probably the alcohol, has me grinning as we make our way through the forest toward the low thrum of bass. This was exactly what I hoped for when I came here. A little bit of room to stretch my wings, have some harmless fun, and figure myself out.

"Do a lot of students usually come to these things?" I ask Bianca as we pick our way through the trees, trying not to trip on anything and end up face-first on the forest floor.

"From what I hear, usually, yeah. Especially the first one of the year."

The rest of the group is ahead of us, and someone must have said something funny because they all burst out in laughter.

"How does the school not know about them? We can already hear the music from here."

Bianca grabs my shoulder when she almost trips on a small branch. "I think the administration probably knows about them and turns a blind eye, but who knows? Could be they think it's a good idea to let us blow off a little steam this way rather than letting it get pent up and have violence erupting in the dining hall or something."

"Makes sense, I guess."

The music grows louder, and we continue to push our way through until we reach a clearing where the forest opens up and reveals our destination. Inside the large clearing is a mash of students. Some dance in the center to the thrumming beat of the Tiësto song, and others on the outskirts are watching or having conversations in their own groups.

It's only members of the Italian houses here. I'm not sure what the Irish or the Russians do for fun, but it obviously isn't attending forest parties with their enemies.

Lasers project up onto the canopy of trees surrounding the space, and between that and the electric energy coming from everyone, exhilaration sizzles through my veins. Tonight is exactly what I've been looking for. No worrying about Gabriele and the hold he still has on me for some unknown reason. No worrying about what it means to be Marcelo's sister and whether he'd try to marry me off sometime soon. No thoughts of figuring out who and what I'm meant to be. Just fun.

Bianca hooks her arm through mine and leans in close. "Want to grab a drink? The keg is over there."

I nod. "Absolutely."

We push through the crowd until we reach the far side where some kegs are set up. I've never poured a beer from a keg, so I let Bianca do the honors, and she passes me a red plastic cup filled to the brim.

When I take a sip, I avoid cringing. This is my first beer, since I usually opt for champagne or wine. But beer will work tonight, so I suck back some more and swallow.

"Where did everyone else go?" I ask, realizing everyone we walked here with is gone.

She shrugs, seeming unconcerned. "Who knows. Who cares!" She laughs, earning looks from some of the people surrounding us. "We're going to have fun either way." She holds her cup out in front of her. "To new friends."

With a smile, I push my cup forward and press it to hers. "To new friends."

We each gulp down a heavy amount of beer, and that's when I see him over the rim of my Solo cup.

My brother.

"Shit."

Bianca's forehead wrinkles. "What's wrong?"

"My brother is here. If he sees me, he's going to put an end to my night."

"Well then, we can't let him see you." She grabs my hand and hauls me off the way we came, both of us giggling.

I assume my brother thinks I might be here and will be on the lookout for me. I can't avoid him forever, but I will for as long as I can. I'm not in the mood for one of his lectures.

We end up finding the rest of the group we came with and hang out with them on the edge of where everyone is dancing. Because

I don't want to go back in the direction my brother was in, Dom agrees to grab me another beer when I finish mine.

I haven't seen Marcelo again, but all night, I can't shake the sensation that someone is watching me. Every time I glance around, though, I don't spot him, so I shake off the feeling.

Dom returns with a beer for both Bianca and me.

"Thanks so much," I lean in to say and stumble a bit. I faceplant into his chest, and he chuckles, helping to right me. "Sorry."

Heat swamps my face. I'm embarrassed that I clearly can't handle my alcohol. It's not like I never drank before, but I don't have the tolerance others do.

"No worries." Dom's hands drop from my arms as soon as I'm steady.

Unlike his brother, Dom is a gentleman. I only met Dante briefly in the elevator this week, but his reputation had preceded him. Everyone says he works his way through women pretty fast.

A shiver runs up my spine when I remember Gabriele's surprised gaze on me as I entered the elevator.

"Are you cold?" Dom asks.

I shake my head. "No, I'm good." I bring the beer to my lips.

Dom stands next to me, his shoulder against mine. Is he interested in me? Is Dom someone I could like? I don't know. He seems like a decent guy. Marcelo would certainly approve as far as his lot in life—second in line to the Accardi throne.

But even as I consider, a persistent nagging in the back of my head tells me that he might be attractive, but he's not Gabriele.

I chug the rest of my beer at the thought I'll be hung up on Gabriele forever. I'm so sick of not being able to get him out of my head. He made his feelings, or lack thereof, perfectly clear in Miami. The attraction is not mutual. He only sees me as a child.

"Woah, girl," Bianca says from behind me when I finish off my drink.

Dom merely arches an eyebrow. "Thirsty?"

"Something like that," I mutter.

A Florence and the Machine song plays, and Bianca squeals, rushing up beside me. "We have to dance."

She drags me onto the makeshift dance floor, and somewhere along the way, I drop the empty cup on the ground. Once Bianca finds a space for us, we sway to the beat. Our hands are up in the air as we chant, "I am free," laughing with one another.

I'm not sure I've ever felt this uninhibited.

That's not true. It was back at the club in Miami.

The feeling of that rope of imprisonment being gone is addictive. I want to chase it like a bird following prey from the sky.

And I do.

We dance for a few more songs, and I'm living entirely in the moment. My mind isn't thinking about a million things at once, wondering what's to come or how things might work out. It's just me in the middle of a forest, dancing to the beat and surrounded by people with the same quest.

Eventually Dom approaches. Bianca is busy chatting with a girl I don't recognize so I turn my attention to him.

He bends and whispers into my ear, "Let's go smoke a joint."

My eyes widen. I've never smoked weed before, but I'm not against it. I'm already pretty drunk and not sure I should push it much more. But when I spot Mira pulling my brother into the fray through the crowd not far from us, I whip around to face Dom. "Let's go."

He takes my hand and leads me off the dance floor. I have the brief thought that maybe I shouldn't go off into the woods with a guy I just met, but I push it away. I honestly don't think Dom is a threat to me.

Maybe he'll put a move on me, but I can handle it. At least I can once I sort out how I feel about him. Right now, the alcohol has my thoughts muddled, but isn't that what I wanted so that I wouldn't think of Ga—

Nope.

Not going to even grant his name space in my head.

Dom leads us to the outer edge of the party. We're not in the woods, but we're right at the edge of the forest line. He pulls a joint from the pocket of his shirt, lights it, and takes a pull. I watch while he holds the smoke in his lungs for a beat before exhaling. The earthy, skunk-like scent fills the air around us, and it's not displeasing.

Dom extends the joint in my direction, and I bring it to my lips, mimicking what he did. Only I can't hold the smoke in for more than a second before I'm coughing into my arm.

"First time?" he asks with no judgment in his tone.

"How can you tell?" I say when I finally stop hacking.

He chuckles. "Try again. It'll get easier."

I do as he says, and he's right. I hold it for longer and manage not to cough up a lung this time before I pass it back to him.

We chat for a few minutes until the joint is a small roach in his hand that he drops on the ground and stomps on until he's sure it's out. He's obviously not into me since he didn't make a move.

"Want to see if we can find Bianca on the dance floor?" Dom asks.

"Sure." I shrug. I'm pretty sure I'd agree to just about anything. My head feels fuzzy, but I have a permanent smile. My limbs are heavy in a way that makes me comfortable in my own body.

Domenic doesn't reach for my hand this time, instead stepping up to the crowd a few feet ahead of us, before sliding through a gap between two groups.

I'm following him, but I step into a hard chest instead. Even in my current state, I don't have to arch my head back to look at who it is that's stepped in front of me. The scent alone tips me off that it's Gabriele.

My only question is—why?

CHAPTER EIGHT
GABRIELE

Aria bumps into my chest, and it's all I can do not to steady her. But that would only lead to me wanting to put my hands on her again and again and again.

This woman might be the death of me.

Still, I've watched her drink and smoke pot with Dante's little brother all night, and each time I notice her lose her footing, a little thicker layer of protectiveness flares inside me because she's drunk and vulnerable.

Why do I care? I have no fucking clue.

But it's clear I do.

So here I am. Separating her from Dom because, of course, he's continued off into the crowd, not even keeping an eye out to make sure she's still behind him after he got her stoned.

What I should do is make sure what he's done gets back to her brother.

But then you couldn't use the excuse to step in yourself.

"What . . . what are you doing?" Aria's beautiful, yet naïve, doe eyes are wide, staring at me while her head flops, causing a tendril of hair to slide over her face.

I'm this close to tucking it behind her ear when she does it herself. Her dopey smile would be cute if I wasn't so pissed.

"Getting you out of here."

Her reaction is slower than it would normally be, but eventually she scowls. "I'm not going anywhere. I'm having fun."

"I'll bet your brother would want to know just how much fun you're having."

Her mouth drops, and she juts out her hip.

Bull's-eye. I know just where to hit to make her do my bidding. As usual, information is the most valuable asset. And while Aria might be annoyed by how overbearing her brother is, she loves him and doesn't want to make things harder for him or create a bad reputation for the family.

"Now, let's go." I motion for her to turn around before she argues.

Her shoulders slouch, and she makes her way out of the crowd. I don't bother saying a word as I pass her, knowing she'll follow.

I lead her the long way through the forest. It's not the most direct route, but there's a path, and it appears to be hard enough for her to walk in a straight line, let alone trek through a forest. At least this way I won't have to put her over my shoulder or lay a hand on her at all.

We're quiet for the first few minutes of our walk, but she shatters the silence.

"You're not really going to tell my brother, are you?" She looks at me, tilting those plush lips of hers down into a frown.

"Not now I'm not."

She doesn't respond. It takes everything in me not to lecture her about being more careful, but she wouldn't listen to any advice from me. I don't know if she'll even remember this conversation tomorrow.

"I just wanted to have fun," she murmurs loudly enough for me to hear. "Why's it so bad that I want to experience life?"

That last question is directed at me.

We emerge from the forest onto the sprawling lawn of the school grounds, and I stop. "When you pull this shit, you make yourself accessible, and there are a lot of people in the world who would happily take advantage of you. Even without being who you are."

She studies me, taking a few lazy steps toward me. "You worry about me."

I stiffen. "I don't worry about you. I'm just not some asshole who's gonna sit and watch while an innocent young woman gets taken advantage of because she's put herself in harm's way."

She grins, and if it weren't so irritating, I may consider it sexy. "Nuh-uh. You feel it, too. This pull." Her finger waves between us.

I scoff and start to walk again. *Jesus, I can't be that transparent. Especially when she's drunk and high.*

She stumbles a bit as she catches up to me. I clench my hands so I don't turn around to make sure she's okay. For whatever reason, she doesn't say anything else for a while. Thank Christ. She just struggles to keep up with the pace I set, which is fast. All I need to do is get her safely to her room and leave before I do something rash and stupid.

When the Roma House comes into view, the tension dissipates inside me.

"Why do you say I'm too young for you? I'm only three years younger than you are."

All the stress and strain returns as if it never left.

She's crazy if she thinks I'm having this conversation with her. No way in hell. There's shit a girl like Aria doesn't need to know.

"You're just going to ignore me? Real mature." I hear her annoyance and assume she's rolling her eyes.

Again, I don't say anything, just continue to walk while she lags behind.

"I'm just going to keep bugging you about it until you tell me."

"I'd expect no less," I finally say as we near the doors of Roma House.

A few more minutes, and I'm free.

"What were you even doing there tonight if you weren't there to have fun? What was the point of going?" Judgment laces her tone.

Not as if I could give her the truth. *Because my particular brand of fun isn't offered at this school, and it was a feeble attempt at letting off some steam.*

I don't normally attend the forest parties, but since my contact in security was fired a week before school started, I'm having a harder time getting my shit smuggled in this year than I had last year. Lucky for me, he had a gambling problem that made him susceptible to bribes. Unlucky for him, the school found out about his addiction and fired him.

Now I need to make inroads elsewhere or I'm fucked.

And so, when Alessandro came by my room to harass me into joining him, I caved. Figured it might be a good chance to unwind a bit, get my mind off things.

I pull open the door and motion for her to go inside the building. Surprisingly, she steps through without argument but with a rigid back. The moment the door closes behind us, and we start on our way to the elevator, she's pestering me again.

"Tell me why you say I'm too young for you."

Lucky me. Alcohol seems to loosen her lips. Awesome.

Thankfully, everyone must be at the party because no one is in the lounge area to overhear her.

"I told you, we're not talking about this." I stab the up button for the elevator with my finger.

She stands next to me, and I feel her eyes on me. "But I want to know. It makes no sense."

I push a hand through my hair, frustration boiling in my blood.

The elevator doors ding, open, and we step inside, then I turn to face her.

"Just tell me. C'mon, Gabriele. Why do—"

"Maybe young isn't the right word."

A small grin tugs at her lips as though she's gotten her way.

"The better word might be innocent." I hit the button for her floor, and the doors slide closed.

I turn back to face the doors, willing the elevator to hurry so I can escape this confined area with her. But in the space of a breath, she's plastered herself against me—her firm breasts pillowing against my chest, her sweet scent filling my nostrils.

"What makes you think I'm so innocent?" she purrs and trails a hand down my chest.

She rests her hand on my belt. I stab the stop button on the elevator, and it comes to a lurching stop. Aria's eyes light up with lust as though I'm going to finally live out all her fantasies. But within a blink of her long, dark lashes, I have her back to the elevator wall and her wrists high above her head in my hand.

"Don't," I hiss at her in an effort to scare her.

Her breath heaves so hard. Instead of cowering as I want her to, she arches her back as if this is turning her on.

"Or what?" Her gaze drops to my lips, and fuck me, I want so badly to lean in and kiss her. Suck the air from her soul until all that's left is her unyielding need.

But I do not need the wrath of both my father and her brother coming down on me. Someone like Aria wouldn't be able to handle being with someone like me. She'd probably gape at me in horror if she knew what I really want to do with her, what plays in my mind late at night.

"You need to stop this bullshit, Aria. Nothing is going to happen between us, no matter the reasons. Got it?" I stare into her dark eyes glazed from the weed, her lids heavy from the need swirling between us.

"I see through you. Why can't you just admit you want this? You want me?" Her tongue grazes over her bottom lip.

God, help me, I lean in. Not much, maybe an inch. But I should be backing up, not considering giving in to temptation. Aria tilts her chin up in invitation to kiss her. And as I'm considering taking what I've been thirsting for, her chin drops and she throws up, covering both our shoes.

The stench of vomit fills the air, and my eyes close with a sigh. I turn and hit the button for my floor.

I choose not to be annoyed by what just happened because she did me a favor. I was about to do the stupidest thing I could have.

CHAPTER NINE
ARIA

I groan. One part from mortification, the other part from my stomach turning over on itself. My head spins, the elevator's dinging rings through the small space, and Gabriele's dragging me down the hallway. It's not until I step foot inside a room that I realize that we're not in mine, we're in his.

If I wasn't feeling so queasy, I'd probably rejoice that he's allowed me into his inner sanctum. I'd be cataloging everything in here, but there's only one thing on my mind. I rush further into his room, locate the bathroom door, and collapse in front of the toilet seconds before the next round of vomiting erupts.

A few seconds later, large hands pull my hair back away from my face.

When my stomach is done purging itself, I remain there, catching my breath. I'm so embarrassed to face the man I've been trying so hard to impress for the past year.

"I suppose you think this just proves your point," I say into the toilet bowl, reaching for the handle to flush it.

He doesn't say anything, and I slowly right myself. He lets his hands drop from my hair. I still feel a little dizzy, but my stomach settles a bit now that it's empty.

He ignores my question. "How do you feel now?"

"Better than a few minutes ago."

He nods, lips pressed into a thin line. "Let's get cleaned up. We should shower." Quickly, he adds, "Not together." He clears his throat.

I temper my disappointment. It's not as though I'm in shape for anything other than bed anyway. "Okay, I'll head back to my room."

Gabriele steps forward. "That's not what I meant." He appears conflicted, but he says, "You go first, then I'll go."

"I don't like being where I'm not wanted."

"You're not leaving." His voice brokers no argument. "You can't be by yourself tonight, and everyone else is still at the party. If you pass out, you could choke to death on your own vomit."

"I'll be fine." I push up off the floor to stand and stumble.

Gabriele's hands are on my shoulders to steady me. "You're spending the night here so I can keep an eye on you. That's the end of it." When I don't say anything, he lets his hands drop and steps back. "I'll get you a T-shirt or something to sleep in, then you can have a shower."

I nod, and he leaves the bathroom.

This man is so confusing. One minute he's being nasty and pushing me away, and the next he's worried about protecting me. It doesn't make any sense.

Maybe he's worried about starting trouble with my brother if he were to hear that Gabriele saw me in the state I was in and didn't do anything about it.

I hear him open one of his dresser drawers, then he's back with a plain black T-shirt that he sets on the counter.

"Are you good to shower on your own, or are you too dizzy and need help?" He swallows hard as though he doesn't know what would torture him more.

If I were feeling better, I'd lie and say I need his help, but I don't want to reward his kindness with dishonesty. "I'm good on my own."

He gives me a terse nod and leaves the room, closing the door behind him.

After I've peeled off my vomit-soaked clothes and shoes, I turn on the shower and step under the warm spray. There's something intimate about being in Gabriele's shower. His expensive shampoo has a masculine smell instead of flowers like women's. I lather it in my hair, thinking of not washing it for a while as if I'm a stalker now. I pick up his bodywash and inhale the woodsy and spicy scent that filled the car that night, the one that lingered in the elevator before I threw up. I run it over my body as if it's his hands cleaning me. Oh God, I need major help.

I hurriedly finish the shower and still feel slightly dizzy once I'm done. My stomach isn't quite right, but I don't feel like bowing to the porcelain god anymore so, progress.

I slide my panties and bra back on since they aren't covered in vomit, then I grab the T-shirt from the counter, bringing it to my nose and inhaling. When I pull it over my head, it slides down to settle just above my knees. Even though I shove down the flutter in my chest from smelling like him and being draped in his shirt, my heart betrays me and beats out an uneven rhythm in my chest.

I hang the towel back up and emerge from the bathroom, feeling nervous. This isn't at all what I ever expected to happen between us. My hair is wet, but it's not dripping down onto the T-shirt. My drool might, though, because Gabriele is undressed down to a pair of black boxer briefs.

Which makes sense of course, because he was covered in vomit, too, but I didn't prepare myself.

This is the first time I've seen him anything other than fully dressed. He's fucking hot. His wide chest is muscled, and the ridges of his abs show a trail of dark hair leading down to the thick band of his boxer briefs. Gabriele's shoulders are rounded with muscle, as are his biceps.

Part of me wants to continue to stand there and ogle him, but I remind myself that I'm trying not to lust after this man tonight, so I clear my throat. "Thanks for letting me shower."

"No problem." He walks past me as if he isn't in boxers and I'm not standing here in his T-shirt. I'm sure he really believes I'm some naïve little girl now. "I won't be long. You take the bed."

The bathroom door closes behind him. I've been hoping to hear those words from him for a long time. Just in a different context.

Though I want to use the time alone in his room to be nosy, I still don't feel great, so I do as he says and slide under the navy-with-white-striped covers on his bed. His scent surrounds me as I listen to the shower run, imagining what he looks like naked with water cascading down the dips and valleys of his muscles.

That becomes too tedious because there's no point in getting myself all riled up when I can't do anything about it, so I close my eyes, hoping to fall asleep. I keep them closed when I hear the bathroom door open. It's only when I hear the creak of his weight on the couch that I open them.

His large frame is sprawled across the couch, head turned and looking at me.

"What are you doing over there?" I ask.

"This is where I'm sleeping."

I scowl and try to sit up, but the room blurs, and I return my head to the pillow. "Don't be ridiculous. Get in here."

He pins me with a stare, but I can't tell what's behind it.

"It's a queen-size bed. We won't even be sleeping next to each other."

He flops his body so he's on his back and staring at the ceiling, bringing his forearm to rest over his forehead. "I'm fine where I am."

"If you don't come sleep here, I'm going to leave and go back to my room." I make sure to inject steel into my tone, so he knows I'm serious. Although I'm sure he's not scared of me.

He must realize it, because with a sigh, he sits up from the couch and faces me. "Are you always this much of a pain in the ass?"

"According to you, yes."

He slides in under the covers on the other side of the bed. I lie there in darkness, listening to the sound of his breathing for a minute. The tension between us ratchets even higher. I feel as though I'm in tune with every micro movement he makes. I can almost *feel* the space between us in the inky black. We're not touching, and yet, the foot or so between our bodies feels as if it's connecting us.

"I'm sorry," I whisper into the dark room. "Thank you for making sure I was okay."

He shifts on the bed. "You're welcome."

"I just wanted to have fun. Sometimes I feel like I was locked up for so many years, people always watching every move I made." I roll over and tuck my hands under my pillow.

He's staring at the ceiling. "I know."

But he doesn't really know. Growing up as a boy in our world is the complete opposite. They're shown the world, taught to mature way before they're old enough, while we're sheltered, meant to be pure and innocent until we're handed off to someone to benefit the family.

"I know tonight doesn't mean anything, but I appreciate it. I won't make you regret it by reading into it."

He doesn't say anything. Eventually my eyelids grow too heavy, and I fall asleep.

CHAPTER TEN
GABRIELE

I rouse to consciousness slowly, so it takes me a moment to figure out that the weight of some*thing* on my chest is actually some*one*.

Cracking one eye open, I find Aria moved beyond the invisible barrier between our bodies and rolled on top of me. Her cheek is mashed into my bare chest, her long mocha hair splayed over my skin. When she shifts in her sleep, her knee inches up, and I realize that she also has her leg splayed over mine, and it's now too close for comfort to my morning wood.

Self-preservation tells me to push her off of me, but I allow myself the pleasure of feeling her body against mine while she's none the wiser. I catalog the rhythm of her breathing and how the silky strands of her thick hair feel on my skin. The warmth of her leg seeping into mine. Her small frame compared to my large one.

And then my morning wood hardens further, and I roll her off me in one swift moment.

She grumbles and turns so her back faces me but doesn't wake up. My T-shirt has risen up her body and her black thong is on display. Fucking great.

It takes herculean effort not to smack her perfect ass so that I can watch her olive skin turn pink.

Why did I ever think this was a good idea? Not only do I already know what her tits look like, thanks to Miami, but now I'll have her ass seared into my brain, too.

So many times since that night in Miami, I've stroked myself and that image came to mind. Her sprawled across that couch, about to let strangers do whatever they want to her.

My cock twitches in my boxer briefs.

"Fuck me," I murmur.

I turn and grab my phone from the nightstand to check the time. It's still early, which is good. I don't want anyone seeing her leave my room like this. They'll get the wrong impression. At least she wasn't sick again in the night, though it seems rousing her out of sleep and into what's sure to be a hangover will take some effort.

I set the phone back down and collapse onto my back, staring at the ceiling. Aria rolls over, and once again, she's splayed across from me, only this time her thigh rests directly over the hard ridge of my cock. A shuddering breath leaves my lips. I should push her off—immediately—but the weight of her feels too damn good.

I allow my arm to wrap around her and rest my hand on her head. Her hair is as thick and soft as I thought it would be all those times I imagined yanking it as I drove into her from behind. My dick twitches again at the thought, and Aria shifts further on top of me.

Push her off, you fucking idiot.

I grip her hair a little tighter, and a low moan sounds from Aria's throat. Her hips shift against the ridge of my cock, and my hand tightens further. She moans again, this time a little louder, and drives her hips a little deeper.

What are you thinking?

Her cheek shifts off my chest, and she turns her head, looking up at me as she shifts her hips again. She's not asleep.

Fuck me. I'll never forget that look in her eye—a mix of lust and yearning, need and desperation to give her what she wants.

So instead of pushing her off of me, I don't do anything.

Aria must see the acceptance in my eyes because she presses her hips harder and firmer, pushing up on my chest with her hands and sitting up, straddling me while she circles her core over my hard cock. We're separated by my boxer briefs and the thin scrap of fabric between her legs, but it doesn't matter. My cock grows stiffer with each swipe of her center overtop of it. Aria's top teeth bury into the pillowy expanse of her bottom lip, and her breath grows shallower while I do nothing but watch her.

Her eyes slide closed, and I use the opportunity to study her, memorize her, singe her into my memory. Thanks to Miami, I can assemble a decent picture in my mind of what she'd look like without my T-shirt and actually riding me, and it is fucking glorious.

Her breath hitches, and she moans. She must be close. God knows I am, which is beyond ridiculous. I'm not even inside her.

But watching her take what she wants from me—it stirs something inside me I didn't know I was capable of. I thought the only thing that really got me going was being in control, but with her . . . with Aria, it's different somehow.

With a final few jerks of her hips, she comes on a shuddering gasp. I fist my hands where I've kept them above my head the whole time to prevent myself from dipping them between her legs to see what she feels like coating my fingers. She opens her eyes and meets my gaze, and what I see there has me snapping to my senses—adoration. I take her by the waist and push her off of me.

"You need to go." I roll out of bed, keeping my back to her as I walk to my dresser and pull out a pair of athletic pants to conceal my throbbing erection.

When I turn back around, she's kneeling on the bed, mouth agape. And there it is, that hurt in her eyes—the same hurt I saw in Miami. Which is exactly why I need to shut this down. I'm only ever bound to hurt her. There's no way that we can be together.

"You need to go, Aria." My voice is firm.

Her hurt transforms into rage. It's in the set of her jaw, the flex of her fingers at her sides, the way her eyebrows draw down.

"It's still early. If you're careful, no one will see you. Take the stairs." Then I turn and walk into the bathroom, closing and locking the door behind me. I'm not sure if it's to keep her out or me in.

Only after I hear the door to my room close do I leave the bathroom.

She's left, gone, but the ghost of her will forever remain in these four walls.

*　*　*

I KNOW WHAT I have to do, if only to save me from myself.

I cannot stop thinking about Aria. About the look on her face when she came, about this insane need to protect her, about how persistent she can be. If it were directed at anything but me, I'd admire her tenacity.

And that's why I'm knocking on Marcelo's door after my Sunday phone call with my father.

Every Sunday, we're allowed one ten-minute phone call to the outside world on a secure line. Mine is always with my father so he can update me and let me know if there's anything I should be aware of back home.

Mirabella swings the door open, surprise registering on her face. "Gabriele. Hi."

"Hey, Mira. Is your fiancé here?"

She swings the door open wider, and Marcelo steps up behind her.

"I knew you'd come calling for that favor sooner or later," he says, clearly not happy.

"I'm not here for that. I'm actually here to do you a favor. Can we talk for a minute?"

He arches a brow but steps back and ushers me in. I walk past the two of them until I reach the center of the room, then turn to face them.

"What's this about?" Marcelo asks.

My gaze darts to Mira.

"Whatever you have to say you can say in front of Mirabella."

Usually, the women leave when two men need to discuss something, but I guess the rumors are true. Marcelo and Mira are changing the ways of Mafia relationships.

I nod. "It's about Aria."

The muscles in his jaw flex, and he crosses his arms. Mira slides a tad closer to him as he says, "Go on."

"Did you see her at the forest party last night?"

He shakes his head. "Who was she with?"

He's asking because she should have been with him and his crew.

"Bianca and Dom Accardi, some other first and second years I think."

Mira sends a concerned glance her fiancé's way. "Why would she have gone with them and not us?"

Marcelo doesn't answer, just looks at me expectantly.

I swallow hard, guilt seeping through my pores at what I'm about to do. It feels akin to cutting off a bird's wings. "Your sister was a mess. Trashed, high, too, I think. Figured you'd want to know what she was up to and who she was with."

I wouldn't have thought it possible, but Marcelo's jaw hardens even further. "For fuck's sake. What the hell is she thinking?"

"Marcelo—"

He whips around to face Mira. "No, Mirabella. She needs to get her shit together. This taste for adventure cannot continue." Then he turns back to me. "Is this going to cost me another favor?"

He's referring to when I helped him and Mira out last year and collected a favor from him in return, to be turned in for any request of mine whenever I want.

I shake my head. "Consider this a freebie. A token of goodwill between our families if you will."

He frowns. "What gives? You don't do anything without an ulterior motive."

I chuckle and move toward the door, the two of them staying where they are. When I have the door open, and I'm about to step out, Marcelo calls my name. I slowly turn back around.

"Thanks. I appreciate the heads-up," he says.

I nod and step out into the hall, feeling like a complete asshole. Aria is going to hate me, but she has to understand—I'm doing this for both our sakes.

CHAPTER ELEVEN
ARIA

"Cut the shit, Aria. I mean it." Marcelo glares at me from across my dorm room.

"How do you even know what I was up to last night?"

My brother showed up here a few minutes ago as judge and jury for my behavior last night, and he's making the headache that was already lingering thunderous.

"I have eyes and ears everywhere here."

I roll my eyes. "You're trying to sound like you're in a mob movie or something?"

He steps toward where I sit on the couch. "Mob movie? I'm the don of our family. You're my sister. Not only is it dangerous for you to be so out of your mind you can't watch out for yourself, but you represent our family. Hell, you represent me." He pokes himself in the chest with his thumb.

I sit up quickly and wince from the throbbing in my head. My brother smirks as though he enjoys seeing me pay the price for my fun last night.

"Why is it always about the family? When do I get to decide what I want for myself?"

He pinches the bridge of his nose. "Jesus Christ, I can't take two women like this in my life."

I assume he's talking about Mira. "I mean it, Marcelo. When does my life get to be about *me*?"

He drops his hand and looks at me with something akin to pity. "I know what it's like to be groomed your entire life to play your role in something bigger than you. You know I do. But this is our lot in life. It could be a lot worse. All I'm asking is for you not to take any unnecessary risks and remember that all your actions reflect on me. And if people see you acting out, they're going to question how strong I am, how much power I have, because if I can't keep my little sister in line, they assume I can't keep my men in line. And that's when people get killed."

I shudder at the reminder that our father was murdered in a car bombing. He wasn't the best human being on the planet, but he was still my father. And I can't imagine feeling responsible for Marcelo's death. I would never be able to live with myself—not to mention I'm not so sure who would take over the Costas.

So I nod. "Okay, I'm sorry. I'll do better."

He blows out a breath, and his shoulders sink. "Good."

We're both quiet when I ask, "Do you ever think about him?" I finger the locket hanging off my neck.

He shrugs. "You and I knew very different versions of him."

I suspected. I knew Marcelo was groomed, and he probably saw a version of my dad that I never did, but sometimes I wonder if Dad hadn't been murdered, what would our lives be like now? Would Marcelo have come to the academy and had a little more fun before having to take over his duty? Would I have a little more freedom here?

"He'd be saying the same thing to you," he says.

"I know. He'd just say it louder and with more curse words."

We share a laugh before he makes for the door.

"You didn't tell me how you knew about last night—and don't feed me some lame line again."

He turns to face me before he makes the turn into the short hallway that leads to the door. "Gabriele Vitale spotted you and could tell how wrecked you were. He did me a solid by telling me."

Anger ignites inside me. It was obvious he was shell-shocked after what happened in his bed this morning, but to sell me out to my brother? What an asshole!

"I'll be sure to thank him," I sneer because that's what my brother would expect from me.

"No, you won't. Stay away from Gabriele Vitale, you understand me?" His eyes narrow, and he pins me with a glare.

I huff. "Fine."

He nods, thinking I'll listen to his wishes, and leaves happy.

But I have no plans to stay away from Gabriele. At least not until after I give him a piece of my mind.

* * *

MY OPPORTUNITY COMES a couple days later when he's leaving the dining hall on his own after breakfast.

I'm quick to make an excuse that I have to ditch breakfast early because I forgot something in my room, and no one questions me or pays me much mind when I get up. Once I'm outside, I look both ways down the path and spot Gabriele to my left. I hurry to catch up with him.

"Gabriele!" I call.

He looks over his shoulder but keeps walking.

My molars grind to dust at his obvious dismissal. The sun is hot, and by the time I catch up to him, there's a thin sheen of perspiration on my face. He's just outside a set of double doors that lead back into the school when I tug on the arm of his dress shirt, forcing him to stop.

"What?" he snaps and whips around to face me.

I cross my arms. "You told my brother I was drunk and high? I knew you were an asshole, but I never took you for a rat."

There's a flash of something in his eyes that I can't decipher. "Why are you tracking me down like a bloodhound? I made it clear I'm not going to fuck you."

His voice is cold and devoid of emotion, and it only makes me more angry. "You won't fuck me, but you'll let me use you to get off and then tattle tale on me, is that it? What do you think my brother would do if he found out that I came all over your hard cock?"

He grips my upper arm. "Keep your voice down."

My eyes narrow. I don't know why I'm taunting him. But when I watch his nostrils flare, I get a sick satisfaction that I've affected him.

In a heartbeat, he has me pushed up against the brick wall, hand over my mouth as he towers over me with an expression of fury. He leans in close, his eyes filled with rage. "Careful, little girl. You don't know the beast you're riling up. Keep at it, and I might let it out of its cage."

He's trying to scare me, that much is obvious, but my body reacts as though he just told me he wants to fuck my brains out.

Our gazes lock for several moments, and there's so much swirling there in his eyes . . . I wish I had the code to know what it all means. In the time I've spent with him, it's clear to me that Gabriele's mind is rarely still. There's so much he thinks but doesn't say.

Eventually, he drops his hand from my mouth and steps back. "I know you don't want to hear this, but I'm actually doing you a favor keeping my distance."

I roll my eyes. "Whatever. You can pretend all you want, but I was in that bed, too. I know there's something between us, just as much as you do." He opens his mouth—to deny my words I'm sure, but I don't give him the opportunity. "Don't worry, Gabriele. This is the last you'll have to deal with me. You stay out of my business, and I'll stay out of yours."

I hike my bag up over my shoulder and head back the way I came, leaving my obsession for this man behind.

* * *

A COUPLE OF days later, I'm hanging in the lounge with Mira and Sofia after dinner to pass the time.

"You're pretty quiet tonight. Everything okay?" Sofia asks.

I shrug and slump back into the couch. "I wouldn't want to say anything that could be construed as fun."

Mira tilts her head and frowns. "He just worries about you."

"I know. But he can't actually expect me to have zero fun when I'm here, can he?"

"I'm sure he just wants to keep you safe," Sofia says, ever the peacemaker.

I turn my attention back to my future sister-in-law. "Can you talk to him? Get him to see reason?"

I don't relish putting her on the spot. I really like Mira, and I'm glad she's going to be marrying my brother. But if anyone has the best chance of changing his mind about something, it's her.

"I can, but I don't think it will do much good. Maybe just don't be so public about it next time."

I straighten in my seat. "Are you telling me to sneak around?"

She holds her hands up in front of her. "I'm not telling you anything. I'm saying I understand the need to push against the role this life has carved out for you. And if it were me . . . I'd make sure I'm safe, but anything I was doing that I thought might come back to reflect poorly on Marcelo . . . I might keep it on the down-low, that's all. Hypothetically speaking, of course."

"Of course," I say with a grin.

Sofia shakes her head. "Marcelo is going to be gray by the time he's thirty with the two of you."

Just then, Gabriele enters Roma House and makes his way across the lounge, but I refuse to watch him. In fact, I make a point of not even glancing in his direction. But it's hard. Really hard, in fact. Because for some inexplicable reason, that pull to him—even after he's been a complete hot and cold jackass—hasn't diminished.

Once he's safely in the elevator, I stand. "I need to go work on my homework."

"Me, too." Mira flops back into her seat with a sigh. "But I'm going to procrastinate a while longer until Marcelo gets back."

I don't know what my brother is doing and whether he's with Antonio since he's not here, nor do I care. "All right, I'll see you two later then."

I give them a small wave and head over to the elevator. I'm alone on the way up to my room, which gives me time to think. And as they have every day since Sunday morning, my thoughts drift to my time spent in Gabriele's bed.

How sweet I thought he was when I woke up and remembered how he'd taken care of me the night before—even if he was a jerk about it. Then my mind inevitably moves to me straddling him and the way his steel length felt between my legs. How big he is and the way he watched me with a predatory gleam.

And while I enjoyed having him let me do what I wanted while I was on top of him, my breath hitches when I think of the times he's had me pressed to a wall with my arms above my head. I . . . I liked it. A lot. I enjoyed the helplessness. It turned me on and made me want to please him. What the hell does that mean?

The ding of the elevator snaps me from my thoughts.

I'm pretty sure my face is flushed when I step out of the elevator. But before I can reach my room, Bianca's there.

"Hey," she says with a bright smile, though she looks a little startled, as though maybe she wasn't expecting to find me here.

I smile back. "Hey there."

"Just the woman I was looking for. I just knocked on your door."

"Really? What's up?"

"They're supposed to be doing bingo at Café Ambrosia on Friday night. Was going to see if you wanted to go."

"BINGO?" I almost laugh.

"I know it's kinda lame, but that's what the volunteers are running. I mean, it's not like there're that many options around here if there's not a party going on."

"True enough."

She shrugs. "Maybe they'll have cool prizes or something."

I chuckle. "Let's hope so. But yeah. That sounds like fun. Let's do it." I'm sure Marcelo will be happy I'm playing some senior citizen game.

"Awesome. I'll see if anyone else wants to join us."

I nod. "Sounds good. Where are you headed now?" I do have homework to do, but after the way my thoughts strayed in the elevator, maybe it's better not to be alone, to keep my head where it needs to be.

"Just back to my room. Want to hang out?"

"Sure, let me grab my stuff from my room. I have some homework I need to get done."

She smiles and walks toward the elevator again. "Cool. See you down there."

Something like relief fills me as I make my way back to my room. At least if I'm hanging out with Bianca, I won't be obsessing about Gabriele. I unlock my door and enter my room, going to my desk to get my things. But something catches my eye.

A manilla envelope is lying in the middle of the bed.

I stare at it for a beat, confused. Then I walk tentatively to it, as though it might leap up and attack me.

Where did it come from?

Maybe it's papers from the administration? But how did they get it in my room?

I look around. I don't know why. Instinct maybe? To check if whoever left the envelope is still here? Then I lift the envelope from the bed and slowly open it to pull out what looks like a single sheet of . . . oh, it's a photograph.

I frown, gently pulling it all the way out. My blood turns to ice in my veins, and the photo drops from my hand, fluttering to the floor and landing face up.

I run to the bathroom and, for the second time in a week, empty the contents of my stomach into the toilet.

CHAPTER TWELVE
GABRIELE

Aria hasn't spoken to me, hasn't looked at me since our altercation the other morning. Which is exactly what I wanted. Right?

So why does it feel so fucking terrible?

No matter, it's for the best. Soon she'll forget about me and find some other guy to be hung up on, as much as that pisses me off. It's the reality.

I've just finished changing out of my school uniform and into athletic pants and a T-shirt when there's a knock on my door. Alessandro mentioned he might come by when I saw him in the dining hall. But I'm unable to hide my shock when I swing open the door to find Aria.

She shoves past me into my room while I'm still recovering and trying to armor myself.

"Is this your idea of a threat?" she says behind me.

I close the door and spin around. She stands with fire in her eyes, holding up a manilla envelope.

"What are you talking about?" Within a few steps, I'm in front of her. It's like I can't resist the pull, even when she's pissed off. Hell, it might be stronger when she's mad.

"You're telling me this wasn't you? Who the hell else could it be?"

When I grip the top of the envelope, she grips it tighter. But on my second tug, she releases it. I open it and pull out what feels like a photograph, only I'm looking at the back of it, so I flip it over to see what she's so pissed off about. My stomach drops, and I look at Aria, who is staring at me. To judge my reaction, I assume.

"What the fuck?" I whisper.

Because I'm looking at a still shot of Aria in that club in Miami. Topless on the couch. That woman sucking on her neck and the man kneeling between her spread thighs. And then there's me, off to the side, standing in profile as though I'm directing the entire scene playing out on the couch.

I look back up at Aria, whose eyes are wide and full of distress.

She snatches the picture from me. "You mean you really didn't send me this?"

"Why the fuck would I send you that?" I push a hand through my hair and pace the room. This is bad. This is beyond bad.

"I don't know." I stop moving and look at her, her arms flailing. "As a message to keep my mouth shut about what happened between us in your bed? As a way to tell me that if I don't stay away from you, you'll let this get out?"

Anger, swift and fiery, fills my chest. "You really think I'd intentionally hurt you like that? Jesus, Aria. Everything I've done has been in an effort *not* to hurt you."

I clench my mouth shut. I'm saying way too much.

"Where did you get that?" I ask before she can respond.

"I came back to my room, and it was in the middle of my bed."

My eyes widen. "Someone broke in and left it in your room?"

She nods. "Who would do this?"

I glance again at the photo in her hands, but she shoves it back into the envelope.

"I don't know." I sit on the couch, elbows on my knees, hands in my hair, head facing down. "That was all that was in the envelope?"

"That's it."

With a sigh, I slump back in the seat. "Whoever it is definitely wants something. You don't leave something like that without having an end goal. The question is, who left it and what do they want? If I had to guess, I'd say they'll make their demands clear soon."

"So what? I'm supposed to sit around and wonder what the hell is going on? Not worry that someone is going to blow up my life at any moment?" Aria paces the room, one hand on her stomach as if she's about to be sick.

"Come here." I pat the space beside me on the couch.

She looks at it for a beat before sitting.

"We're going to figure this out. Whoever it is will not get away with this."

"Gabriele, if this gets out, my brother will kill me. And probably you."

I take her hand. It's instinct to offer her comfort. "We'll figure it out."

She shakes her head. "I can't be responsible for someone trying to overthrow my brother or kill him." Unshed tears line her eyes, and it's nearly impossible not to pull her into my chest, but I deny myself.

"That's not going to happen."

"How can you be so calm?" She rips her hands from mine. "Aren't you afraid of what will happen if this gets out?"

I push a hand through my hair again, my tell that I'm stressed. Because of course I am. This could very well start a war between our two families and upset the ever-fragile peace between all sectors of the Italian Mafia.

It won't matter that I showed up there to help Aria. That picture makes it look as if I'm a willing participant. It would be one thing altogether for Marcelo to hear that I'd slept with his sister, but it'd be another entirely to think that I dragged her to a sex club to do deplorable things in front of strangers.

"Of course I don't want this to get out. That goes without saying."

"So you'll help me figure this out?"

Of course, just when I've managed to untangle myself from everything having to do with Aria Costa, somehow I'm yanked back into the spider's web. "You have my word."

She visibly relaxes, knowing that in our life, word is bond.

My chest might broaden if I let my ego think about the confidence she clearly has that I can get to the bottom of this. But without all my gear, it'll be difficult. I'm going to have to make a greater effort to find a weak spot to smuggle my computer shit into this place.

"Thank you." Her voice is soft and a little tentative. "Where do we start?"

"Let's start with the obvious. Did you see anyone leaving your room, hanging around, or acting weird? Do you still have your key on you?"

She nods. "I have my key. And no, I didn't see anyone like that. When I left the lounge and came up, I ran into Bianca Accardi in the hall, and we made plans for Friday and—shit, that reminds me. I have to text her and tell her that I won't be coming by her room."

She leans forward and pulls her school-issued phone from the back pocket of her jeans, quickly typing out a message.

"What are you going to tell her?"

She shrugs. "I said that dinner upset my stomach so I'm not going to be able to make it." Aria slides the phone back into her pocket.

"What was Bianca doing on your floor? Her room is on the second floor." When she arches an eyebrow, I add, "I make it my business to know where everyone's room is."

"She said she'd come from my room. Came to invite me to Café Ambrosia on Friday night."

"Do you believe her?"

Her forehead wrinkles. "Of course I do. What? You think she's the one who planted the envelope?"

"I wouldn't put it past her. The Accardis are known for their hunger for power."

She shakes her head. "I don't think so."

"Why not?"

"I don't know. I just don't. My gut is telling me that it's not her."

"Well, your gut could be wrong." My voice is snippy, but seriously, has she not yet realized that she always has to have her guard up?

She crosses her arms. "Is this what it's going to be like this whole time? You telling me who should and shouldn't be a suspect?"

I sigh and let the Bianca thing rest. I'll do some digging into her on my own. As soon as I get some of my fucking computer equipment here. "Who invited you to the club in Miami? Did you ever find out? Did they ever make themselves known?"

She shakes her head.

"Is that the same kind of envelope that the invite came in?" I ask.

"No. That one was in a classy black envelope. Very formal."

"You don't still have it, do you?" I'm sure the answer will be no, but I have to ask the question anyway. When she hesitates, I tilt my head. "What?"

"I kept it." She lets her hands fall in her lap and looks at them.

"Shit, that's great news, Aria. Why do you look like it's a bad thing?"

"It's nothing." She stands from the couch. "Want me to go get it?"

"Yeah, there's a good chance whoever sent it is the same person who sent this picture. They probably lured you there for the express reason of getting this picture."

Her face crumples. "So I walked into a trap? Like the naïve little girl you said I was would."

I frown, wanting to disagree with her, but she's not wrong. This wasn't what I had in mind exactly—I thought someone had lured her there so they could kidnap her for ransom or kill her outright and send a message.

So rather than try to comfort her and tell her that no, she didn't walk into a trap, I stand from the couch. "I'll come with you."

That draws her from her thoughts. "Why?"

"Because someone got into your room. Who knows what else they did there? I want to make sure there're no bugs or cameras anywhere."

"I don't need you for that," she snipes.

I cross my arms. She's back to being her usual self. "Do you know what to look for? Where to look?"

"No," she says in a snotty tone.

I walk toward the door. "Exactly."

"Fine." She stomps toward me.

If the situation weren't what it was, I'd reflect on how cute she looks.

"You take the elevator and I'll take the stairs. Leave your door unlocked so I can slip in quickly."

She nods and pushes past me without a word, cracking the door open to check the hall before she slips out.

Obviously she's not over everything I said to her.

It's then I realize that she's left the manila envelope on my coffee table.

She may not like me, but apparently she trusts me.

CHAPTER THIRTEEN
ARIA

I step into my room, and for the first time since I've been here, I don't feel comfortable. I feel violated.

Someone was in my private space doing God knows what. Were they here for a long time? A short time? Did they look around, or did they drop the envelope on the bed and make a run for it?

The little hairs on the back of my neck stand on end. When the sound of the door opening behind me registers, I whip around to find Gabriele entering, an intense expression on his face as he surveys my living quarters. It's not until this moment that I realize that he's going to be looking through all my things. Awesome.

I guess it's no more embarrassing than the topless photo of me he was looking at.

"Anything seem out of place now that you're looking at it through a different lens?" he asks.

I shake my head and walk over to the desk to grab the invitation. I'm glad he didn't ask why I kept it. It was supposed to serve as a reminder of what a bastard he could be—with his little speech in the car—but instead every time I pulled it out, all I could think of was how he'd come for me. Thought I was in trouble and came to pull me out of it. Who does that for someone they care nothing about?

I open the bottom drawer of the desk, where I keep the invitation, dig to the back of the drawer, and . . . nothing.

"It's gone." I whip back and look at Gabriele. His face is set in a stern expression. I scour the drawer—notebooks and school supplies. Some books I'd planned on reading this semester. No black envelope. I settle back on my heels, shoulders sagging. "It's not in there."

"Obviously whoever it was didn't want you examining it any closer. Damn it."

I push myself off the floor and stand in front of him. "What do we do now?"

"First thing we have to do is make sure there's no surveillance in this room. Who knows what else they did."

I nod numbly, wondering if I'll ever feel comfortable in this room again.

Gabriele grips my upper arms. "You go sit on the couch and relax while I do this. It's going to take a while for me to do a thorough job."

I manage a small smile, walk over to the couch, and settle in.

"I'm going to start in the bathroom."

A long shiver runs down my spine at the thought of someone putting a secret camera in there. I hear the sounds of Gabriele opening and closing drawers, shifting things around, and I curse myself for making the decision to follow adventure that night in Miami. If only I hadn't let myself get so butt-hurt about what he'd said to me, maybe I wouldn't have been so desperate to prove I didn't care.

Eventually, he emerges and heads over to my dresser.

"Find anything in there?" I ask.

He shakes his head as he opens the first drawer. "Nothing."

As he's pulling out some sweaters I brought for later this year, I ask, "Would someone really put something in a drawer? Doesn't that defeat the purpose?"

"Bugs these days are small and can pick up sound quite easily. You'd be surprised what they can hear even from a closed drawer."

I finger the necklace around my neck, thumbing the locket.

He moves from one drawer to the next until he reaches my underwear drawer, where he pauses. I watch him swallow hard but continue to go through it. Even given the circumstances, it's hard to watch him thumb through my lace thongs without being turned on by them. I've imagined him bringing them up to his nose and sniffing or pulling them down my legs.

I'm deep in thought, trying to think of anything other than the direction my mind is heading, when I realize too late that he's opening the bottom drawer of my nightstand.

"Wait!"

But I'm too late. He is already staring into the drawer, mouth open. He licks his bottom lip. My cheeks heat, but I force myself to bring my chin up to appear unaffected.

"Quite the collection." He pulls out my favorite vibrator—the unicorn cock. And a magical unicorn it is, because no man—not that I've had many—has ever made me come with his cock the way that thing has.

"I'm not ashamed of it if that's what you're trying to do."

He looks me in the eye. "I don't think it's shameful. I think it's fucking hot when a woman knows what she wants, knows what brings her pleasure, and isn't afraid to seek it out."

I want to call bullshit on the statement because it certainly doesn't seem that way, at least when it comes to me, but I keep my mouth shut, more concerned about whether someone is listening in or watching us. "Can you finish up what you're doing?"

Without another word, he returns the vibrator to the drawer.

Gabriele methodically goes through the rest of my room, taking hours to do so, and by the time he's finished, he's confident that if something were here, he would have found it.

"You're sure?" I warily ask again.

"You're safe, at least in that regard."

His words don't exactly fill me with a warm, fuzzy feeling.

"What is it?" He steps up to me, resting a hand on my shoulder and looking down at me with a furrow in his brow.

"It's just . . . this means that someone at this school has it out for me. That's the only explanation for how that photograph got in my room."

He frowns for a beat. "True. But I don't think they're out to hurt you. Not yet anyway."

I scoff. "Great, that makes me feel so much better."

"Listen, whoever it is they're going to contact you at some point. They want something, and they're going to let you know what it is. When that happens, you need to let me know right away. We'll go from there."

"So we do nothing until then?" My eyes fill with unshed tears.

"No, I want you to be vigilant about watching your surroundings. Is anyone paying more attention to you than normal? Did anyone say something odd? I'm going to work on getting some of my equipment here. It will help with tracking down whoever this is."

I nod, pressing my top teeth into my bottom lip.

"We're going to figure this out, okay?" He bends down so that we're eye to eye.

I nod.

"Okay?"

Looking into his deep hazel eyes, I almost believe him. "Okay." My voice sounds small.

"If anything happens, let me know right away, okay?"

I nod.

"What do you want me to do with the photograph?" His gaze flits up and down my body as if he's remembering me topless in it.

I decide to lighten the mood, having had enough of all this seriousness. "Keep it, destroy it. I don't care. I thought maybe you'd want it in case something about it could lead back to whoever's doing this. But don't be a perv and beat off to it or something."

Gabriele takes my lead and lets his mood shift, too. He grins. "No promises."

Then he leaves. I stand, staring after him for the space of a minute because I've never seen him smile like that. It actually reached his eyes.

The result was stunning.

I wish I could see more of his smiles rather than all his scowls.

CHAPTER FOURTEEN
GABRIELE

The next morning, I skip breakfast and head to security in an effort to suss out who might be the person to aid me in getting some of my computer shit in here. I may have lost my contact, but everyone has either a price or a vice.

I rub my eyes before I head through the door that leads to the security office. I'm exhausted. My insomnia was worse than normal last night—mostly because I kept replaying the moment I opened that drawer full of Aria's toys. There was something sexy as hell about the way she owned it. Didn't make excuses or act shy about the fact that she enjoys pleasuring herself.

What I wouldn't do to see her with that unicorn cock vibrator.

I shake my head and adjust myself in my dress pants before I push through the door.

"Can I help you?" the woman in uniform behind the main desk asks me.

"Morning. I was wondering if I could talk to Scott?"

Scott was the guy with the gambling problem who helped me out last year. I already know he's not here, but it's as good of a lead-in as any.

The corners of her lips tug down a bit. "Scott is no longer employed here. Is there something I can help you with?" Her tone suggests that she wants to do anything other than help me.

"Not sure. Scott used to provide me with some . . . assistance. Maybe you're able to do the same?" I arch an eyebrow.

Her judgmental gaze flits up and down me. "Pretty sure I won't be able to assist you in any way. I need this job."

The woman's voice is full of censure, and I have to fight back the part of me that wants to exert my will over her and force her to do what I want, the way I might in the real world if it came down to it.

"I see. Maybe there's someone else I can talk to that would be of more help."

She leans over her desk. "There's not."

I'll give it to her. This woman has a backbone. Little does she know I enjoy breaking them. But that will get me nowhere here.

I nod and turn to leave. I've got to figure out an in with this department.

When I pull open the door to leave the security office, a middle-aged woman is about to walk in. She startles and steps back, motioning for me to leave first. Something about her demeanor tells me that this woman has been through some shit. Her hair isn't as polished as most of the other women who work here, and her roots are growing in. There are bags under her eyes, and she has a general world-weary appearance.

I don't spare her any further mind as I walk past her, already considering my next move. Because I'm not going to give up that easily. Not when there's any kind of threat to Aria.

She puts on a brave face, but she's scared. That much I could tell. Though she seems more worried about what this will mean for her brother if it gets out than she is for herself.

Once again, my protective instincts roar to life where she's concerned. I will get to the bottom of this and eliminate the threat to her.

If only I could figure out how.

***

IT COMES TO me in the middle of my stock manipulation class. I'm barely paying attention because I'm worlds ahead of the shit this professor is trying to teach us, though no one knows it yet.

While I was letting my mind wander about the best way to get an in at security, I realized that what I need is information. Information I can't ask my father to gather for me without involving him in my business. But this is exactly why I collect information and in turn, ask favors for divulging that information.

And Antonio La Rosa owes me two favors.

Last year was challenging for him at the Sicuro Academy, between his sister and his now-wife, and he came to me twice to get him out of a jam. The time has come to collect one of those favors.

It's late in the evening when I knock on Antonio's dorm room door. He shares the room with Sofia now that they're married. This is his last year at the academy, as it is mine, and I have no doubt that next year, Sofia will not be attending. She'll stay with Antonio in Miami to start their life. From all I know about her, she's looking forward to being a Mafia wife in the truest sense.

The door swings open and Antonio stands shirtless and wearing a pair of dark navy sleep pants. His forehead wrinkles when he sees me. "Vitale . . . what's up?"

"Time for me to call in one of your favors."

His face drops, going blank, as he probably wonders what the hell I want, and knowing he can't refuse. Lucky for him, this one is easy as fuck. If I had any other choice, I wouldn't use it to scratch a favor, but time is of the essence.

"Aren't you going to invite me in?" I arch an eyebrow.

He opens the door wider and motions for me to come in.

I look around the room, surprised to find it empty. "No Sofia?" I casually shove my hands in my pockets and turn around to face him.

"She's with my sister. Cut to the chase. What do you need?"

This is always my favorite part—when I have them on the edge, waiting to hear my demands. The control is addicting as fuck, and I find myself slowing the process because of my enjoyment.

"I need to find a way to get all my computer stuff onto campus. My previous contact is no longer available. What I want from you is information. Have your people dig up everything they can on the staff here, especially the people who work in security. I need to find a weakness I can exploit."

He blinks a few times, looking surprised. "That's it?"

I nod. "That's it."

"Why wouldn't you ask your dad to have someone do it on your call this weekend?"

"That's none of your concern."

He holds my gaze for a beat, likely wanting to challenge me but knowing I'm right. He wouldn't offer up any additional information that might make him vulnerable down the road either.

"And when I do this, we're square? One of the favors I owe you is eliminated?"

"Correct."

He nods. "Consider it done then. I hate having those favors hanging over my head."

I smirk. "I'm sure you do. But I'm also sure you'd say it was worth it given that your sister and your wife are still breathing." Pulling my hands from my pockets, I brush past him to the door. "Don't take too long."

Without another word, I leave the room and head for the elevator. I punch the button and wait, noticing a colorful poster that's been tacked to the bulletin board on the wall beside the elevators.

The War Games.

I hadn't given them any thought, forgetting they were next weekend. They're an annual tradition here, and each house has their own version. All the Italian families from the Roma House will compete next weekend on four separate teams—one for each of the four quadrants with the highest-ranking member of each family acting as the leader. In essence, myself, Marcelo Costa, Antonio La Rosa, and Dante Accardi are all competing for bragging rights.

I've never given much of a shit whether I win or not. In the end, it doesn't mean anything tangible. But the idea of Aria watching me lose fires up some competitive streak inside me. Maybe I'll actually try this year.

The elevator dings, and I shake my head, stepping in.

I have to keep reminding myself that it doesn't matter what Aria thinks of me. I'm only helping her because I have something to lose, too, if that picture is leaked.

CHAPTER FIFTEEN

ARIA

By the time Friday rolls around, I'm thoroughly creeped out and questioning everyone who looks at or talks to me. Could they be the person who left me the picture?

I'm even uncomfortable being in my room. Sure, Gabriele went over the place thoroughly, but without whatever machine he and every other Mafia guy I know uses to detect bugs, can he really be sure?

I try to push all of that aside as I step into Café Ambrosia to meet Bianca. It's Friday night, and all I want is to be a normal academy student. Bingo sounds fun, and I've never actually played before, so I'm sure it will be a good time.

Bianca smiles and waves at me, and I can't help but wonder whether she's befriending me as part of some bigger ploy. We don't come from the same family after all, and while it's not unheard of for members of different families to be friendly while at the academy, being friends is something else entirely.

But rather than keep my distance, I decide to lean in. Bianca and the Accardis in general are the only real lead I have, and I need to explore it fully before ruling them out.

I sit across from her, and Bianca pushes a red bingo card over to me. "I grabbed you one from the front."

I look over and see two students onstage passing them out to participants. One is from the Accardi family, and the other is from the Vitale family. They must be two of the student volunteers assigned to run activities at the café this semester.

"Thanks." I smile at her. "Have you played before?"

She shakes her head.

"Me either."

"Hopefully that means we'll have beginner's luck."

I chuckle. "Here's hoping."

She leans in. "I heard that one of the prizes they're giving away is a day pass off of campus."

My eyes widen because I can't even believe they would do that. "Really?"

"Apparently the administration okayed it as long as a chaperone accompanies them."

"Them?" I tilt my head.

"Winner gets to bring a friend. Promise I'll bring you if I win."

A warm feeling invades my chest, even though I'm supposed to be suspicious of Bianca. "Aw, thanks."

"I want to win so badly. Can you imagine getting out into the world, even if it's for a short time? Even if it's in the middle of nowhere?"

I consider that Bianca might be like me. Up until now, she hasn't had a chance to live her life and discover who she really is. She's eager to get out in the world, but my brother did strike a chord with me the other day, and the last thing I want is something to happen to him or our family.

"It would be pretty cool." I push back my chair. "I think I'm going to get a drink before we start. Do you want anything?"

She shakes her head. "I'm okay."

"Be right back."

By the time I'm back with my latte, Dom is seated in one of the free chairs at our table. He's studying his bingo card as I approach, and when I pull my chair back out to sit, he looks up.

"Hey. Hope you don't mind me joining. Bianca mentioned that you two were going to get your old lady on tonight."

I chuckle and sit, though I'm wondering whether that's true. Maybe he's here because he's behind the picture, and he wants to throw me off by acting like my friend.

I hate this. Used to be that I took everyone at face value, but now I'm questioning everyone who interacts with me.

"Bingo's not for old ladies anymore. We're going to make it cool, right, Aria?"

I nod and laugh. "Right. Besides, we both want to win a day off campus."

His eyebrows slant down. "What?"

Bianca and I explain the rumor she heard.

When we're done, Dom leans back in his chair. "Guess I'm here for more than the view then." He looks directly at me when he says it, and I feel my cheeks heat.

Bianca puts her finger in her mouth and makes a gagging sound. "Give it a rest, cuz. Stop trying to charm our new friend."

He shrugs and gives me a smile. "I can't help it. I have natural charm."

"Yeah, well, Aria is not a conquest to be had, so back off." Bianca narrows her eyes at her cousin.

"No, she's much more than that."

I want to believe Bianca's being a good friend and looking out for me, I do. But maybe this is some preconceived plan they have in place. They're working together.

Jesus, Gabriele has made me paranoid.

Thankfully, I'm saved from having to respond to Dom's obvious come-on when the girl onstage welcomes everyone to bingo and explains the rules of play.

* * *

AN HOUR AND a half later, it's time to start the final round for the grand prize. Bianca was right. They announce they're giving away a day pass to leave campus.

The room goes crazy. The energy in the room is electric, everyone eager to win this one.

So far, neither Bianca, Dom, nor I have won anything, but that's okay. This is the only one I want to win. Throughout the evening, daydreams of me winning and taking Gabriele with me off campus for some fun have been running through my mind, but that's ridiculous.

He may be helping me, but that's only because he has as much, maybe more, to lose if that picture gets out. It's not because he has any kind of feelings for me, even if I get the vibe that he is at least physically attracted to me.

"All right, guys. Think good juju so one of us will win this one," Bianca says, kissing her marker and holding it ready to dot the boxes.

Dom rolls his eyes. "You and your juju bullshit."

"Hey!" She smacks his arm. "It's not bullshit."

I shush them. "It's about to start."

I'm not usually a competitive person, but I really want to win this. I need a win this week.

The girl onstage calls out the numbers. I have all five of the first numbers but then don't have the next two. This game is a full card game, meaning every number on my card has to be called to win.

She continues calling out the letter-number combos, and a quick glance at Dom's and Bianca's cards tells me I'm doing better than them. Excitement bubbles in my stomach, and I wiggle in my chair.

"Holy shit, Aria. You're close," Bianca says, peering over.

I nod, not taking my eyes off my bingo card for fear I'll miss her calling one of the numbers on my card. That is, until the back of my neck tingles with the sensation of being watched. I look over my shoulder to figure out who it might be. Is it the person who left the picture?

But I'm met with Gabriele's blank stare as he grabs something to drink. He's impossible to read. I can't tell if he's pissed, curious, or nothing at all.

The feeling of someone squeezing my hand has me turning back around.

Dom has his hand over mine, and his other one is pointing at my card. "She called B-six. Mark it off on your card."

I blink rapidly then do what he says, returning my attention to the game. I have two more empty spaces to go. The next one she calls I have. I grow antsy in my chair, my heart leaping. A quick glance around, and there's a table in the back cheering on a guy who I assume is close to winning, too.

Bianca and Dom get up from their seats, leaving their cards where they are since they have at least half of their cards to fill still, and crowd behind my chair. As if I don't already know by heart what I need.

The next one she calls I don't have, and I look at the guy in the corner. He shakes his head to his tablemates. Our eyes meet for a moment before she calls the next number.

"G-sixty," she announces, and I barely mark the box before my chair pushes back, and I stand.

"BINGO!" I shout, holding my card over my head.

Everyone else in the room groans, but Bianca and Dom jump up and down, cheering with me. They each draw me into a hug.

When I pull away from Dom, I spot Gabriele by the exit, watching us, eyes narrowed, right before he turns and leaves. Just like that, my excitement wanes slightly.

CHAPTER SIXTEEN

GABRIELE

Sunday night, I'm leaving the dining hall after dinner with Sandro when Antonio follows us out.

"Gabriele, wait."

I turn to face him.

"Can we talk?" Antonio eyes Alessandro, who looks at me.

I nod at Sandro. "Give us a minute."

His lips form a thin line, but he reluctantly nods. "I'll see you back at the Roma House."

Once he's far enough away that he won't overhear us, I tip my chin up at Antonio. "What's up?"

"I have some information for you."

I cross my arms. "That was fast. Let's hear it."

"I took the first call this morning and had Sofia take the last one so she could use it to see if they'd been able to gather any information. I'm sure you know how little time that takes when you know what you're looking for."

I nod. "Thank Sofia for me for wasting her call."

"She did it for me. She doesn't like me being beholden to you any more than I do."

I smirk. What it must be like to have someone on your side like Sofia is to Antonio and Mira is to Marcelo. It's not something I've ever wanted. Sure, I'll be arranged at some point, but other than having an heir, I won't have to interact with my wife. But these two couples are really making an honest and truthful relationship in our world. Seems unreal.

"What'd you find out?" I ask.

"Your best bet is Rachel Proctor. Works in security. Only been with the school for, like, six months or something. Single mom of three. Husband doesn't pay child support. One of her kids has a chronic illness that requires a lot of care. Probably took the job here because it pays better than most. From what my guys were able to find, she's squeaky clean. No arrests, no priors, not so much as a speeding ticket."

"Good work."

He nods. "My guys are going to mail all the info to the school for me. Hopefully it makes it through, but since it's papers, it shouldn't flag anything. Figured you'd want that in case you can't figure things out with this Rachel."

"Great, thanks. Pass it on when you have it."

"Will do. So we're even now?" He arches an eyebrow.

"We're not even, but you can cross one favor off your list."

He smiles. "It was worth a shot."

As he heads back into the dining hall, I chuckle and walk along the path.

Good. This is good. Now I have a weakness I can exploit. I've been going stir-crazy all weekend with nothing to do. Usually I'd be gathering intel on my classmates or working on my secret project, trying to figure out if it'll make us money. But since I don't have my equipment, I've spent the weekend replaying over and over in my head the look on Dom's face when he was hugging Aria at the café.

Is she into him?

And if she is, I have no reason to care. I turned her away.

You know why.

I've managed to steer clear of her since I saw her on Friday, but it's inevitable that I'll see and speak with her again. I need to be over this constant yearning for her before I do.

I walk into the Roma House. Rather than wait at the elevators with everyone else who's returning from dinner, I opt to take the stairs. When I push out of the stairway doors on the fourth floor, I come to a stop as though my feet are stuck in quicksand.

Aria's standing outside my door.

There's no one else in the hallway, thank God. The last thing I need is rumors circulating about the two of us. Hell, I don't want anything tying us together. That's the whole point of me helping her.

"What are you doing here?" I ask as I stalk over to her, fishing my key out of my pocket.

When I reach my door, I quickly unlock it and pull her in right before me, then I look both ways for any prying eyes.

"We can't be seen together, Aria." My voice is full of censure.

I've irritated her, by the way her eyes narrow ever so slightly. "You told me to come to you if something came up."

"And?" I arch an eyebrow.

Aria's wearing jeans and she reaches into her back pocket and pulls out a cell phone. It's not the student-issued one either. It's a burner phone. "I was about to head out to dinner when I heard something beeping in my bag. Turns out it was this."

I take it and open it. There's only one message, and I'm sure if I tried to trace the number, I'd come up empty. It's likely another burner phone that's texting her. I open the message and read:

YOUR FATHER HAD SOMETHING OF MINE. IF YOU DON'T WANT THAT PRETTY PICTURE OF YOU BEING LEAKED THEN YOU'LL FIND IT. AWAIT FURTHER INSTRUCTIONS.

I frown at the screen. At least now we know for sure that someone wants something—the question is who and what.

"Well . . ."

I glance up at the sound of Aria's voice. She's looking at me with wide, concerned eyes and biting her bottom lip. Her long, dark hair is styled in a braid that hangs down over one shoulder. What I wouldn't give to wrap it around my hand and use it as leverage.

"It's bad, right?"

Once again, her voice draws me from my thoughts.

"It's what we figured. Did your dad ever say anything to you that makes this make sense?"

She shakes her head. "My dad never talked about business with me. Only Marcelo. Why would they send this to me? My brother is the one who this would make sense to."

"Because you're the easier mark." I read the message on the phone again, and when she doesn't say anything, I look back up at her to find her scowling. "It's true, Aria, and you know it."

She huffs out a frustrated breath and crosses her arms, which only pushes her tits up more past the edge of her white tank top. "Well then, why wouldn't they at least tell me what the hell it is they want me to find? I mean, it could be anything."

That's the more puzzling part. "My guess would be to frighten you. Make you more likely to cooperate when the time comes."

She thinks about that for a minute.

"Did your dad leave anything to you when he passed away?"

Again, she shakes her head. "Besides daddy issues, no."

I frown. I can't imagine having Sam Costa as her father was easy. His reputation as a fiery, womanizing sleaze preceded him.

"Then we'll have to wait until they contact you again. In the meantime, keep that phone on you but out of sight. They'll reach out soon enough. They've gone to all this effort, so whatever it is they want, it's important to them."

"Okay." She nods fast.

I put my hands on her shoulders and stare into her eyes. I know the answer before I ask the question. "You all right?"

She bites her lower lip. The one I'd do about anything to suck. "I'm scared. What if I can't find what they're looking for?"

I squeeze her shoulders. "One thing at a time. Let's see what it is that they want you to find first, okay?"

She nods, but none of the tension leaves her shoulders.

"I'm not going to let anyone hurt you, got it?" I lower my head so that our eyes meet.

"Okay." Her voice is soft and breathy, but there's fear all over her pale cheeks. This has shaken her.

"Now, how do you think someone got the phone in your backpack?"

"I don't know. I've been thinking it must've happened either in one of my classes or at the café right after school."

I let my hands drop from her shoulders, getting too comfortable having them there. "Did you leave your bag with anyone else or by itself?"

She worries her lips. If I weren't so annoyed with what is obviously a yes, I'd probably think it was cute.

"Seriously?"

She throws her hands up at her sides. "What? I can't keep an eye on the stupid thing twenty-four seven."

I blow out a breath and push my hand through my hair. "Jesus. Okay, well . . . what's done is done. Try to be more observant from now on, okay?"

Aria nods. "Yeah, okay."

"Let me know if anything else happens." I walk toward the door in order to show her out, making it obvious that I want her to leave.

Not want really, more like *need*. Before I do something stupid again.

"Next time, don't rip my head off if I do." She follows me.

"We can't be seen together. You know that."

She does this cute little pout thing with her lips.

"Text me next time, and we can figure out when and where it's safe to meet up."

She doesn't argue, much to my surprise.

"Don't leave me unread." She breezes past me and leaves without bothering to check whether anyone is in the hall.

I don't know why I'm even surprised. She challenges me at every turn.

CHAPTER SEVENTEEN
ARIA

It's the morning of the War Games for the Roma House, and everyone is buzzing about which family will win. Not only is it a small bit of excitement in our regular lives, but this evening, there's a Vegas Night event being held in the gymnasium.

It used to be that the girls could choose to either put their names in the hat to be picked to participate in the War Games, or they could help prepare the feast for afterward. But that's changed as of this year. Mira did a lot of campaigning, and now the usual staff in the dining hall will be preparing the meal, and the girls are free to participate or cheer on the participants.

Going in, I'm pretty sure I know who each of the guys will pick. My brother will pick Mira. To everyone's astonishment, he picked her last year—the first time that had ever been done—and they won. Antonio will pick his best friend, Tomasso, because Sofia likely has no interest in doing an event that's pretty much a Spartan race. Dante could pick his best friend, but I think he'll choose his brother, Dom, based on what Dom was saying earlier this week. And Gabriele will choose his cousin, Sandro.

I'm right on all counts.

Once the selection is complete, the guys and their seconds stand onstage while Chancellor Thompson explains how the event will work. "Our events team has been hard at work and has changed up the stations again this year. Participants will have to contend with a rope climb, an A-frame cargo climb, a slackline, and a mud pit, among other things. I'll remind everyone that you're welcome to cheer on your favorite team, but no unsportsmanlike behavior will be tolerated."

We all know that we're each going to be cheering on our own family, though a part of me wants to also cheer on Gabriele. Still, my loyalty lies with the Costas, and that's who I want to win.

Once the chancellor is finished with his speech, the participants make their way to the starting line while the spectators head to whatever station they want to find for the best view of the course. I decide to stay near the start. After the starting pistol is fired, I'll go sit on the hill because it gives me a decent overall view of the course.

Everyone lines up and are shit-talking each other about how they're gonna kick the other's ass. Dante has the biggest mouth.

"Go, Mira!" I shout with my hands around my mouth.

She looks at me and gives me a thumbs-up and a smile. When she turns back to look at the course, she gets an intense expression on her face, and it's clear to me how she and my brother won last year.

My gaze heads to the end of the line where Gabriele is, and I find him already looking at me. Our eyes meet and hold before his cousin grips his shoulder and says something, stealing his attention away from me. Gabriele nods, agreeing with whatever it is.

Then the chancellor counts down the start of the race with the starting pistol raised. A shot rings out, and they're off.

The first event is the barbed wire crawl—probably because it forces everyone into the mud, thereby making the rest of the race more difficult and unenjoyable.

The first people through are Dante and Dom, followed by Marcelo and Mira, then Gabriele and Sandro, and finally Antonio and Tomasso. Everyone watching is yelling and screaming, rooting for their favorite team. I'm one of the few sitting on the hill overlooking the raceway.

As the race goes on, who's in first changes many times over. It's a tight race, and no one team is dominating, so I'm not sure who might win. They all reach the final event—the Olympus wall. It's a ten-foot wood wall they have to climb with only small holes or chains as the holds. It's neck and neck when they reach the wall, and since I'm on the back end of it, I can't see who's making the best progress until they pop up on top of it.

Disappointment flares in my chest when Dante's first to crest the top, not my brother or Gabriele. He reaches down, presumably to help his brother up, and Dom climbs over the wall. Gabriele is right behind them, then my brother.

I stop paying attention to everyone else and watch as Gabriele's and Dante's teams make it back onto the ground. But Sandro lands funny off the wall and falters before he stands back up, costing them time.

Dante and Dom race ahead to the finish line and cross it first, Gabriele and Alessandro a close second. Dante and Dom are immediately surrounded by a swarm of people, including Bianca, but my attention diverts to Gabriele. I'm surprised to find that he actually doesn't seem upset that they came in second, while Alessandro is clearly enraged.

I stand, brushing off my butt, then make my way down the hill toward the celebration. Though I want to go over and talk to Gabriele, I can't, so I head toward my brother and Mira. They're both covered in mud, so I don't hug them or anything, but I do tell them they did a great job.

Marcelo doesn't say much, and Mira gives me a wan smile. They're clearly disappointed in the result. Especially since they kicked ass last year, from what I heard.

"I guess I'll see you guys later at Vegas Night after you clean up?" I say.

Mira's gaze darts over to my brother, who's now talking to Nicolo, Andrea, and Giovanni. "I'm not sure if we'll make it. He's going to be in a mood all night, and I may have to . . . make him feel better."

I pretend to choke. "Please don't elaborate on that."

She laughs. "You're going to go, though, right?"

I nod, though I don't know who I'll tag along with now. I could always force myself on my brother's friends, and they'd let me tag along, or I could see what Sofia and Antonio are doing, but neither of those options sound fun. I'd be a third wheel with Sofia and Antonio, and I'd cramp the guys' style, even if they'd never say so because of who my brother is.

I spot Bianca over Mira's shoulder. Maybe I'll go see if she plans to attend. I do still want to make sure the Accardi family isn't behind the photograph.

"Well, you two have fun doing whatever it is you're going to do. I'll catch you later," I say before walking away.

I walk in Bianca's direction, but before I reach her, Dom steps into my path. "Hey, Aria, aren't you going to give me a congratulatory hug?" With a big smile, he holds his hands out at his sides.

I rear back. "Not likely. Who knows what's in that mud?" We both laugh. "Congratulations, though."

"Thanks. What are you doing later?" he asks.

I shrug. "Thought I might check out the Vegas Night thing. You?"

"Same. Want to head there together?" He arches an eyebrow.

I'm not sure what to say. I like Dom, but I'm not into him in that way. I know nothing's going to happen between Gabriele and me, but I can't help how my heart feels. It doesn't feel fair to lead Dom on by saying yes. At the same time, maybe spending more time with him will give me a better opportunity to find out if he knows anything about the photo.

"That sounds like fun, but would this be a *date*?"

He gives me a grin I'm sure works on a lot of women. I'm just not one of them. "Do you want it to be a date?"

"Honestly, I'm not looking to date anyone. I'm still getting over someone." He doesn't need to know the details, nor the fact that the someone is standing twenty feet to his left.

"Fair enough." He sets his hands on his hips. "Friends then. Let's make it a friends date. But if you ever want to go on a *date* date, you say the word."

I laugh. "Sounds good."

"All right, I'll swing by your room at eight." Right then, Dante shouts his name. Dom rolls his eyes. "Better go see what His Majesty wants. See you later."

When I chance a glance at Gabriele, he's watching me again. What I don't know is whether he's doing it because he's trying to suss out whether someone I'm talking to could be the person behind the photograph, or for another reason entirely.

* * *

I OPT TO wear a cobalt blue bodycon dress with my hair down in waves, and as I primp for the hundredth time in front of the mirror, I tell myself that it's because I want to look nice and not because I'm hoping Gabriele will be there. There's a knock at my door as I slide my room key and the burner phone into the small bag I'm using tonight.

I walk over and swing the door open. Dom stands there in a navy suit. As good as he looks, my body doesn't buzz or react at all.

"You clean up well," I say.

He laughs and steps past me into my room. And it's then I realize that Dom knows where my room is. I mean, it's not as if it's classified information, but I didn't tell him my room number. So how *did* he know where my room is? I make a mental note and list it under the category of things that make me suspicious.

"Hey, how did you know where my room was?" I ask, trying to keep my voice from shaking. I'm way more on edge than I'll admit.

"Bianca told me," he says, looking around my room. He doesn't look as if he's been here before, but any good Mafia guy has been trained at the art of hiding.

"Where is Bianca? Is she coming tonight? I didn't get a chance to meet up with her after the War Games."

He nods. "Yeah, she wanted to arrive with us, but I told her to back off—we had a friends date planned." He laughs.

I chuckle. "Can't imagine she liked that."

He grins. "Not at all."

I grab my purse off the desk. "Let's go then."

"Let's." He waggles his eyebrows up and down, but despite his teasing, I get the sense he understands that nothing is going to happen between us tonight.

We make our way to the gymnasium, and when we step inside, the entire space has been transformed. Black, white, and silver balloons arch over every doorway, and gambling tables have been set up everywhere around the perimeter of the room. Music pumps through the space, and a line of food and drink tables runs along the far wall.

The vibe is upbeat, and a trill of excitement runs through my blood. Until this moment, I hadn't realized how much I need to relax and have fun. How badly I need to get out of my head with everything going on.

Dom's hand is at my back as he walks us farther into the room. My eyes scan the room and catch Gabriele's.

You were hoping to find his, so you shouldn't be surprised he's watching you.

His eyes are narrowed, and he looks pissed off. If I didn't know any better, I'd say he looks almost jealous. Which makes no sense. Why would he be jealous when he wants nothing to do with me romantically?

I considered telling Gabriele my plan to attend the dance with Dom is a way to get closer to him and try to figure out whether he has any part to play in the drama swirling around me. But there's no point in telling Gabriele. He'd only get pissed off that I'm doing something he hasn't approved of. And if he is upset because he thinks I'm on a real date with Dom? Well, good. I hope it makes him jealous. Though I don't think I'm that lucky.

I turn my attention away from Gabriele and let Dom lead me farther into the room. I have a mission tonight, and it doesn't have to do with me fawning all over a man who doesn't want me.

CHAPTER EIGHTEEN

GABRIELE

I don't drink often, but I wish it were a shot in my hand rather than a soda. What the fuck is Aria doing here on a date with Domenic Accardi? Are they a thing now? First he's a possible suspect, and now he's her date?

I slam my drink down on the green velvet of the blackjack table. "What are you looking at?"

I glance at my cousin, trying to school my expression. "Nothing."

Sandro motions for the dealer to give him another card. "Bullshit. Something's got you pissed off, and it should be the race. Dante is a dirty fucking player."

He's still pissed about Dante pushing ahead of us at the wall, knocking Sandro down and causing him to twist his ankle. Sandro has always been more competitive with things like that than me. I'm competitive on outsmarting people, not who can run the fastest.

I split the pair of eights I have, and the dealer hands out two more cards. "It is. I am."

Through my peripheral vision, I see Sandro study me, but he doesn't say anything else. Which is good. I'm not in the mood to explain myself to him.

The rest of the evening, my eyes stray to Aria. So far I've clocked her laughing with Dom, putting her hand on his forearm, and watched as he removed something from her long, luscious hair. Each instance felt like more weight being dropped on my chest.

Two hours into the event, I can't take it anymore. I have to get out of here before I lose my shit and let everyone know how badly I want Aria Costa.

There's not much I value more than control, and Aria pushes me to the brink of losing it every damn time.

"Here." I slide the rest of my chips over to Sandro. "I'm done with this shit. See you tomorrow."

I don't wait for him to respond. Instead, I get up from my seat and walk through the gym to the hallway. Of course, fate has other plans for me because the moment I step out of the gym, Aria comes out of the bathroom. Her steps falter as she walks toward me, but she raises her chin like the proud woman she wants everyone to believe she is.

I'm not sure what happens. One moment we're walking toward each other, and I'm telling myself I won't do or say anything to her, and the next I have her pinned against the wall. But rather than protesting, she stands there breathing heavily, her lust-filled eyes on me.

"What the fuck do you think you're doing?" I spit at her, angry at myself for giving in to my need for her.

"What do you mean?" Her voice is breathy. My gaze skirts over her from top to bottom, memorizing her curves in the tight-fitting dress.

"You're here with Domenic. Why?" I press my body into hers, and she opens her legs, making room for my thigh to rub against her core as I brace her hands above her on the wall.

The spark in her dark eyes says she's not going to let me get away with this. She's going to fight me. "What do you care? You made it perfectly clear that you want nothing to do with me in that way."

"I don't care. Not for the reasons you want me to."

Liar.

"But if he's involved at all in this scheme, you need to watch yourself. You're not the only one with something to lose here." I press my thigh between her legs and she inhales, but shows nothing.

Her eyes narrow, and a small smirk shapes her full lips. "You keep pretending that's why you're pissed. You're lying to yourself because deep down, you know it's more than that."

She holds my gaze, not backing down.

With a curse, I push off the wall, releasing her, and walk away. She's right, and we both know it. I'm not fooling anyone.

* * *

I LIE IN bed unable to sleep, considering all the possibilities.

First, continue to beat off to thoughts of Aria and never be fully satisfied. Less than appealing.

Second, talk to her brother and come clean with him that I have some interest in his little sister and ask for his blessing to date her. Less appealing than my first option. Do I really want my ass kicked tonight?

Third, give in to the pull between us and hope that once she sees what I'm into, it doesn't scare Aria off for good. I fucking wish.

Will my dominating side prove too much for an innocent girl like her?

But then I remember her reaction when I had her pinned to the wall earlier tonight . . . the way her lids grew heavy and her nostrils flared. How she squeezed her thighs around my leg. The way her nipples pebbled under the fabric of her dress.

Is it possible she likes being controlled? Does my dominating side turn her on?

If I was with her, would it feel less like corrupting her and more like coveting if I were giving her what she really needs, what she desires?

After lying in bed for another hour, I decide there's only one way to know for sure. It's late, and as I climb the stairwell up to her room, I tell myself that I'm not going to hell for what I'm about to do. Because there's little doubt in my mind that Aria will be into what I'm offering tonight. The issue becomes, what happens after?

I peek out the small window in the door of the stairwell and see no one in the hallway, so I step out and walk over to her room, where I knock softly on the door. She doesn't answer, so I knock again. The door whips open to Aria wearing only an oversized light purple T-shirt. At least in my mind, she's not wearing any underwear.

"Gabe?" She must have been sleeping because her eyes look sleepy, and her hair is mussed in a way that makes me wish it were my hands that had done the mussing.

Her shortening of my name makes me feel even more possessive than I already do over her. She's never done that before. Very few do, at least to my face.

I don't say anything and instead step past her, telling myself it's because I don't want anyone to catch me here, when really it's because I need to be closer to her.

I need the answers to the questions in my head.

I need to know if I'm right about her.

"In Miami, when you figured out what that place was, why didn't you leave immediately?"

She sighs behind me, and I whip around to face her, taking her by surprise. She blinks and looks as if she's trying to remember what I asked. Then her lips thin, and she gives me her pissed-off eyes. "Did you really come here in the middle of the night to lecture me?"

"Answer the question, Aria."

She throws her hands in the air, seemingly exasperated. "Because I was curious. Because I was turned on. Because I wanted to explore my sexuality. I don't know, take your pick." She walks toward her bed. "Now save me the lecture about how I got us into this whole mess and leave. I'm going back to bed."

I've never met anyone like her—at least not in my world. She's sweet, but when it comes down to it, she has a backbone. Like kicking me out of her room, or how she called me on my shit earlier. The way she's so open about her sexuality and doesn't seem to have any shame about wanting to explore it.

The women in my world are raised to service their husband, sure. But they're meant to be mothers and guileless. Rather than have their own needs that get satisfied, they work to satisfy those of their partners.

But Aria isn't like that. Whether that's because she's always been this way, or if it's a by-product of her father being dead and not being able to lord over her any longer, I don't know. Don't care either.

Before she can pass me, I snag her arm and yank her into my chest. Her breath escapes her in a whoosh, and I crash my lips to hers. I'm not sure if she'll accept the kiss at first, because she freezes. It would serve me right if she pushed me away and told me to fuck off.

But within a few seconds, her hands weave around my neck, and her chest presses to mine as I slip my tongue past her lips. I grow hard as I push a hand into the hair at the back of her head, angling it the way I like. She groans as I taste her, exploring her mouth and biting her bottom lip before I pull away.

"I'm done fighting, Aria. I can't do it any longer. But before we start anything, I need to know that we're on the same page."

She doesn't say anything, looking up at me as if she's in a daze.

"I like to be in control. That doesn't mean I won't provide you with pleasure—that's always the goal. But I need to know that you can handle my dominant side. You say you want to explore your sexuality, and I'm on board for being the one to do that for you, but that's all it can be. You and I . . . we can never be more than that." I think of her brother and my father and frown. "No one can ever know about us. There's no future for us. I need you to know that before anything else happens."

A flicker of disappointment shines in her eyes when I say we have no future, but she must hear the truth because she's quiet for a few moments before she nods. "I'm okay with all of that. But I have a condition of my own."

I arch an eyebrow, impressed that she's pushing back. "What?"

"You can't be with anyone else while we're doing this. I don't want to have to worry about some other girl crawling into your bed."

My hands drift down past her waist and squeeze her ass over her long T-shirt. "That goes for you, too."

She nods. "Deal."

"Seal it with a kiss. Then I have plans for you."

CHAPTER NINETEEN

GABRIELE

I pull away, ending our kiss. "Go sit on the edge of the bed."

She does as I ask without a word, which makes my cock thicken in my lounge pants.

Then I study her for a minute, deciding which scenario I want to play out here. So many have been running through my mind since Miami—what I'd do to her if given the chance. And now I'm finding it hard to choose.

But we should probably start off nice and easy—no sex. I want to be sure this is what she wants, that this is what gives her pleasure. If I ever felt like I was a regret to this woman, I think I'd want to off myself.

I picture all the ways in which I've wanted to take her, and once I've decided on my course of action, I stalk over to her dresser, remembering where she keeps all the tights she'll wear with her uniform during the colder months. I'll have to improvise a little since there's no rope, which isn't a problem. If nothing else, I'm wise with my resources.

After yanking open the drawer, I pull out two pairs of dark tights and turn back to face her. Aria sits on the edge of the bed, big doe eyes wider than normal, her chest heaving. Whether from arousal or fear, I'm not sure. Hopefully both.

"If you change your mind, if it becomes too much at any point, you say stop, and I will."

"Don't we need a safe word or something?" Her voice trembles.

"I know what the word stop means. You say that, and it ends. Immediately. No judgment. Not everyone wants to be controlled, and that's fine. But I need to be sure you're not going to go along with something you're not into in an effort to please me. What pleases me"—I take a few steps forward so that we're only a foot apart, and she looks up at me from below—"is pleasing you. Is delivering you pleasure *when* and *how* I want to. Or denying you pleasure when and how I want. It's not just about me, though, even if I covet the control. You understand?"

She nods slowly.

"I need you to say it, Aria."

"I understand."

"What are you going to say if it becomes too much?"

"Stop."

"Good." I give a sharp nod. "Now take off your shirt."

She sucks in a breath, whether at my command or at the change in my voice, the authority commanding her to do what I want, who knows? But that hitch of breath makes my cock twitch.

Her hands go down to the hem of her T-shirt, and she pulls it up over her head.

Fuck me.

Her body is a work of art. The way her tits are the perfect size for her frame, perky with dark nipples, taut with arousal. Her waist dips in before her hips flare out in a way that makes me anxious to have my hands on them as I drive into her from behind. But all in good time.

I want to ease Aria into this arrangement. Make sure it's really what she's into before I impale her with my cock.

"Sei così bella," I say, palming one breast.

Her back arches into my touch, and her eyes drift closed when my thumb traces over her nipple. I linger longer than I planned.

I step into her and mold her other breast into my other hand. She opens her eyes, her nostrils flaring when she realizes my hard length is right in front of her. Hidden behind the fabric of my pants and underwear, but obvious nonetheless.

I love learning what turns her on. While I play with her tits, her breath becomes more rapid, telling me she likes it. But when I twist her nipple between my thumb and forefinger, she lets her head drop forward so that it rests on my erection.

I groan, looking down and seeing her there. So close and yet so far.

As I continue my ministrations, she nuzzles her face against my cock, rubbing and providing only a small amount of friction, but enough that I can no longer hold off.

My hands drop from her body, and I step back. "Turn around and lie across the width of the bed. Leave your head hanging off the end."

She looks at me quizzically for a beat, then does what I say, positioning herself so that she lies across the bed, her head hanging off the end directly in front of me.

I pick up the tights from the floor and grab one of her wrists. Aria's pulse thrums wildly under my fingers as I pull her arm straight out from her side and fasten the tights around her wrist then around the headboard. I repeat the action with her other arm and the footboard. Her hands pull against the restraints—testing them maybe—but she doesn't tell me to stop.

My cock throbs now, demanding some attention, so I slowly get undressed. All the while, I take in her curves, the rate of her breathing, how that locket she's always wearing glistens in the light where it lies against her collarbone. The scent of her arousal fills the air. I'm sure if I delved my fingers underneath her white lace underwear, I'd find she's soaked.

I hold back a groan at the thought.

Once I'm undressed, I step over to her nightstand and open the drawer that holds her treasure trove. While I'm certainly going to get off tonight, I'm not going to leave her behind. Not yet.

After a few seconds, I find what I'm looking for—a vibrator.

I look back at Aria, whose head is hanging off the bed and turned toward me now.

"What are you doing?" she near-whispers.

"I'm going to satisfy you while you satisfy me."

Her back arches against the mattress, and she squeezes her legs together.

A dark chuckle echoes out of me as I look back at her over my shoulder. "Ti piace quello?"

"Yes," she says in response to me asking if she likes that.

I turn and face her, watching her as she takes me in. *All* of me. Her breathing picks up again as I step toward her, stroking my dick. She licks her lips, and my cock twitches in my hand. Fuck, I can't wait to know what it feels like to be inside her warm, wet mouth.

"I'm gonna fuck this pretty mouth of yours, Aria. Would you like that?"

"Yes," she says without hesitation.

"Have you done this before?" I assume she's not a virgin by how forward she's been with me in the past and the fact that I found her half naked in the middle of a sex club. But I don't know how much experience she has. Not much, if I had to bet.

"Just twice. And not like this."

I can't help the half grin that tilts up the corners of my lips.

"I may not be your first, but I'll make it memorable." I flick on the vibrator and the buzzing sound fills the room. I want her to anticipate it, though, so I don't bring it to her panty-clad pussy yet. "Let me see that tongue, bella."

She opens her mouth, sticking out her tongue. Still fisting the base of my cock, I step close enough that her tongue is on the underside of my balls. Without me having to tell her, she licks and worships them, pulling one into her mouth and sucking gently, then the other. It feels phenomenal.

I decide to reward her for her efforts and bring the vibrator to the juncture of her thighs. She jolts from the surprise, moaning instantly. Her back arches, and her head twists, so I pull the vibrator away.

Aria makes a disappointed sound. "Please don't stop."

"You stop, and I stop, understood?"

"Yes." The word is desperate and breathy.

"I'm going to tuck this in your underwear, between your pussy lips. Do you think that will feel good, cara?"

"Oh God, yes." She moans as though she can already feel it.

"And then I'm going to fuck this mouth. And if you stop, it stops, got it?"

"Yes, please, Gabriele. Please don't make me wait any longer."

Jesus Christ. The way she says my name when she's hot and bothered is almost enough to make me erupt.

Leaning forward, I slip the vibrator under the waistband of her panties and wedge it between her legs so that it rests on her clit.

"Oh God." Her back arches, and her mouth opens wide.

Bending my knees so I'm lined up, I feed her my cock, pressing it between her lips. "Perfetta."

A satisfied moan traps in her throat as I push myself farther in before pulling my hips back. I pump in and out a few times, impressed that she's able to take my full length and marveling at how her throat bulges when I'm fully seated inside her.

I push in and hold myself there, gripping her throat and jaw and wiggling her side to side on the base of my cock. Fuck, that feels like heaven. I pull out when I don't think she can take anymore, and she sucks in a big gasp of air.

Aria's legs squirm. She must be close.

Leaning forward while I push back into her mouth, I yank the vibrator from between her legs. She groans around my cock. With my hands on either side of her body, I fuck her face in earnest, as though it were her pussy. I look between the length of our bodies and moan when my length disappears into her waiting and eager mouth.

She's so beautiful sprawled out, tied up, and at my mercy. Puffy lips spread wide around my cock shoved down her throat. There's nothing she can do but take it. Take what I'm offering her. And the trust that requires, especially when she knows me. Knows the life I'm in and what I'm capable of. Fuck.

I groan. I could come thinking about it.

I'm not going to be able to hold off much longer.

When I fuck her face even harder, I expect that she might do something to get me off of her. I'm ready for it. But she doesn't. She takes it willingly. God, she's fucking perfect.

"I think I'll let you come now, Aria. Would you like that?"

She can't answer me with my cock down her throat, but she makes some sound that could be interpreted as a yes. Supporting myself with one hand, I reach beside her for the vibrator still vibrating on the bed and increase the tempo.

"This should help." I slide the vibrator back between her legs, and she bucks underneath me, pulling at the restraints on her arms. "Look at you. At my mercy. I could do anything I want to you, and you'd take it, wouldn't you?" I continue pumping into her mouth, then stilling to hold myself there.

When I can tell she's on the edge, I turn the level of the vibrator up again, and she cries out around my cock.

As much as I want to paint the inside of her throat, I want to mark her in a way that I'll be able to see. So I pull out of her mouth and rest my balls on her lips. She sucks one into her mouth and arches up off the bed, crying out as she comes in wave after wave of pleasure. After a few quick pumps, ribbons of my release lash over her face, painting her in the prettiest way possible.

We're both panting as we come down from our releases and I remove the vibrator from between her legs. I wipe the sweat from my brow and watch as her breathing slows, watch as my cum slides down her face.

Beautiful.

Without a word, I walk into her bathroom and wet a washcloth to clean her up.

First things first. I quickly free her of the makeshift restraints so that she can sit up. Once her arms are free, I help her spin around and slowly help her sit up.

"Not too quick, or you'll be dizzy."

Once she's sitting on the edge of the bed, I wipe her face. Only once she's cleaned up do I return to the bathroom to clean myself. When I'm done, I rejoin her, picking up my pants from the floor and sliding them on before I sit beside her on the bed.

She's still nude, but she makes no effort to cover herself. I love that she's so comfortable in her own skin. I pull the hand closest to me onto my lap and gently massage her wrist.

"Are you sore?" I ask.

She shakes her head. "Not my wrists." When I frown, not understanding, she adds, "You're packing a lot of heat in those pants." She wiggles her jaw side to side.

I throw my head back and laugh. "I'd apologize, but I'm not really sorry."

She smiles, a sparkle in her deep brown eyes. "I'm glad you finally gave in to this thing between us."

My amusement fades. "I didn't know if you'd be into what I like."

She holds my stare. "I'm totally into it. I like when you're in control."

Fuck, this woman is perfect.

But she's wrong . . . I may have the illusion of control, but there's no doubt she's got me by the balls.

CHAPTER TWENTY
ARIA

I practically float through the hallways of Sicuro Academy for the next two days after Gabriele leaves my room Saturday night.

What we did . . . suffice to say it was even better than what I imagined it could be, and we didn't even have sex. Our encounter was a little filthy, a tad bit demeaning, but at the same time, he took such good care of me before, during, and after that it was impossible not to feel spoiled in some weird way.

I'm trying not to read too much into it, enjoy myself and explore what I'm into, but that's easier said than done. I'd be a liar if I said I wasn't hoping that at some point, he'll change his mind. But for now, I'm content to see what happens. As long as more of what we did that night is coming my way.

I've always thought that Gabriele was hot, but when he towered over me, in control and oozing power—the depths of my fascination with him reached a whole new level.

The sound of a chirp echoes from the bag set at my feet and makes me still. It's the middle of class, and some sixth sense tells me that it's not the academy-issued phone that's received a new message.

For the remainder of my Intro to Embezzling class, I'm on edge and anxious. I want to see what the hell it says.

The moment class is finished, I don't wait for Bianca, instead telling her I have to hit the bathroom before my next class. I rush off to the closest ladies' room and lock myself inside a stall, hanging my bag off the hook and searching through it for both phones.

As I thought, it's the burner phone left by the mystery person with a new message. I pull up the message and read:

YOUR FATHER HAD A USB WITH SOME VERY IMPORTANT INFORMATION ON IT. WE WANT IT BACK.

What the hell?

I suppose it's good that I finally know what they want, but how the hell am I going to find a USB my dad had? He's dead. It could be anywhere. It could have been on him when he was blown up in the vehicle. And if it had something important on it, I doubt he would have left it lying around somewhere.

Stashing the burner phone back in my bag, I pull out my academy-issued phone to text Gabriele.

ME: Just got another message. When can we meet?

His response comes immediately.

GABRIELE: Come to my room after your last class before you head to the dining hall for dinner. I'll leave the door unlocked. Just walk right in so no one sees you.

ME: See you then.

I put my phone back in my bag and take a deep breath in an attempt to calm my racing heart. I've been distracted for the past couple of days by what happened between Gabriele and me, putting this whole situation to the back of my mind. But now I'm really worried. What will happen if I can't find what they're looking for?

* * *

THE MOMENT MY palm closes around the handle to Gabriele's dorm room, my stomach feels as if there's a team of synchronized swimmers inside. I'm here for something other than being physical with him, but I wonder what might happen with him once we're done with that.

When I slip inside his room, I'm met by the sound of music playing softly. It's a song I recognize but can't place. Gabriele is sprawled across the couch, reading a book.

"What group is this?" I ask.

He straightens on the couch, closes his book, and tosses it onto the side table. "It's by Cigarettes After Sex." Then he stalks over to me, hand outstretched. "Let me see the phone."

I frown at his businesslike tone but quickly stop, not wanting to seem like some needy girl. So I walk over to the desk and set my bag on it, unzip it, and pull out the phone. When I hand it to him, he reads the message.

His gaze flicks to me. "Don't suppose you have any idea what they're talking about?"

Shaking my head, I say, "None at all."

He blows out a breath. "At least we have a little more information than we had."

I tilt my head. "How so?"

"There's a good chance that whatever your dad had on this USB, he was using it to blackmail this person. So now we have to ask ourselves, who could he have been blackmailing?"

"I have no idea. My dad didn't ever talk to me about business stuff. I could ask Marcelo, but—"

"No. I don't think your brother knows anything about whatever this is. If he did, they probably would've gone straight to him with their threats. But they came to you because you're the one who is easier to manipulate."

My lips press into a firm line, irritation pawing at me like a cat. "How do they expect me to find some USB my dad had while I'm stuck here on campus? It would be hard enough to find even if I were at home."

Gabriele palms the back of his neck and stares at his feet. "Not sure. Maybe they think it's on campus for some reason. You said your dad didn't give you anything to hold on to, but what if he gave it to your brother, and he doesn't even know he has it?"

I shift in place. "I guess that's possible."

"We need to find out." He holds the phone back out to me, and I take it.

"Maybe we should just text whoever this is and tell them I have no idea where to find what they want."

He's shaking his head before I'm even done speaking. "Nope. Do not engage. Nothing good will come from it. You'll either piss them off or let them in on the fact that you have no idea how to get them what they want. Better to keep them guessing until they reach back out. In the meantime, we need to find out whether your brother knows anything."

I frown, not entirely agreeing but trusting that Gabriele is more versed in this stuff than I am.

"How am I supposed to do that?" I swallow hard. I can't go to my brother and be honest about this. He'd send me home and probably have his goons keep an eye on me twenty-four seven. I'd be miserable.

"First, talk to him and see if you can get a sense whether he knows anything. If that doesn't work, we'll break into his room and have a look around."

My eyes widen. "We can't do that. We're doing all this so that he won't find out about Miami. If he catches us, we'll have no option but to tell him what's going on. And even then, he might kill you for breaking into his room."

Gabriele reaches out as if he's going to put his hand on my shoulder but drops it before he does. "He's not going to find out because I'm getting my equipment back tomorrow." He grins wide. I've never seen him so excited.

"You are?"

He nods. "Yep. I'll hack into the security feed and be able to see his comings and goings, so we'll make sure he's nowhere near his room."

A relieved breath rushes from my mouth. "Okay then, sure."

"Now that I have my stuff coming in, I want to ask you something, but I'm not sure how you'll feel about it."

My head tilts. "Okay . . ."

"I want to put cameras up in your room."

I blink a few times at him.

"I don't think whoever left the picture in your room will come back, but on the off chance they do—either to leave you something else or to search your room themselves—I want to be able to see who it is."

I nod. Makes sense. But that would mean that he can look in and see what I'm up to whenever he wants. Why the hell does the idea of that turn me on? "Okay, you can put the cameras up."

His eyebrows rise. "I thought you'd put up more of a fight than that."

I shrug. "It's a means to an end. The sooner this whole thing is over, the better."

He nods as if it's settled.

Good. Maybe now we can get to the part where we get naked.

"If that's all settled, then I have to run. Told Sandro I'd meet him for some sparring before dinner."

I frown. Why is he acting as if nothing has changed between us? He had his cock shoved down my throat a couple of days ago, and I *know* he enjoyed it. The evidence of that was all over my face.

When I don't say anything, he motions behind me toward the door. "You should probably go first. I'll follow behind in a few minutes." His expression doesn't give away anything.

Anger is like gasoline flowing through my veins, ready to ignite. But I bite it back. I don't think Gabriele is into drama queens.

For whatever reason, he's backing away, creating some distance between us. Distance I need to build a bridge between. Then an idea takes form in my head, and I smile.

"Okay, I'll see you later. I'll try to prod my brother to see if he knows anything and get back to you."

He nods, and without another word between us, I leave his room. But when I do, I'm confident I'll be back and in his bed next time.

CHAPTER TWENTY-ONE

GABRIELE

Rachel in security came through, and it's a win-win for all. Now she won't have to work double shifts, and she'll be able to pay off most of the medical debt that's been piled on her.

The moment the last of the boxes containing my computer equipment are in my room, it feels as if one of my organs is back in place.

Finally, I'll have something to do besides sit around in my fucking dorm room obsessing about Aria Costa. Since Saturday, she's been running on a loop in my head—the way her mouth spread for me and how her throat constricted around the end of my cock. What her tongue felt like on my balls or the way she looked up at me as though she trusted me fully and would do whatever the fuck I asked of her.

I groan thinking of it and adjust myself in my pants.

Enough of that. I have to get all my stuff set up.

In favor of getting this done sooner than later, I skip my classes for the day, citing illness.

It takes most of the morning to get my computer through the back door of the network at the school in a way that no one will notice and set up the cameras outside my room so I have a direct view of anyone who approaches.

Around lunch, I text Aria that I want to come by her room tonight to set up the cameras. She tells me that she has plans to hang out with Bianca, but she'll text me once Bianca has left her room. I want to ask whether Dom will be tagging along, but I don't.

I could tell Aria was pissed with me when I essentially dismissed her and told her to be on her way last night when she visited my room. She probably showed up thinking there'd be a repeat of Saturday night, but I needed some space.

Space to get my head on straight and remember that I cannot fall any further for Aria. Not only will it be an issue with her brother, but the bigger problem is my father.

It's not that I'm scared of my father, though most people would be. Angelo Vitale is a man to be reckoned with. But he's old school and reluctant to change. He wants to live in a world that doesn't exist anymore.

I've tried to talk to him over and over and decided six months ago that the best thing to do would be to show him. If I cross him with this thing with Aria, there's a good chance his pride won't allow him to concede that I'm right about my little pet project I've been working on.

Once it's settled with Aria, I get to hacking into the Miami hotel's security files. I want to see if I can find a video that shows exactly who slipped into Aria's hotel room and left her that invitation to the sex club.

Whether I'm trying to back off of Aria or not, one thing is certain: I'm going to make whoever is threatening her pay before I slit their throat and watch them bleed.

She may not be mine, but no one gets to do this to her and live.

* * *

I PULL THE glasses from my face and rub the bridge of my nose. I don't need prescription lenses, but I began wearing blue light glasses when I'm on the computer over the summer, hoping it would help with my insomnia. So far, I don't think it's done jack shit, but I keep wearing them anyway, hoping they'll eventually make a difference.

My phone chirps on the desk beside me, and I pick it up to see a text from Aria.

> ARIA: Coast is clear.

> ME: On my way. Leave the door unlocked.

> ARIA: Oooh, starting the control thing before you even get here. I like it.

Shaking my head, I set down the phone and ignore her innuendo. It'll take a herculean effort tonight not to strip her bare and strap her to the headboard. But at this point, rather than exert control over her, I need to show her that I can control myself where she's concerned.

I gather everything I need, shove it in my bag, and take the stairs up to her floor. When I peek out the window on the stairwell door and don't see anyone, I exit and walk to her room, going straight inside.

Aria's in there wearing a tight-fitting crop top and baggy, light gray jogging pants. Her hair is assembled in a messy bun. I try not to follow the V of her necklace to where the oval locket rests at the top of her cleavage, but that proves impossible.

"Hey." I nod and set my bag on the edge of her bed to go through it. Flashbacks from the other night flit through my memory. "What'd you do tonight?"

She shrugs. "Nothing much. Worked on our homework."

"You still think maybe she or Dom might have something to do with all this?" I unzip my bag to pull out everything.

"Nah, I don't think so. She never acts weird or asks me really personal questions. Same with Dom. I saw him during lunch today, and the more time I spend with them, the more I think they have no part in any of this."

Hearing her say Dom's name makes me grind my teeth as I pull the last of the equipment from my bag and turn around. "Well, hopefully all this will help us figure out who is behind everything."

"I'm not sure whether I hope some strange person breaks into my room again or whether I don't want them to."

I chuckle. "Fair enough. This shouldn't take too long. These little guys will link to my computer, and they're small enough that no one should even know they're here."

"Except me. I'll know they're here." There's a sultry note to her voice that I ignore.

"Once I get them in place, I'll make sure the angles work so that we've got the whole room covered."

I take the first camera and walk to the far side of the room, opting to place it between two of the record albums on her bookshelf. I noticed her vinyl collection the day I was in here looking for bugs.

"I'm going to put this between your Florence and the Machine and girl in red albums. Okay not to listen to those until this is settled?" I turn and look at her over my shoulder.

"Yeah, sure."

"You must really like music. You've got a lot of vinyl here." I look around to decide where I'm going to put the other two cameras.

"I have double that at home." There's pride in her voice.

"What started your obsession with albums?" I ask, walking past her to the other side of the room.

"It's not an *obsession*. I just spent a lot of time in my room in high school. My dad, like my brother, was overbearing and protective—even where friends were concerned. He didn't trust people at all. Music became my company. Made me feel not so alone." She shrugs. "It's dumb, I know."

I shake my head. "Not dumb. I understand it in a way."

She's quiet, waiting for me to continue.

I don't even know why I'm telling her this. "I have trouble sleeping, so I'm up through the night a lot. Computers and hacking kind of became my companions."

She smiles in a way that makes her deep brown eyes sparkle like the night sky. "Exactly."

Our gazes lock and hold until I look away, feeling as though I'm exposing too much. I get back to work installing the cameras, and we're both quiet for a while.

She says, "You mentioned sparring the other day. That's the Krav Maga?"

Something a lot easier to talk about. "Yeah. I started taking martial arts when I was younger. So did my cousin, so we still spar sometimes."

"Wow. That's cool. What belt are you?" She sits on the edge of her bed while I pull my laptop from my bag and open it on her desk.

"Started with Taekwondo and got my black belt in that, then moved on to Krav Maga and some judo."

"Is that where your need for control in the bedroom started?"

My head whips in her direction. She's grinning, and though it's clear she's half joking, it's also obvious she really wants the answer.

"I don't know where it came from. Since my first experience, I just knew I liked to be the one controlling things, telling the other person what to do, and no matter what it was, having them obey."

She nods slowly, taking in the information. "Have all your partners been into that sort of thing?"

"If they weren't, they weren't my partners."

"I see," she says and, to my surprise, lets the subject drop. "Who won your sparring session?"

I smile at her. "Who do you think?"

I get back to testing the cameras' connection with my computer, perfecting the angles so the entire room is covered. When I'm done, I shut my laptop and shove it back in my bag.

"That should do it." I stand from the desk and sling the strap of my backpack over my shoulder. "Meant to tell you, after I got everything set up today, I spent the afternoon hacking into the hotel's system in Miami."

Her eyes widen. "Were you able to find out who left the invite in my room?"

I shake my head, irritation clawing at my chest, the same as it did earlier today. "Cameras were already scrubbed. Either they don't keep footage that far back as a practice or someone else got there before I did."

Aria frowns. "It was worth a shot." She steps closer. "Are you leaving already?"

The innuendo is clear in her voice, and though my dick twitches when I think of all the things I could do to her, I force myself to ignore it. I need to remember my priorities.

"Yeah, it's getting late, and I'll be up early to go to the gym." I walk toward the door. "Let me know what you can find out from your brother."

I don't bother waiting for her to respond, knowing that every extra second I remain in this room is one second closer to my willpower caving.

CHAPTER TWENTY-TWO

ARIA

Two hours after Gabriele left my room, I lie in my bed, unable to sleep. Sexual frustration mixed with irritation puts my body on edge.

I suppose I shouldn't have been surprised when he left my room—he's kept his distance since the night we fooled around. It's not as though we expressly said that it would be an ongoing thing, but I thought it had been implied. Apparently, I was wrong.

When I can't take the frustration any longer, I whip off the covers and sit upright in bed. Then I remember my brilliant idea from yesterday and decide to put my plan into action. First, I slip off my panties so I'm only wearing my T-shirt. Next, I open my nightstand drawer and pull out my vibrator, setting it on the bed beside me. Last, I grab my phone off the nightstand and type out a text to Gabriele.

> **ME:** I think there's something going on in my room. Check the cameras.

Setting down my phone, I lie back on top of my covers, legs spread wide, and bring the vibrator between my legs. When I flick the switch and the vibration starts right where I need it, I moan.

I don't know how, but I know he's watching. It's as though I feel his gaze roaming over my body, admiring it from way too far away.

It doesn't take me long to work myself into a frenzy. When I can hardly take it any longer, my legs clamp down around my hand and the bright pink piece of machinery as I cry out, arching my back as my climax races through me.

I lie there panting and spent.

But instead of the euphoria I should be feeling having just come, there's only bitter disappointment and frustration because there's no text, no knock on the door, nothing.

Maybe Gabriele really is well and truly done with me after one time.

* * *

THE NEXT MORNING at breakfast, I don't allow myself to glance at the Vitale table to steal a glimpse of Gabriele. I might not have a lot of pride, but I have some.

I'm forking my eggs around my plate when my cousin and my brother's right-hand man, Giovanni, sits beside me.

"Hey, cuz, how's it going?" He wraps an arm around me and pulls me into a side hug.

"Hey, Gio. Not bad."

I like my cousin, but he's loyal to Marcelo first.

"You getting used to campus life?" he asks before shoveling some porridge into his mouth.

"Beats being at home." And that's the truth. At least I have some freedom here and know where I fit.

Just then, my brother and Mira sit across from us. Perfect. I can work my father into our conversation this morning without being obvious.

The four of us chat about nothing in particular for a few minutes. I don't want to be too obvious. Then I steer the conversation to my dad.

"Dad's birthday would have been next month," I say.

Marcelo's fork pauses halfway to his mouth. Mira takes my hand, thinking I'm upset about it. I'm not sure how I feel about it. We had a complicated relationship.

"Don't tell me you're missing him." Marcelo raises a skeptical brow.

We both know our dad was no saint. In fact, he was a bit of a deranged asshole. Especially to Mom.

"Not missing him per se." I shrug. "I've just been thinking a lot about him lately." I move my hand to my necklace. "This is all I have left of him. It's weird when people die, they're just . . . gone."

Guilt coats my insides like tar. I hate having to put on this act and lie to my brother. He might drive me crazy sometimes—okay, a lot of times—but I'm loyal to him. So I remind myself that he's the reason I'm doing all this. Because if that picture got out, it would look like the head of another family pulled one over on him and corrupted his little sister, turning her against him. Everyone would think it's their time to strike.

And I cannot be responsible for that. I have to protect my brother.

"That may be, but we're better off without him," Marcelo says.

Mira gives him an irritated look, then turns her attention to me. "It's normal that you'd be thinking about him with his birthday coming up."

"I guess, yeah." I look at my brother. "Did Dad leave you anything?" I try to keep my voice as even and innocent as possible.

"Just a bunch of messes to clean up." Marcelo goes back to eating his breakfast.

"That seems strange," I press, hopefully not so much as to make him suspicious.

"Nothing strange about it. Everything gets passed to me anyway as the head of the family. Mom keeps the houses, of course, and everything in their personal bank accounts, but anything to do with business is mine automatically. Did you think he'd leave some sweet note for me in his will?" A dark laugh leaves Marcelo, and he and Gio make eye contact before his laughter dies quickly. "Not a chance."

Guess that answers my question about whether or not my dad passed on the USB and a note. It's not like my brother would be specific with me if he did, but he'd say something along the lines of "Nothing you need to worry about."

I'll have to let Gabriele know, something I'm not looking forward to after last night. I can't say for sure that he saw my little performance, but the sting of rejection is still lingering.

I'll deal with it tonight. Today, I'm determined to clear Gabriele from my mind and focus on my classes.

* * *

It was a nice try, I think as I leave my first class to head to the other side of campus for my next one. Removing Gabriele from my mind proved impossible during class, but I'm determined for my next one.

Bianca and I don't have our next class together, so after I chat with her outside the classroom door for a few minutes, we say our goodbyes and head in opposite directions. I'm walking past a doorway that's cracked open when I'm yanked to the side and pulled into the room. A hand clamps down over my mouth before I have a chance to scream, and my back is pressed against someone's hard chest. The door in front of me is kicked closed by a big, booted foot. I jerk around, but the band across my chest tightens.

"Did you enjoy teasing me with your little performance last night?"

Gabriele. I instantly still in his arms, and he drops his hand from my mouth.

"Did you know I was watching you? Watching as you rubbed that vibrator all over your wet pussy? Do you have any idea how hard I was lying there watching that?"

My only answer is the swift intake of air at the image his words evoke and the hammering of my pulse.

"I jerked my cock so hard to that last night and again this morning. Perhaps I should thank you, but you've been a bad girl, dolcezza. I thought I made it clear that pussy is mine. *You're* mine. Unless I make you come or tell you to make yourself come, there's no release for you. And now you're going to learn a lesson."

My nipples become tight peaks in my bra, and I almost moan at the promise in his words.

He spins me around, and I realize we're in a large custodian's closet. Without a word, and without removing his gaze from me, he undoes his belt.

Holy shit. Is he going to spank me with it or something? I swallow hard. Will I let him? Hell yes, if that's what he wants. Maybe I'll like it. I have a feeling I probably will.

Once the belt is free from his pants, he stands there holding it to his side. "You trust me?"

I nod.

"You remember what to say if you want this to end?"

I nod again.

"Good, now get on your knees."

Again, the command in his voice has me doing just that. It's like a switch is flipped when he takes control, and he oozes even more power than he does normally.

The concrete floor bites into my exposed knees, but I don't complain because he's unbuttoning his pants and lowering his zipper. He loops the belt around my neck, holding it together with one hand behind my head. The leather bites in on my throat, but not enough so that I can't breathe.

"Now open that beautiful mouth, bella." His voice comes out as rough as sandpaper.

His free hand pushes down his boxer briefs so they rest under his balls, then his cock springs into view when he pulls up his dress shirt.

"Put it in your mouth and make me come like you made yourself come last night."

I groan as I take his hard length in my hand, pulling down to expose the head from under his foreskin, then wrapping my lips around it and swirling my tongue. His head falls back on a groan, which urges me on. He's in control, but I'm the one providing him pleasure.

I stroke him as I move my head up and down, forcing myself to get as far down as I can. He's so hard in my mouth, and when I pick up the pace, he pistons his hips.

He uses the belt to control me. Pulling me off him and watching saliva drip down my chin with a satisfied smirk, then pulling me toward him and back onto his cock. When he pulls me on and off over and over again, I think I might come without even touching myself.

My clit is swollen and aching for relief. I'm more desperate than even last night.

He lets me return to my own pace again, easing up on the leather around my throat, and I work him fiercely. If I can't make myself come, I'm sure as hell going to make him come, and I want to make sure it's spectacular.

No more of him denying me and trying to act as though there's not something between us.

I push him to the back of my throat, and he uses the belt to hold me there until I'm on the edge of panic, thinking I won't be able to draw my next breath when I need to. But then he eases up, and I pull back, sucking in air. We do it a few more times until he pulls up on the belt, forcing me to stay in place while he fucks my face.

This should probably feel like degradation—I'm getting face-fucked in a cleaning closet—but it feels closer to praise and satisfaction and worship.

With a final few thrusts, Gabriele empties himself down the back of my throat with a groan, holding himself there for a beat until he pulls back so just the tip remains in my mouth. Then he looks at me with softness in his eyes and whispers, "Bellissima."

Some instinct in me knows not to move, not to say anything until he tells me to. Even if I'm still so turned on that all I want to do is take care of myself.

He watches me for a few heartbeats, then lets go of one side of the belt so it falls to hang in front of me. He helps me up off the floor, bends to dust off my knees, and wipes the saliva off my chin with his thumb.

"You okay?" He arches an eyebrow.

"Yeah," I say in a soft voice.

"Ready for your own release?" he asks as he puts his cock away and zips up his pants.

I nod, probably appearing a little too eager, but I don't care. "Definitely."

He slides his belt back through his belt loops and does it up. "Good. Stay that way. You don't come until I say you can. And when you do, I'll be the one to give it to you." Gabriele kisses my forehead. "Have a good day."

Then he leaves the closet. I turn and grin at his back as the door closes behind him.

Sure, I might be sexually frustrated, but it's worth it because Gabriele Vitale just all but said we'd mess around again.

CHAPTER TWENTY-THREE
GABRIELE

I return to my room, frustrated after searching through Marcelo and Mira's room for a USB drive and coming up empty.

Aria is sitting in front of my computer because I put her in charge of being the lookout. I pulled up all the cameras she'd need to know whether Marcelo or Mira were returning, and she was to text me immediately if I needed to get out.

She was excited and kept saying she felt like she was on a stakeout when I gave her the job, though her disappointment was evident when I told her she couldn't go to the room with me. Her pout was cute as hell, although I wish it weren't.

She spins around on my chair when she hears the door to my dorm room open, and a relieved look washes over her face when she sees that it's me. "No luck, huh?"

I shake my head and sit down on the couch. "Nope."

"What do we do now?"

I heave out a breath. "I'm not sure. Short of getting off campus somehow and searching your dad's old office, there's not much we can do here at Sicuro."

She frowns. "Speaking of getting off campus . . ."

I arch an eyebrow at her.

"I won a day off campus during that bingo game."

I'd forgotten all about that.

"It's this Saturday. Mr. Smith is escorting me, but I'm allowed to bring one person with me, and I thought . . . well, I thought maybe you might come with me."

I stare at her for a beat. "Aria, you know I can't do that." There's no part of me that wants to hurt this woman, and my chest tightens when disappointment flashes through her eyes.

"Because you don't want to or because you're worried about what my brother will say?"

Am I honest with her? Do I tell her how much I enjoy spending time with her? How interesting I find her and how I want to learn everything about her? But . . . there's no future for us.

No. That will probably only encourage her to think there could be something more than what we are at the moment. "Both."

She frowns, and the tightness in my chest feels as if someone stabbed me multiple times. "I really want to go do something fun, and I could bring Bianca, or maybe even Dom, I guess . . ."

My hands tighten in my lap.

"But I'd feel safer if you were around. You're the only one who knows what's going on. I know you'd keep me safe."

Damn it. She's got my number, doesn't she? First, she mentions Dom, then her safety. Does she know how much I yearn to protect her—from everyone but me?

Before I can answer, there's a buzzing sound on the desk behind her, and she stills.

I stand from the couch. "Is that the burner phone?"

She slowly turns and picks it up. By the time I make it over to her, she's looking at the message, so I read it over her shoulder.

TICK TOCK.

My blood pumps faster, and I fist my hands at my sides. I can't wait to end whoever is threatening her.

"I'll come with you," I say before I think too much about it and the headache it'll bring.

She spins around in the chair. "Really?"

It's then we both notice that she's eye level with my crotch since she's sitting and I'm standing in front of her.

I step back. Not because I don't want her mouth on my dick, but because I'm still recovering from the mind-blowing head she gave me earlier today. Aria is a fucking savant with that mouth of hers. Not becoming obsessed with her is proving harder and harder.

"Yeah, but we're going to have to deal with your brother."

She stands from the chair. "Let me deal with him."

I arch an eyebrow. "And what exactly are you going to tell him?"

"I'm not going to tell him you came down my throat earlier today."

I can't stifle my laugh. Her dark eyes glitter as she watches me.

"If you did, I'm not so sure I'd be alive on Saturday."

"Definitely not. By the way, how did you know where I was this morning?" she asks.

I shrug. "Just hacked in to see your schedule. Figured out which way you'd probably go from one class to the other."

She seems to like my answer and steps into me, wrapping her arms around my neck. The press of her breasts against my chest makes my dick twitch.

"Speaking of which, when is it my turn to come? I've been turned on all day." She sticks out her bottom lip in a pout.

I unwind her hands from around my neck and step back. "Not now, that's for sure."

Her forehead creases. "Why not?"

"Because that's your punishment for being such a fucking tease."

She pouts more, but the glimmer in her eyes says that she enjoys the game we're playing as much as I do.

* * *

By the time Saturday rolls around, Aria's a ball of energy. I don't know if it's the fact that she's getting off campus or it's because we're together, but when I slide into the back seat of the blacked-out SUV, she's practically vibrating. Then again, maybe it's because I've refused to let her come all week.

Mr. Smith, our chaperone, teaches the weaponry class at the Sicuro Academy, and one look at him tells you his name is not actually Mr. Smith. He's obviously full-blooded Italian with his dark-olive skin, deep brown eyes, and gold chain peeking out around his neck. With his honed body and the way he's always quietly observing everything around him, some instinct has always told me this guy is a trained killer. I haven't been curious enough to dig into him to see if I can find out his real story, but after today, maybe I will.

He meets my eyes in the rearview mirror. "Gabriele," he says with a nod.

I nod back, then turn my attention to Aria as the vehicle pulls away from the school. "What's the plan for today?"

"Fun. That is the only plan for today, right, Mr. Smith?" She smiles and looks at the front seat.

"Fun, but within reason," he says, glancing at me in the rearview.

"Where are we going exactly?" I ask as the trees lining the drive that leads to the iron security gates whiz by.

"Closest town to the school. It's small, not much there, but it's a change of scenery for you."

True enough. It's not until now, when I'm getting off campus, that I realize how much I needed this. The academy is large and offers enough that you don't feel trapped, but we're stuck here for months at a time, so we itch for anything different.

We ride the rest of the way into town in silence. There's nothing I want to talk to Aria about that I want Mr. Smith to hear, and Aria seems to feel the same. And Mr. Smith himself isn't exactly a conversationalist.

When we pull into town, it's underwhelming. We're driving down what's clearly the main street. The small downtown area looks to only be about four or five blocks filled with mom-and-pop shops.

Thankfully, I spot a tavern. Wouldn't mind visiting that before we head back.

Mr. Smith parks the car, and we all step out. The few people walking on the sidewalk turn to give us the once-over, then quickly whip back around when I meet their stare.

We stick out. Of that I have no doubt. None of us have the laid-back, easy attitude of a person living a simple small-town life, not even Aria.

The community surrounding the Sicuro Academy doesn't know what lies on the thousands of acres the school is set on. I'd love to hear the rumors people spread about what's behind the iron gates.

I look up and down the street. "Well, what do you have in mind?"

"This place is so cute. Let's start at one end of the street and work our way up. We can check out all the little shops."

Definitely not my idea of fun. Based on the look on Mr. Smith's face, he'd agree. But really what are our options?

"Sure," I say.

"Great, come on." She grabs my arm and drags me forward.

Mr. Smith follows us. Close enough to keep an eye on us and make sure we don't bolt or get ourselves into trouble, but far enough away that we have some privacy to talk without him overhearing.

"I've been thinking of what our next steps should be regarding our little . . . problem." I keep my voice low in case Mr. Smith has some kind of superhero hearing.

Aria stops walking and turns to me. "I don't want to think about any of that today, I just want to have fun. Promise we won't talk about it?" She holds out her pinkie finger.

We can't put off the inevitable, but will it kill us to not think about it for one day? No. In fact, I think I'll enjoy the reprieve as much as she will.

I wrap my pinkie finger around her smaller one. "Promise. But after you tell me what you told your brother about today. I need to make sure I back up your story."

She presses her lips together and spins to walk down the sidewalk again.

My stomach clenches. "Aria, don't tell me you didn't tell him we were going off campus together today." I walk after her, snagging her elbow and forcing her to stop.

"I tried, I really did. But then I got nervous that he'd say no and somehow sabotage today, and we wouldn't be able to go, so I figured I'd just tell him about it after."

I let my chin drop to my chest and squeeze the bridge of my nose with my fingers. "That's gonna make it so much worse. You realize that, right?"

"I'm going to tell him that Bianca was supposed to come with me, but she wasn't feeling well—I already cleared that story with her. My brother knows how impulsive I can be. I'll just say I saw you after breakfast, and before I knew it, I invited you."

I cross my arms. "You really think he's going to buy that bullshit story?"

She shrugs. "Doesn't matter whether he does or doesn't. We'll have already had a fun day, and he won't be able to ruin it."

Blowing out a breath, I shake my head. "Sometimes I wonder if you're more trouble than you're worth."

She pokes me in the stomach. "C'mon, you know I'm not." She winks and struts down the sidewalk again.

I glance back at Mr. Smith, whose eyebrows rise in a gesture that reads "Good luck with that one." Shaking my head, I follow her into what is only the first in a long line of shops selling a bunch of shit that doesn't interest me. But watching Aria get excited when she finds a candle in her favorite scent or homemade soap to bring back for some of the girls makes it worth it.

I swear, who am I these days?

CHAPTER TWENTY-FOUR
ARIA

After a long morning and early afternoon of checking out every single shop on Main Street, we end up at the tavern for something to eat.

To my surprise, Gabriele was a good sport as I dragged him around a bunch of stores that really didn't have anything he'd be interested in. I have a feeling the only stores he wants to visit are probably ones with computer and video equipment or a gun shop.

It's been so much fun hanging out with him today in a regular environment. As hard as I've tried, it's impossible to keep my thoughts from straying to what if . . .

What if we could be together and do this kind of thing on the regular?

What if my brother approved of him and let us see each other?

What if we didn't have to sneak around, and we could be more?

But those kinds of thoughts are dangerous because they lead to hope. And I don't want to get my heart crushed—because I'm not sure I could survive it. Things with Gabriele just fit. I don't feel lost like I did when I first came to Sicuro. As if the final piece of some puzzle I didn't know I was working on fell into place.

"I'm stuffed." I push my plate away, unable to eat anymore.

"You barely touched your meal," Gabriele says before taking a big bite of his French dip sandwich.

"I had enough. I don't want to be overfull. I hate that feeling. It takes so long to go away, and you're so uncomfortable. Clearly you don't have that problem."

He smiles around his sandwich as he takes another healthy bite. I guess it takes a lot to fuel his perfect physique.

"I'm a growing boy," he says when he's done chewing, and I roll my eyes.

I glance at Mr. Smith, who took a seat in the far corner of the tavern. It didn't escape me that it gives him the best view of the entire place.

At first, I worried that he'd be on top of us all day, but he's kept his distance and allowed Gabriele and me to do pretty much whatever we want. He even let Gabriele order drinks with our meal and neither he nor the grizzly guy who works behind the bar said anything when Gabriele ordered two and slid one across the table to me.

I look behind me at where a pool table sits unused. "Want to play a round of pool when you're done eating?"

He shrugs. "Sure, if you feel like losing."

"How do you know I'm not a pool shark?"

"Because there's no way your father would let his Mafia princess hang out in seedy New York pool bars, that's how."

He's not wrong. I've never played in my life, but I enjoy trying new things, and this will just be something to add to my roster.

I shrug. "I'm a quick learner."

"You sure are." His eyelids grow heavy.

I press my thighs together and shift in my seat, that near-constant thrum between my legs amping up again.

Gabriele chuckles.

"Stronzo," I snipe.

He just continues to laugh.

When he finishes eating, he orders two more drinks at the bar and meets me at the pool table, setting them on the small circular high-top table set off to the side. The tavern is one of those places that allows patrons to throw their peanut shells on the wood floors, and they crunch under my shoes as I grab a pool stick from the holder on the wall.

"Have you played before?" Gabriele asks me as he racks the balls. I shake my head. "No. You'll need to show me."

He looks at me as if he knows what I'm up to and glances back at Mr. Smith, who's still at the table on the other side of the bar. "You're a fast learner. I'm sure you'll pick it up quickly."

I grin across the green felt table at him. Once he has everything set up, he grabs his pool stick, takes something off the ledge, and rubs it at the end of his pool stick.

"What are you doing, giving yourself an advantage?" I ask, making my way over to him.

He hands me the square-shaped item that has blue chalk on one side. "Chalking my pool cue. Do yours, too."

"Hmm, let me see how fast I pick up on this part." I exaggeratedly rub the chalk over the top.

He rolls his eyes at my antics, but he's amused. Then I lick my lips, imagining it's the end of his cock I'm paying such avid attention to, and his eyelids grow heavy.

He situates himself in his pants. "Careful, dolcezza. You know what happened the last time you were a tease."

I chuckle. "Maybe that's the goal."

He walks away from me, shaking his head. "I'll break them and then show you some things from there." Gabriele bends down and lines up his shot, his hazel eyes focused before he slides the stick through his long fingers and thrusts it forward. The balls scatter in all directions, a few sinking in the pockets. "We won't worry about the rules just yet. I'll just show you how to shoot, how to work the angles to line up your shots, then we can play a game. Sound good?"

"Yep." I take a large gulp of my drink and practically skip over to him. I like when he shows me new things, even if they're not sexual. "So what do I do?"

"Bend over—"

"Okkaayy." I waggle my eyebrows.

He laughs. God, it feels so good to make this serious and stoic man laugh.

I do as he says and bend over, trying to mimic the way he was holding his pool stick. I'm wearing a flirty floral skirt that ends at mid-thigh, so I know the hem is likely sitting right at the crease of my ass in the position I'm in. And because I know this, I wiggle my ass side to side, since it's facing the wall and not the rest of the bar.

I suppress a smile when Gabriele groans behind me.

"You need to adjust your fingers on the pool cue." I change them a bit, and then he says, "Here," and leans in over me.

Our groins are lined up, and his chest presses into my back. I can't help it. I push my ass back a bit and suck in a breath when I feel him hardening slightly. We both pause, breathing heavily before he talks.

"Do this with your fingers." He shows me, and I follow his instructions, but it feels kind of weird. Then he sets his hands over mine, pulling back the pool stick, sliding it through my fingers. "Nice and easy, like this."

He does this a few times before he pistons the pool stick, and his body presses against mine. Oh, if we were naked, this would be a whole other experience. My nipples grow tight, and the space between my thighs tingles, begging for attention. I can't help the moan that crawls up my throat, demanding to be heard.

"Soon." His breath flutters my hair, and goose bumps rise on my skin as it washes over my neck. He punctuates his words with a small jerk forward of his hips.

I'm panting and sink absolutely nothing.

We straighten up, and I miss the heat of his body against mine.

He takes the next shot, then helps me with mine and on and on we go. By the time he sinks the final ball, I feel like a jumbled mess of hormones desperate for release.

Gabriele straightens and glances at Mr. Smith, who's at the table and looking at his phone. "Meet me in the women's bathroom."

My eyes widen. He sets his pool stick on the table, then casually walks in the direction of the hallway leading to the bathrooms.

My breath comes hard and heavy in anticipation, and I send up a small prayer that I'll get to come this time as a result of whatever Gabriele has in mind. When I look at Mr. Smith, he's looking at me. I mouth and motion to the hallway that I'm going to use the restroom. He nods and goes back to looking at his phone with a frown. The poor man is probably bored out of his mind.

Trying not to be too eager, I make my way to the hallway and into the women's washroom. I don't get a chance to even get a sense of what it looks like because the moment I'm inside, Gabriele pins me against the door and locks it.

The sound of the lock sliding into place is like the starting pistol at the beginning of a race, and we're on each other. His lips are on mine, his hands in my hair as I slide my hands around to his back. Too soon he pulls away, staring at my face for a beat and breathing heavily.

Then he drops to his knees in front of me, forcing me to set one foot on the counter to our right and opening me to him. "Don't make a sound. If you do, I stop. Got it?"

I nod feverishly, wanting nothing more than his mouth on me. He hikes up my skirt, tugs my panties to the side, runs his tongue between my folds, then sucks on my clit.

Oh my God! My head hits the door, and I close my eyes. My back arches at the sensation, and he takes my wrist and directs my hand between my legs, wrapping my fingers around my underwear. I pull it to the side and hold it there.

He uses one hand to spread me while the other pushes two fingers into my pussy. I bite my bottom lip to keep any noises from slipping from my mouth. Gabriele always means what he says, and if he stopped, I might just die from lack of getting off.

Gabriele works me fast and hard, cognizant of the fact that we don't have long. The sensation of his lips pulling on my clit mixed with the steady pace of how he fucks me with his long fingers has me on the edge of orgasm within a minute. He primed me so perfectly that I'm surprised I didn't come from just the visual of him between my legs.

His whiskey eyes watch me from below, cataloging my every reaction to how he works my body, and when I'm about to come, it's as if he knows. A gleam of satisfaction glimmers in his eyes. He curls his fingers just right, taking one final pull on my clit, and I combust.

I don't know if I make any noise when I come—I'm too far gone to care.

My body feels as if it shatters into a million little pieces, then those pieces ricochet back, and I'm whole once again, panting and leaning against the door while Gabriele gently tugs my panties back into place and lowers my foot from the counter.

"Worth the wait?" He arches an eyebrow.

A knock on the door behind me startles me, and I go rigid.

"Get the fuck out here, you two."

Shit. It's Mr. Smith.

I hurry over to the dingy mirror in the bathroom to check my appearance. Do I look like I just got off?

One hundred percent. Great.

"Just a minute," Gabriele calls.

I smooth out my hair and straighten my clothes.

He comes up behind me and sets his hands on my shoulders. "Not sure it's going to matter, cara. We've been found out."

I cringe. It's not as though I'm worried Mr. Smith will tattle on me—he'd catch as much or more flack than we would for allowing us the opportunity to mess around—but it's embarrassing.

When I'm satisfied that I've done what I can, I walk over to the door where Gabriele now waits. He unlocks it, and we step out into the hall. Mr. Smith leans against the wall with his arms crossed. He doesn't look happy.

"Because I don't want to deal with your brother, Miss Costa, I'll pretend I'm ignorant to what probably just went down in that bathroom."

My cheeks heat, and I nod my thanks.

"And you, Mr. Vitale, see if you can keep it in your pants until we get back to the academy, and you're on your own time."

Gabriele steps forward and looks as if he's going to say something, so I take his hand and squeeze it. He stops, takes a few deep breaths, and stalks down the hallway. Mr. Smith and I trail behind.

"I've paid the bill. Day of fun is over now," he says loudly enough for Gabriele to hear.

We head toward the door, and Gabriele holds it open for us. I suspect more for me than Mr. Smith at this point, because Gabriele's still glaring at him. We follow behind Mr. Smith, cutting across the street when we approach where the SUV is parked on the other side of the road.

We're halfway across the street, and I can't stop staring at Gabriele's profile. It's too late, and I'm not sure I can keep lying to myself. This isn't about getting off for me. As I realize I'm falling for him, he looks at me with a full smile. Oh, the life I could have with this man.

A loud bang rings out, and Gabriele looks over my shoulder. He lurches forward, throwing me over his shoulder, and scrambles to the other side of the SUV. Our perfect day, perfectly ruined.

CHAPTER TWENTY-FIVE
GABRIELE

My mind isn't on anything but her when the sound of a gunshot echoes through the warm afternoon air.

I look in the direction I assume the shot came from and see another SUV parked well down the street. Windows are tinted full black, but the one on the back driver's side is down partially, and I spot the muzzle of a gun there.

Another shot shatters the silence. Aria screams, and I hoist her up by the waist and drag her behind our SUV, forcing her down to the ground. I frantically inspect her to make sure she hasn't been shot. I tell her to stay put and crawl around the front to check on Mr. Smith. He's on the ground near the driver's door, blood flowing from his right shoulder.

He meets my gaze and reaches around with his hand, cringing and pulling a weapon from the waistband of his pants. I'd clocked it earlier, not at all surprised he was carrying. Being in charge of two students' safety comes with danger, especially when they're Aria and me.

"Here." He slides the gun over the cement to me.

I immediately aim for the SUV, but it's already pulling away from the curb and turning to head in the opposite direction. I fire off a few shots, hitting the back of it, and manage to catch the tail end of its New York license plate.

It doesn't take a genius to figure out that whoever it is, they probably have a connection to what's going on with Aria since New York is the Costa territory. But if they'd wanted, they could've easily taken us all out. They had the jump on us.

Motherfuck. I let my guard down, too consumed by Aria to look around. My assumption is Mr. Smith was pissed about us fucking around in the bathroom and not checking our surroundings. We're both at fault, but protecting Aria is my responsibility, and I failed her today.

People emerge from the storefronts to see what happened.

"Aria, get in the SUV!" I shout, darting forward to help Mr. Smith up off the ground and into the back seat.

I open the back door to get Mr. Smith in, and Aria's eyes are wide, her face pale.

I help Mr. Smith in, and once he's settled, I whip off my shirt and toss it to Aria. "Use this to apply pressure to the wound. I'll drive us back."

She nods wordlessly and does what I say.

Neither of us speaks as I dig the keys from Mr. Smith's pants and get into the driver's seat. He's losing a lot of blood, but he should be fine if we can get him back quickly enough. There are doctors on campus who can help him. Taking him to a local hospital isn't even an option. Not only will the doctors at the Sicuro Academy be better, they won't ask questions.

As I race through the small downtown, I type the school's address into the GPS.

"He passed out," Aria says. Her voice is shaky and scared, and my instincts roar to comfort her and make sure she's okay, but now is not the time.

"He'll be okay. We're almost there." A bit of a lie, and she probably knows it, given that she can likely see the GPS screen from the back seat, but she doesn't argue with me.

The rest of the drive is made in silence. Security is quick to rush us through when they see Mr. Smith in the back seat, covered in blood. I race up the drive toward the school, and when we're still a distance away, I spot Marcelo pacing near the circular drive, no doubt ready to kill me since Aria didn't inform him she'd be leaving campus with me today.

My hands tighten on the steering wheel. I don't have time for this shit.

I slam on the brakes and throw the SUV into park. Marcelo's head whips in our direction. It's then I realize that Mira is with him, because as he stalks over to us, she's tugging on his arm, and her lips are moving. I can't hear her words, but I'm sure she's pleading with him to calm down.

After getting out, I head directly to the door behind me and open it.

"You've signed your death warrant, Vitale." Marcelo's voice comes from behind me as I drag Mr. Smith out of the back seat.

"Later, Costa. Help me get him inside."

He steps up from behind me. "What the fuck? Where is Aria? Is she okay?"

"Oh my God," Mira says, then a few seconds later, she's whipping open Aria's door.

Marcelo's shoulders fall when he sees his sister is alive and not shot.

"We were ambushed right before we headed back. He took a bullet to the shoulder."

"I'll go get someone to help," Mira says and rushes off.

Marcelo helps me get Mr. Smith out of the back seat. He moans as we move him around, likely because we're jostling his injury so much. That's okay, though. At least I know he's still alive.

With each of us on one side of him, we half drag Mr. Smith around the vehicle and up over the concrete toward the school en-

trance. Before we reach it, Mira comes out, holding the door open
for one of the medical staff rushing behind her with a wheelchair.
We get Mr. Smith in it, then we're all left looking after him while
the nurse rushes off. Once the school doors close behind him, Marcelo returns his attention to his sister and me.

"What the fuck?" He steps up to me, and we bump chests.

"Back off!" Aria says, trying to get between us.

I glare at Marcelo, fisting my hands at my sides. I glance down
at Aria, and her eyes are filled with unshed tears. "Now's not the
time. Go see to your sister. She's upset. I have to go see the chancellor."

It's not as though the chancellor has called me in to see him yet,
but it's coming. As soon as he finds out what happened, he's going
to want to speak to all three of us. The sooner he makes the payoffs
to keep what happened in that town today off of anyone's radar, the
better.

"He's right," Mira says, tugging on Marcelo's arm.

His jaw flexes, and finally he steps back.

I'm not afraid of Marcelo, especially when no weapons are involved. I could have him on his back in two seconds flat, but Aria's
been through enough shit today.

I stalk off without looking at her or saying goodbye. Right now,
it's too hard to look into the eyes of the woman I failed and who
could have died as a result.

* * *

ONCE I'VE TALKED to the chancellor and explained to him that we
have no idea who was shooting at us or why, he lets me call my father. I don't fill him in either on what's really going on.

Of course, my father questioned why I was anywhere with Aria
Costa alone, and I lied and said that we each won a day pass off
campus at different school events and that it was a coincidence it

was the two of us. I'm not sure he believed me, but I don't care. I have other things to attend to.

First Marcelo, next Aria, and then seeing if I can trace that partial plate of the SUV.

After I've left the main building, I walk across campus toward the Roma House. The entire way, all I can think of is how close Aria came to losing her life today. They didn't want to hit her—they had the perfect opportunity. But it was a warning. Get them what they want, or suffer the consequences. Shooting Mr. Smith was to prove they're serious.

It's not as if I didn't think whoever it was would try to get what they want at any cost, but being here on campus, it's easy to forget how insulated we are. The time has come to double our efforts and figure out who's behind all this and make them pay. The time has also come to face what I feel for Aria Costa.

The more I have her, the more I want her, and after what happened today, it's been made especially clear that my feelings for her go beyond the physical. If something would have happened to her . . . I shudder. A hollowness fills my heart that I'm pretty sure no one else could ever fill.

I pull open the door of Roma House and make my way through the lounge. I'm not left to wonder if anyone has heard about what happened because all conversation instantly dies down, and everyone turns to look at me. No one's stupid enough to say anything to me, though. Pretty sure my aura reads "fuck with me and suffer the consequences." That is, until I step up to the elevator and press the button, then wait for it to come.

Sandro steps up beside me. "Jesus, you okay? Heard what happened."

I don't turn to look at him but see him give me the once-over in my periphery. I'm sure I look a sight—my clothes are still covered in Mr. Smith's blood, though I did manage to wash my hands. "Fine. Can't say the same for Mr. Smith, though."

"He gonna be all right?"

I nod. "Should be."

"Where are you headed?" he asks.

"To see Costa."

"Marcelo or Aria?"

I turn with a raised eyebrow and narrow my eyes at him.

He raises his hands in front of him. "It's a fair question."

"Maybe so, but it will have to wait." The elevator dings. I step inside and turn to face him. "I'll reach out when I need you."

His expression grows serious, and he nods, then the elevator doors close between us.

When I reach Marcelo's door, I knock, knowing he's waiting here for me, on his turf. The only thing I'm not sure about is whether Aria will still be with him.

The door opens, and Mirabella stands there wearing a solemn expression. "I'll leave you guys to talk."

I nod at her and walk past.

"Try not to kill each other," she says before she closes the door behind her.

Marcelo's in the center of the room, arms crossed, face drawn. I'm not here to be scolded by him, so if he thinks I'll stand here like a petulant child and be berated, he has another think coming.

But I'll let him set the tone, so I stand silent, meeting his gaze.

"Before we start, I need to thank you," he says.

My eyebrows raise to my hairline in surprise. I'm sure he's not thanking me for eating his sister out against the door of a dingy bathroom.

"Aria says you picked her up and removed her from harm's way today. In fact, she says that's the first thing you did without worrying about anything else, so thank you. I don't know what I would've done if . . ." He swallows hard. This is as much emotion as I've ever seen from Marcelo, but I understand it. I had much the same reaction earlier when I let myself think about if things had gone differently today.

"It was instinct to protect her."

He nods. "Which is the only reason I haven't already put my fist through your face. I'm going to let you explain to me what the fuck is going on with you and my sister. She wouldn't say much despite my threat to have her removed from campus. Seems she chooses to protect you." His lips press into a thin line.

I debated earlier on how much to tell him. Do I lie and say we're friends? Do I mention the threat against his sister, and if so, how much detail do I give him?

In the end, I decide to be truthful about my feelings for his sister and only give him vagaries about how the threat against her began. No brother wants to hear about his sister topless in a sex club.

"I have feelings for your sister. Strong ones."

Marcelo's jaw clenches. "So what, you guys have been fucking around?"

He steps toward me, but I remain in place.

"Do you really want the answer to that?" I arch an eyebrow.

He pinches the bridge of his nose. "Fuck no, spare me the details." He looks back up at me with barely restrained fury. "I don't have to wonder how she feels about you. It's obvious from the look on her face when she talks about you or says your name."

My forehead wrinkles. "What's the look on her face?"

"The same one Mira has when she looks at me." He pauses. "Which is what has me so concerned."

"Explain." I nod at him to continue.

"You see, I looked into you when my sister first showed interest in you last year when she came for her campus tour. I could tell she was all fucking moony-eyed, and you've always been a bit of a mystery, so I paid people to do some digging."

My fists tighten at my sides.

"Yeah, I can see you don't like that. But you're not the only one who can dig into other people's lives, Vitale."

"Just say what you have to say." The only reason I'm still standing here listening to this bullshit is because it's a necessary evil to get what I want—Aria.

If I want to be able to spend time with Aria from now on, I need Marcelo on board, or at least not in opposition to us. He knows enough now that he could keep her from me if he wanted.

"Because of my digging, I know that you frequented a few sex clubs in your area this summer. I don't know what you're into, and I don't care. But you keep that shit far, far away from my sister. And if you fuck around behind her back to go get your fix of whatever it is you're into, you and I are going to have a real problem, we clear?"

My jaw clenches, and I narrow my eyes at him. Everything in me wants to push back and tell him to go fuck himself—no one except my father tells me what to do. And even then, it has an expiration date.

"You have nothing to worry about with your sister and me. She's in good hands." There's not much else to say. It's not as if I'm going to betray Aria's trust and tell her brother that she gets off on being controlled.

"You just make sure it stays that way. I'll be watching you."

I nod. "Understood."

Who knows what Marcelo thinks I'm into? A lot of shit goes down in a sex club—BDSM, orgies, swapping, public humiliation, and voyeurism, to name a few. I've dabbled in most of them, and I can take or leave them. I like to dip my toe in from time to time, but I've learned that what I really covet is being the one in control of the scene.

But I would never push Aria into something she's not comfortable with. Never. And he doesn't have to worry because as long as she's with me, no man is ever getting his hands on my woman.

"Now, let's talk about why the fuck someone is shooting at you guys." He sounds even more pissed off now, as he should be.

"What did Aria tell you?"

"Again, not much. She said you could explain."

So she's leaving it to me to reveal as much or as little as I think we need to. One thing's for sure—I'm not telling him about the sex club that started all this.

I launch into a rundown of everything that's happened so far and what it is they're looking for, not explaining what they have on Aria to blackmail her with. Especially after he just issued his decree about keeping Aria far away from my sexual proclivities. He'll never believe that I had nothing to do with her being at that club.

"Any idea what it is they might want her to hand over?" I ask him.

His forehead wrinkles, and he sits on his couch. "No idea. Noticed you didn't mention what they're blackmailing my sister with." His gaze holds mine.

"Trust me when I say it's better if you don't know, but it has nothing to do with the two of us being sexual at all." Not a lie.

He cringes and curses in Italian, looking down and shaking his head. "What happened to my sweet, innocent little sister?"

"Knowing what I know about your sister, she doesn't seem like she was probably ever that sweet or innocent."

"Fuck off," he grumbles to the floor.

Now for the part I know he's really going to hate. "I'm calling in my favor."

About a year ago, I did Marcelo a favor when some shit was going down with him and Mira, and he owes me one in return. In our world, your word is your bond, and there's very little I can't force Marcelo to agree to when I call it in.

His head whips up, and he bolts up from the couch, his hands fisted at his sides and his breaths coming in short spurts. "You can't seriously be asking me to let you fuck my sister because I owe you a favor."

I raise a hand. "Relax, even I'm not that much of an asshole."

Relief washes over his features, but I don't think he'll like my demand any more than the idea of me sleeping with his sister. Not my problem.

"You need to stay out of this thing with Aria and the blackmail," I say. "Trust me to handle it as I see fit, and if I need you, I'll let you know."

His face turns red, probably biting back the words he wants to say to me. But I know him. We're the same. Marcelo's going to want to take over and do things his way, and when there are too many captains steering the ship, it just goes in circles.

"Believe me when I say that no one is more motivated to bring down whoever it is after today."

His jaw hardens, and his lips press into a thin line. "What choice do I have? If I do this, we're even then?"

I nod. "We're even."

"Fine. But nothing better happen to my sister, or you will answer to me."

"Believe me, if anything did, I'd welcome your retribution."

He studies me for a beat then nods. "Tell me what you need."

So I do, and then it's time to tell Aria everything I realized today when she was almost ripped away from me.

CHAPTER TWENTY-SIX
ARIA

There's a knock on my door, and I bolt off my bed. I've yet to see Gabriele since he walked away from me when we arrived back at the school.

I whip open the door and relief wraps around me that it's him. His hair is still damp from a shower, and he smells like that body-wash I love so much.

My stomach sours at his anxious expression. Oh God, did my brother warn him off of me, and he's actually going to listen? I didn't tell Marcelo much of anything when he was grilling me earlier.

"Come in." I open the door wider and allow Gabriele to walk past me. Trying to play it cool lasts about three seconds. I blurt out, "Gabriele, what's going on?" before I've even closed the door.

Once he's in the room, he turns and gives me a puzzled expression.

"You didn't even look at me before you left me at the entrance to the school, and it's been hours and hours since we returned, and I haven't heard from you." I swallow the lump in my throat. "I thought maybe you were mad at me because I got you shot at, all because I went to that stupid club in Miami. I understand if you want nothing to do with me." By the time I'm done speaking, even I hear the spastic panic in my voice.

"Aria . . ." He takes my hands. "I wasn't going to come see you covered in blood, so I had to shower first. Then once I was back in my room, I decided I had to go work out first before I came and saw you."

"Oh." I frown, not understanding.

He sighs. "I had so much aggression and adrenaline flowing through my body . . . I didn't want to risk being too rough with you if we . . . I needed to get some of it out before I saw you."

Those words probably wouldn't sound romantic to anyone but me. My heart flutters. "You're not mad at me?"

He chuckles and tucks a strand of my hair behind my ear. "Of course not. I want to murder whoever shot at us—slowly—but I'm not mad at you. Why would I be?"

I dip my chin and look at the floor between us. "I got us into all this because I was impulsive and didn't think through my actions."

He lifts my chin with his finger, forcing me to meet his gaze. "This isn't your fault, Aria. Someone else set all of this in motion, not you. Understand?"

I nod, trapped by the look of possession in his whiskey eyes.

"I went to see your brother before coming here."

Anxiety flares in my chest again. "How . . . how did that go?"

"I think Marcelo has a good understanding of how I feel about you. Now I need you to know."

"Okay," I whisper, bracing myself in case it's not what I want to hear.

He brings both hands up to my cheeks. "Aria, today when I heard that gunshot . . . before I looked at you to make sure you were okay, was the most terrified I've ever been in my life. I didn't know what I was going to see when I looked over, and all these horrible images of you hurt or worse assaulted me. And in that split second, I knew."

"Knew what?" My gaze roams his face.

"Knew that you were it for me. Knew that despite trying my hardest not to fall for you, you somehow snuck through the cracks in my armor and straight into my heart. Knew that there is nothing I wouldn't do to ensure your safety and your happiness."

Tears well in my eyes.

"Thank you for being you. Thank you for never taking no for an answer when it came to me. You're impulsive and hardheaded and everything I didn't know I needed and wanted in my life, and I am never, ever letting you go. Today I got a glimpse of what I would feel if you weren't in my life anymore, and I refuse to ever feel that way again."

I don't know what to say. Everything he told me . . . it's more than I could have ever hoped for. I'm just . . . stunned. Stunned silent.

"Why aren't you saying anything?" His gaze darts between my eyes.

I shake my head and snap out of my stupor. "I'm sorry, I don't know what to say. You don't understand how long I've waited for you to say those things, to feel the same way about me as I do for you."

His smile starts small, like the sun just peeking over the horizon in the early morning, then it grows wider and wider until it's filled with happiness. I vow to commit the image to memory. I don't know when I'll see a smile like that on his face again.

"You're in this then? We're in this together?"

I nod, not trusting myself to speak again without bursting into happy tears.

He kisses me, hands slipping into my hair from my cheeks. It starts off deep and slow, as though he wants to kiss me thoroughly, commit this moment to memory. But quickly it turns more desperate until we're nipping at each other's lips, needing more.

Mouths still joined, we work at undressing each other. Neither of us is willing to separate from the other. Today's close call has made us both aware of how close we came to never having this.

Once we're undressed, Gabriele pulls away and looks at me with heated eyes. "Go lie on the bed."

My nipples peak at the command in his voice, and I do as he says. Once I'm on my back on the mattress, I spread my legs for his view, wanting nothing more than to tempt him.

Gabriele walks over to his discarded pants and rolls a condom down his thick length, then he stands at the end of the bed, hand on his cock, slowly jerking it while his gaze peruses my body. "Sei cosi bella."

I feel beautiful when he looks at me like this. I'm expecting him to give me an order, tell me what he wants me to do. But rather than taking control, he crawls on the bed so that he's hovering over me. He leans in and runs his tongue between my legs, once, twice, then three times, making me moan.

Instinctively, I reach for my breasts and squeeze them. He groans in response, and it sounds like a growl.

"Please . . ." is all I can say, desperate to finally feel him moving inside me.

He fists the base of his cock and runs it along the same path his tongue just took, brushing the head through my wet folds. When he circles the tip over my clit, my back arches, and I'm panting. My nipples are so tight it's almost painful when he teases me, pushing the tip of himself into me and holding it there.

I know better than to try to force my will by moving to get him inside me. This is just another exertion of his control, and I'd be lying if I said it didn't turn me on. Instead, I bite my bottom lip and meet his gaze. When I do, he slowly sinks into me about halfway, then he slams himself home.

The stretch of him burns in the best way possible. It makes me feel full—of him—and there's no better feeling.

He holds himself in place while I pant underneath him. "You okay?"

His concern sends a warm rush through my chest, and I nod.

Gabriele leans down and kisses me as he moves. Every nerve

ending between my legs lights up in pleasure. I grow wetter, and even though he has a condom on, it's like he can tell because he groans. My legs squeeze around his hips as he moves his lips from mine and trails kisses down my jaw to my ear.

"This pussy is mine now, Aria. No other man will ever be between these legs again. No other man will ever know what heaven feels like."

The care and warmth of his voice is at odds with the possessiveness of his words, but it makes me feel coveted and safe just the same.

He rises over me again, pulling his lips from my skin, and our eyes meet. We maintain eye contact with every push and pull in and out of my body, and suddenly what started out as being about pleasure feels more like an emotional connection, an intimacy I've never shared with anyone else.

My eyes well with tears, I don't even know why. After everything that happened today and then this, I just have too many emotions inside me to keep them contained.

Gabriele doesn't make me feel like an idiot, though. He whispers, "I know." Then he places a soft kiss over each of my eyes.

When he takes my legs from around his waist and pins them up near my chest, it changes the angle of his entrance into my body and strokes something inside me that makes me feel a little crazed. Alive. I pant, trying desperately to stave off my orgasm—I want this to last. I don't want it to ever be over.

But I needn't have bothered. My climax rolls over me like a wave in slow motion. I see it coming, but when it hits me full force, I realize I didn't know the strength of what was headed my way. My back arches, and I cry out Gabriele's name. Before my eyes squeeze shut, I see him watching me, enraptured.

Once I've come down from my high and open my eyes, he's still looking at me, and he moves faster. He groans, panting hard until, without warning, he pulls himself from my body and rips off the condom. Gabriele fists himself, jerks a couple of times, and coats the inside of my thighs with his release.

The sound he makes when he does so will be committed to memory for eternity. It's so delicious.

After he's recovered for a minute and both our breathing is closer to normal, he gets up off the bed, taking the used condom with him to the bathroom. When he emerges, he has a wet cloth in hand and cleans me before returning to bed and pulling me into his side.

We lie there wrapped in each other's arms, and though there's a shitstorm swirling around us, I've never been so happy. My heart is light and giddy with love.

When Gabriele speaks, he doesn't say what I expect. "You should know that your brother has agreed to stay out of this mess for the time being unless I request his help."

I perch myself up on one arm to see him. "How did you get him to agree to that?"

"I have my ways. The other thing you need to know is that the day after next, we'll be taking Marcelo's private jet back to your place in New York, where we're going to search your father's office high and low for what we're looking for. I can't risk taking my plane and tipping my father off on what's going on."

My mouth drops open. "First my overbearing brother agrees to stay out of it, then he's letting you into what is essentially now his private office?"

Gabriele is a Vitale, not a Costa. I can't believe my brother would ever agree to that.

"He said he's already removed anything he thought was of importance and brought it to his own office at his place. None of what he took was a USB."

I frown. "But how are we going to get off campus?"

"We're going to use what happened today to our advantage.

You're going to skip classes Monday, citing being too upset and traumatized over what happened today. I'm going to start a fight with someone in weaponry class so that the chancellor asks me to take a few days away to clear my head."

I rest a hand on his chest. "You can't start a fight, you'll be expelled."

He lifts my hand from his chest and kisses my knuckles. "Not when I can use the fact that the school let us off property without sufficient safeguards in place. You let me worry about that, okay?"

I nod.

I'm going to go home with Gabriele. I never, in my wildest dreams, thought that would ever happen. Maybe dreams do come true.

CHAPTER TWENTY-SEVEN
GABRIELE

We spend all day Sunday in bed, and on Monday morning I awaken with Aria practically on top of me, her dark hair strewn over my chest. It's then I realize that I slept through the night. Had no trouble falling asleep. That never happens. Ever.

Squeezing my arms around the reason why, she stirs from sleep.

Obviously I sleep much better with Aria around. I'd better make sure I sleep with her every night from here on out just to test my theory.

I have a lot to do before we leave on Monday. I have to fill my cousin in on the threat so that he can keep his eyes and ears open in my absence. I have to goad someone into a fight with me in weaponry class, and I have to see if I can track down that license plate.

With all that in mind, I kiss the top of Aria's head and attempt to extricate myself from under her without waking her.

"Where are you going?" she mumbles into the pillow before I've managed to get off the bed.

"Things to do before we leave. I'll be back tonight, okay?" I climb off the bed and find my boxer briefs where they were discarded in our frenzy last night.

I slide them on and turn to face the bed. Aria lies face down on the mattress, no blanket pulled up over her, perfect ass on display.

I groan and adjust my dick, reminding myself all the reasons why I have to leave this room.

"Okay." She turns her head to face me. She's sleepy and has wrinkles on her skin from her pillowcase. Basically, she's cute as fuck, and it makes me want to stay in this room and feel her come around my cock again. "Will you sleep over again tonight?"

I hate hearing the anxiety in her voice, as though she's not sure how I'll answer.

"Depends." I walk closer to the bed and sit on the edge. "Do you want me to?" I arch an eyebrow.

"You know I do." There's promise in her voice, and I somehow prevent myself from groaning.

"Then you have your answer. I'll do whatever it takes to make you happy, Aria, and I mean it." I kiss the bare skin on her back, lingering there.

She moans, and I feel it reverberated through her chest to my lips. I have to leave right away, or I'm going to spend the entire day in this room, worshipping her between her legs.

I stand and make my way to the door, adjusting my erection. "Ciao, bella."

Then I head to my room.

As hard as it'll be after last night, Aria has to be pushed to the back of my head. I have shit to do today, and I won't get anywhere if my thoughts keep drifting to her. She's entirely too distracting. Especially now that I know what the slick heat between her legs feels like enveloping my cock.

I exit the stairwell door and make out Antonio stepping away from my room, large manilla envelope in hand. He's walking away from me, so I call his name.

"Looking for me?" I ask.

He turns around. "Yeah. Got that info packet I owe you." He holds it up and makes his way over to me. "Sorry it took so long.

Took forever to get through the mail room. The first package my guy sent went missing."

I arch an eyebrow, and I know what we're both thinking—it likely didn't go accidentally missing. Someone made it disappear. Someone who works in security most likely.

"Interesting."

"I thought so," he says. "Anyway, here you go. Not sure if it's of any use to you now that you've got your stuff here, but a deal is a deal." He eyes the small security camera I have over my dorm room door.

I take the envelope. "Thanks. Consider your debt paid. One down, one to go." I smirk.

His body tenses, but he nods, knowing I'm right. "Let me know when I can close out my remaining debt. The sooner, the better."

I chuckle and unlock my door before going inside my room.

After I'm showered and dressed for the day, I check the time. I have about half an hour before I need to get going. That's plenty of time for me to track down the owner of that partial plate from the vehicle that was shooting at us yesterday.

Within fifteen minutes, I have the answer I expected to find— the plates were stolen. No New York plate ending in those three numbers is registered to a black SUV.

Though it's what I expected, it's not what I'd hoped for.

At least if I can figure out *who* is threatening Aria, I can better protect her because I'll know from what direction the threat is going to strike.

Frustrated, I close my laptop and set off in search of Alessandro. I don't know whether he'll be surprised to hear about what's going on with Aria or not, but I trust him not to say anything. I also trust him to keep an eye out on campus for anything suspicious. And after that, I have a fight to start and some leverage to dangle in front of the chancellor.

***

ARIA AND I join the Mile High Club an hour before we touch down at JFK airport. From there, we take a helicopter into Manhattan.

"Does my mom know we're coming?" Aria asks as the driver Marcelo arranged for us drives us in the direction of the penthouse suite her mother used to share with her father.

I shake my head and take her hand. "No. She's away."

Her head whips in my direction. "She is?"

"That's what your brother said. He said she's on an extended vacation in the Caribbean."

She frowns.

"What?" I ask.

"It's just weird, I guess. I don't really think of my mom as having a life outside of the one I grew up around, but I guess now that my dad is gone, and my brother and I are both out of the house . . . that makes sense. Weird that she didn't mention it, though."

I squeeze her hand. "Aria, when your brother heard what was going on with you, he *sent* her on a vacation." I'm not sure why it bothers her so much that she wasn't in the loop about her mom, but it clearly does. Something to dig into later.

"Oh." She nods, seeming to ponder something. "Why are we staying at a hotel then? You mentioned you'd booked a suite. We can just stay at my place."

"Because we're not going to stay anywhere associated with you or the Costa family. We're here under an alias using cards that no one can trace back to me. We're safe. If anyone goes snooping, they'll just find Mr. and Mrs. Cavalli staying in the hotel suite."

She smirks. "You made us a Mr. and Mrs.?"

I shake my head with a laugh. I guess I did. Didn't even think about it when I did it either, it just felt natural.

"Don't think I'm romantic, Aria. You'll only be disappointed." I place a chaste kiss on her lips.

Her eyes sparkle when she looks at me. "You're more romantic than you think."

I chuckle and squeeze her hand. "I'll take your word for it."

I've already changed so much since I've met her. I can't imagine who I'll be soon.

CHAPTER TWENTY-EIGHT
ARIA

I almost feel like a stranger in my family's penthouse. Although I haven't been gone that long, it feels as if it's been longer. Everything is still and silent. None of the lights are on, and our steps echo as we walk through the foyer.

"So this is where you grew up . . ." Gabriele steps in front of me once we reach the expanse of the combination living and dining room.

"Yup. Moved here when I was seven. We had a house, too, but the majority of our time was spent here during the school year. Mom sold the house right after my dad died and bought a house in the Hamptons." I don't mention I think she goes there to forget the memories these walls and the ones of our mansion held.

He nods absentmindedly. I swear he's studying the layout, committing it to memory. "Show me your bedroom."

My pulse flutters, thinking maybe we're going to get naked, but when we step inside, he puts his hands on his hips and looks around. I try to take in the space through his eyes—the bedspread with ruffles on the bottom, the ornate furniture, and the cross on the wall over my dresser. It probably all looks juvenile to him.

"This is what I expected," he finally says.

"It is?" I step up beside him, and he nods.

"If I had a sister, I suspect her room would be decorated just like this by my mother. This room isn't you at all. There's no personality, no life."

I can't suppress the smile that comes to my lips. That's oddly one of the nicest compliments anyone has ever given me.

"Where does your family live?" I ask.

"I don't live with my family anymore. I'm north of downtown Seattle, in a house in Broadmoor."

I blink a few times, surprised.

"Does that shock you?"

I chuckle. "I just pictured you holed up in some super-techy condo downtown full of computers. Like a hacker hidey-hole or something."

He barks out a laugh. "A hacker hidey-hole?"

Smiling, I shrug. "You asked."

"That I did." He presses a kiss to my temple. "Let's go to your father's office. I don't want to be here too long, just in case."

I lead the way. The door is unlocked, and it's clear my brother already took a lot of things. I was only permitted in here whenever my father summoned me, and it's odd to be here without him. Being hit with such a blatant reminder that my dad is gone makes the ache in my chest intensify.

I can still smell the tobacco of his cigars. I see him behind his big ornate desk, leaning back in his chair, his belly stretched under his shirt, lecturing me about expectations and how to be presentable for our family. I should thank Marcelo, because I'm not sure my father ever would have let me go to the Sicuro Academy.

He could be a mean man. I grew up hearing the fights, the demands he made on my mom. Although I never saw him with another woman, I'm not stupid enough to think there weren't some. But Mom always handled it with such secrecy.

"Did your dad give you that necklace?" Gabriele asks, coming to stand beside me and nodding down to where I'm fingering it.

"How'd you know?"

He shrugs. "You play with it a lot when your dad is mentioned or when you're stressed. Figured it was sentimental, and since it's the first thing you did when we walked in here, I put two and two together."

It should probably scare me how observant he is, but I remember how observant my brother is. They're both men trained to see what others don't. In order to keep their family and their men safe, they have no choice but to notice and decipher things before others.

"I think it was the only present he ever chose for me himself. Everything else . . . birthdays and Christmas were all my mom's efforts. I thought as I was getting older, our relationship might develop."

Gabriele wraps his arms around me, letting them hang loosely around my waist. "I understand why it's special then."

A lump forms in my throat, and I swallow hard. "It probably sounds weird, but sometimes I forget that he's dead. There were lots of times I wouldn't see him for days when he was . . . working or doing whatever else he did. And now that I'm away at school, it's not like I'd see him there anyway. It's easy to forget, which makes the guilt heavier."

His forehead creases. "Why would you feel guilty?"

"My dad and I had a strained relationship. He didn't treat my mom well at all, and I resented him a lot for it. And because of how I am—"

"Willful and headstrong?" He arches an eyebrow.

I roll my eyes. "We used to bump heads a lot. Maybe I thought we'd have time to fix our relationship or maybe I didn't, I don't know, but that's the thing. I never considered how I might feel if he were gone, and now it's too late to change anything. Although I'm not sure he would have ever changed."

Gabriele cups my face and brushes his thumb over my cheek. "You are perfect. If he couldn't see that, it was his loss."

My smile is sad, but my chest warms at his words nonetheless. "Let's get looking around," I say to change the subject.

He nods, apparently seeing that I need a break from talking about my dad. "Why don't you take that shelf, and I'll take the desk? Pull the books out to make sure there's nothing behind them and rifle through the pages."

I nod and get to work.

It takes hours, but we go through every inch of the space, including the safe my brother gave me the code for. Nothing.

I plop down on one of the chairs and let out a long breath. "Now what are we going to do?"

"First, we're going to get out of here." Gabriele steps around the desk and moves to stand in front of me. "Then we're going to go back to the hotel and eat. You haven't eaten since we left campus. Then I'm going to go through that file Antonio gave me to see if I can figure out who might have intercepted the mail his people sent him for me, and last . . ." He holds out his hand to help me up. "I'm going to make you come—a lot."

I lick my bottom lip and squeeze my thighs together.

He frees my bottom lip between his thumb and forefinger. "Careful. I'm liable to bend you over the desk and fuck you if you keep it up."

"That sounds good to me." I'm not even embarrassed at how breathy and needy I sound.

A dark chuckle sounds in his throat. "I don't need your father haunting me until the end of days because I defiled his daughter on his desk. Let's go." He slides his hand in mine and leads me to the door.

When we're at the door, I turn around one last time.

"Are you going to miss it?" Gabriele asks.

I shake my head. "I thought I'd miss New York more when I left, but being back here . . . it's nice and all but . . . I was ready for a new adventure." I look at him, sure that he can see in my eyes that he's all the adventure I need.

"Seems so was I." He kisses me deeply.

By the time we're walking toward the elevator, I'm able to worry a little less about the state of my life.

* * *

AFTER WE'RE FINISHED eating, Gabriele pulls out the envelope Antonio gave him and gets on his laptop to dig into the people who work in security at the Sicuro Academy.

I love watching him work. He's wearing his black-framed blue light glasses, and he looks like a sexy professor. If a professor would bend you over the desk and smack your ass when you were late to class. His focus is intense, and it reminds me of the way he looks controlling me. Like nothing else exists outside of what he's doing.

"What are you looking for exactly?" I ask, turning down the TV.

"I won't know until I find it. But it will be something that's not obvious, if there is anything. Something that requires digging. Someone intercepted that first envelope, and they're either working with or being paid off by whoever is threatening you."

As if he spoke the words into the universe and willed it to happen, the phone in my bag dings. It's the burner phone.

My eyes widen, and Gabriele meets my gaze.

Suddenly my chest is tight, and I'm frozen. He must realize I'm stricken because he gets up and walks over to my bag to retrieve the phone.

When will this ever end? I feel as if I'm walking on perpetual eggshells. It's never-ending wondering if someone is going to shoot at me again or if that phone is going to ding. Though I've been doing my best to focus on the good—Gabriele—and push all this to the back of my mind, it's been near impossible.

Everyone I talk to at school, I wonder whether they're secretly plotting against me. Since the shooting, I've had low-level anxiety thrumming through me all the time. And now, being back here in New York and being in the space that was my father's, that I was never permitted access to unlike my brother, has brought up more feelings than I care to deal with because they'll never be resolved— he's dead. I have to live with them.

"What does it say?"

Gabriele walks toward me, looking at the phone in his hand with a scowl. When he reaches where I'm sitting, he holds it out.

I take it and read the screen.

TIME IS RUNNING OUT. WHAT DO YOU THINK YOUR BROTHER WOULD THINK IF HE SAW THAT PICTURE?

Gabriele told me not to engage, but I can't help it. Rage is like lightning in my veins, and I type my own message back.

How am I supposed to get you something I don't have?

"Aria!" Gabriele goes to grab the phone, but I'm too quick and hit Send, holding the phone away from him.

It's clear he wants to punish me, but before he can say anything, the phone dings again.

IN CASE THE BULLETS DIDN'T MAKE IT CLEAR, WE'RE SERIOUS. HAPPY TO SEND YOU ANOTHER MESSAGE THOUGH. FIND THE USB. DON'T TEXT AGAIN UNTIL YOU HAVE IT.

My stomach sinks. Gabriele rips the phone from my hands, reads the message, and curses. His lips thin, and he looks as if he wants to launch it across the room but throws it onto the couch cushion instead.

A sense of dread pushes down on me, and my chest tightens, making it hard to breathe.

"Aria." Gabriele must sense my panic because he drops to his knees in front of me in a flash. His hands land on my shoulders, and his eyes search my face. "Calm down. What can I do?"

My answer is likely not what he's expecting, but it's what I need. And he's the only one who can give it to me. I meet his gaze and whisper, "Make me forget."

The line at the bridge of his nose deepens. "Are you sore from earlier?"

I shake my head, unable to speak. The truth is that I am a little tender—I've yet to grow used to the way he stretches me—but I welcome the small sting of pain. I have to get out of my head before I go crazy.

He nods once and stands, looking down his nose at me, every bit the powerful made man he is. I shiver in anticipation.

"Stand up and take everything off below your waist."

I do so, wordlessly standing and shoving off my leggings, underwear, and socks until I stand there wearing only my bra and my fitted short-sleeved shirt.

Gabriele wraps his hand around my upper arm, leading me around to the end of the couch, then applies pressure between my shoulder blades, forcing me to bend over and expose myself to him. My pulse jackhammers. I'm equal parts excited and nervous.

"You stay like that. Don't move unless I tell you."

I nod my agreement. A few moments later, I hear the sound of his belt jingling as he pulls it off his pants.

My core clenches in anticipation. What is he going to do with it? The same thing as last time? No, he wouldn't have me in this position.

He doesn't make me wait long. He slips the belt between the front of my thighs and the side of the couch, then tightens it so that my legs are pressed together, and I can't move them apart. In a weird way, it makes me feel more exposed and restrained than if he'd spread my legs and tied each one to the bedpost.

Gabriele dips a finger through my exposed folds. "Always so wet and needy for me, cara, aren't you?"

"Yes," I moan as he pays particular attention to my entrance, swirling his finger around but never in.

"Look at this beautiful pussy, and it's all mine. I think it's time I worship her again."

He must get on his knees behind me then because the next thing I feel is his tongue as he swipes it from my clit up to my entrance, dipping it inside. Gabriele works me over, and the dynamic of being so exposed below the waist but completely covered above ratchets up my desire to another level.

He laps at me, making me desperate and needy, getting me exactly where he wishes. Then he tongues me *there*.

Oh God. I didn't realize it would feel so good. No one has ever done that. Before long, I'm panting and feel as if I'll go out of my mind if I don't either get him inside me or come.

"Please, Gabriele. Please." I beg when I shouldn't, but I don't care. My existence has been whittled down to the need for release, and it's the only thing that matters.

"You like that?" he asks before biting my ass cheek.

My yelp turns into a moan when the tip of his tongue plays with my puckered hole.

"Yes, yes. More please let me come." I grind into his face as much as I can in this position. And when he brings his fingers to circle my clit once, I'm so primed and ready that I come on a scream.

Before I have time to recover, Gabriele slams into me from behind, to the hilt in one brutal thrust, and somehow my orgasm goes on even longer.

"Fuuuck," he groans and holds himself still, twisting my hair around his fist, tugging my head back.

Brutal, hard thrusts that are no longer about my pleasure. They're about sating his animalistic need, and that alone sends me spiraling toward another orgasm.

"Fuck, you should see how good I look disappearing into you, bella." His voice is rougher than concrete.

Before I can inhale, I come again on a scream and a sob, it's so intense. Moments later, Gabriele pulls out and spills his seed all over my ass cheeks.

It's only as I'm catching my breath that I realize we didn't use a condom.

CHAPTER TWENTY-NINE

GABRIELE

I watch my cum drip down her ass cheeks and onto her thighs, satisfaction flooding my chest.

"Gabriele, the condom," Aria's soft voice says.

I still. Fuck. We didn't use protection.

It's the first time I've ever been bare inside a woman. No wonder it was fucking phenomenal. How did I not realize I didn't have one?

But after that last text, I lost myself—could feel my control slipping. All because I can't control the situation we're in. I can't control whether she gets hurt or not. Or whether she dies. At least that's how it feels. And that uncertainty drove me forward, urging me to control what I can. Her.

She'd needed an escape as badly as I needed the control.

"Let me clean you up, then we'll talk about it."

I go into the bathroom and wet the cloth, pondering how I would feel if Aria were pregnant with my child. Probably not how I should, because the idea of her belly swollen with my child isn't upsetting.

Yeah, I don't think I hate the idea at all. But it would cause a lot of issues for the two of us given that we're not married, not engaged, and haven't even been given the blessing to be together from the heads of our families.

I return to the living room and remove the belt from around Aria's thighs, letting the leather drop to the floor, then I wipe her skin with the washcloth. After I go back into the bathroom and clean myself.

By the time I return, she's dressed and is sitting on the couch, biting her bottom lip, looking nervous.

After pulling my boxer briefs back on, I sit beside her, taking her hand. "It's going to be okay. We can stop and get Plan B on the way to the helipad tomorrow."

"I just don't want you to think I was trying to trap you or anything."

I scowl, taking her chin between my fingers and turning her toward me. "Are you serious? Aria, I was as much a part of that as you were. No one put a gun to my head and told me to fuck you bare."

Some of the tension leaves her body. "Okay. I just didn't know how you'd feel once I realized what we did."

"Exactly, *we*. We're in this together. That said, we do need to get you on some birth control."

She nods. "I'll make an appointment with the doctor at the academy when we get back. I'll have to say my periods are irregular or heavy. I'll figure something out."

"Okay. Feel better about it now?" I raise my eyebrows in question.

She nods. "Much, thank you."

I place a chaste kiss on her lips, afraid if I do more, we'll just end up naked again, and I have things to do. Things that could keep Aria safe. "Good. I'm going to go through those files and see if I can find out who's being paid off in security."

The obvious place to start is the same contact I'm using. I already know she'll take a bribe and that she's in need of money. So once I get myself set up on the large dining room table with the file and my laptop, that's what I do. But Rachel Proctor has no hidden bank accounts and hasn't had any other large sums of money deposited into the accounts she does have. Some of her medical debt still remains, and I'm certain if she did have extra money, she'd be using it for that.

At some point, Aria goes to bed, telling me not to stay up too late. I'll admit, though I'm used to insomnia, I do want to join her in bed. But more than that, I want to figure out who is doing all this so that she's safe.

I work for hours, going through every security person and digging down past the surface-level shit to find the things they don't want people to know. Everyone has something. None of us on earth are saints.

And then I reach Andy Bathgate. At first, nothing seems amiss, but then I stumble upon something. Andy was adopted. Interesting.

Something in me urges me farther down this rabbit hole. My gut tells me there's something here, and it's usually not wrong. It takes a while—too long if there's going to be nothing to find—but eventually I get a breakthrough and find that Andy's birth parents legally changed his name when he was still an infant. Andy Bathgate was born Andrei Babayev.

My fingers fly over the keyboard, and I find his original birth name listed in a few Russian community organizations as a member while he was in high school. Seems Andy is pretty proud of his Russian heritage. And when I find the secret bank account where a large sum of money has been deposited, I'm sure I now know who's behind the threats to Aria—the Russians.

The question now is whether it's the Pavlovas, the Vasilievs, the Aminoffs, or the Volkovs.

* * *

In the morning, I fill Aria in about my findings, and she seems to feel some sense of relief.

"You still need to be careful. We don't know which family is behind it, and there's a chance I could be wrong, so you need to stay vigilant."

She nods, shoving the last of her things in her bag. "I know. I'm just happy that now I don't have to worry about Bianca or Dom. I can relax when I'm around them and just be with my friends."

My jaw clenches at the mention of Dom's name, but I don't say anything. Aria needs stress-free happiness in her life, and if that means having a friendship with a guy, I need to shut down the instinct that demands she not be friends with him.

"We should get going. The car will be waiting downstairs." I take her bag.

We ride the elevator to the lobby of the hotel and step out onto the sidewalk where the same driver who picked us up is waiting. He opens the back door for Aria, then takes the bags from me. Before I get in the back seat, I glance around the street. Not seeing anything concerning, I slip in beside Aria.

My instincts are on even higher alert now that I'm certain who our foe is.

When the vehicle pulls away from the curb, I glance out the back then turn to Aria. "I messaged the driver last night to let him know that we need to make a stop on the way to the helipad for the Plan B." Her cheeks pinkening, I add, "He doesn't know what we're stopping for, just where we're stopping. There's a pharmacy close to the helipad."

"Okay," she says softly.

She still seems so shy and unusually quiet about the whole incident. I'd like to tell her that I don't care if she were to get pregnant, but I don't want to scare her off. She's younger than me, and though I already know she's it for me, she may not feel the same. I don't want to push her away by scaring her.

I glance behind us into traffic and notice the same maroon sedan I saw after we first pulled away from the hotel still two cars behind us. I lower the privacy screen between us and the driver. "Take the next right and then the next right."

The driver doesn't ask why, just meets my gaze in the rearview mirror and nods.

"What's going on?" Aria asks.

I hate the thread of fear in her voice.

"Just testing a theory," I say.

The driver makes a right, and the vehicle follows. I meet the driver's gaze in the rearview mirror again, and he nods, obviously having spotted my concern for himself.

"Put your seat belt on," I tell Aria, pulling my own across my chest.

"Is everything okay?"

I take her hand. "It will be."

When the vehicle once again follows us as we make another right turn, essentially taking us in the opposite direction we were originally heading, I silently curse.

"You know what to do," I say to the driver, and he accelerates.

Aria's hand tenses in mine, and I give it a squeeze. "What's happening?"

"We have someone following us. He's going to lose them."

There will be no stopping now, and I wonder how Aria will feel about that. It doesn't matter, though. My first concern will always be getting her out of harm's way.

It's not rush hour, but it is Manhattan, so the traffic is still thick. Regardless, the driver does an excellent job of weaving in and out of traffic.

"Not sure we're going to lose him. We can't get enough distance with all this traffic," the driver says.

"Just get us to the helipad, and we should be fine."

It's not as though some Russian goons are going to whip out their guns and shoot at a helicopter in broad daylight. They may have some cops in their pocket, but not the entire force and not the entire New York City press.

Being that the car never pulls up beside us, I assume that this is once again an intimidation tactic. Still, I'm not going to take any chances.

Aria whimpers every time the driver takes a sharp turn. By the time we pull up to the helipad, her face is pale and drawn. I make a vow to rain down vengeance on whoever is doing this to her.

"We're going to make a run for it. The driver will be watching our backs, and it's not likely they're going to try to shoot us with this many witnesses, but we have to be fast, okay?"

She nods without saying anything.

"We got this." I lean in and kiss her forehead.

A few seconds later, the driver opens the door, and I take her hand, stepping out onto the sidewalk first. She follows, then we're running to the entrance of the building with the helipad. I glance to my side and see the sedan parked at the curb farther down the road, but I can't make out who's inside.

But I'll find out. Then I'll hunt them down and watch them bleed.

CHAPTER THIRTY

ARIA

I'm really tired of having people out to kill me.

While I'd been freaked out and fearful after the car ride to the helipad, I'm now angry and wanting retribution.

Gabriele and I arrive back on campus to a bunch of stares and whispers. It doesn't surprise me that everyone knows we ventured off campus together, but I have no idea what they think. It isn't as though he and I have discussed what we are or what we'll tell others.

It's something I want to bring up, but I'm afraid if I do, I won't like the answer, so I keep pushing that boulder down the road.

"What's the plan?" I ask him as we walk into the Roma House. Everyone turns our way, but I ignore their interest.

"We need to go talk to your brother first. Fill him in on our trip home. Then I'm going to have a little chat with Andy in security."

I can only imagine what he means by a little chat. Right now, I'm nervous about going to see my brother *with* Gabriele.

Before we reach the elevators, Bianca and Dom approach.

"Are you feeling better?" Bianca asks, looking concerned.

It's easier to believe her concern now that I know it's the Russians after me and not the Accardis.

"Much, thank you." I put on what I hope is a genuine smile.

"Glad to hear it. Missed you around here," Dom says.

Gabriele stiffens next to me but doesn't say anything. I'm sure that's costing him every bit of his willpower.

"It's good to be back." I smile at them. "But I have to go talk to my brother."

"I'll bet you do," Dom says and glances at Gabriele.

"Can we catch up later?" I ask.

"Come by Dom's room tonight. Some of us are going to be hanging out," Bianca says.

"Sounds good. I'll see you then." I give them a small wave and accompany Gabriele to the elevator, where he stabs the button on the wall as though it's personally offended him.

He doesn't say anything as the elevator moves up, but when we step off of it and walk down the hall, he grabs my hand and links our fingers together. My heartbeat triples, and I fight the grin that wants to emerge. A few people lingering in the hallway gawk at our joined hands.

When we reach my brother's door, Gabriele knocks, and a few seconds later, Marcelo opens it. His gaze darts down to where our hands are interlaced and his jaw tics, eyes narrowing on the man at my side.

"So it's like that, is it?" My brother arches an eyebrow.

"It is." Gabriele lets go of my hand, placing it on the small of my back for me to step into their room first.

I walk in, avoiding my brother's gaze. Mira is in the room, sitting on the couch.

"Hey, Aria. How are you doing?" she asks.

"I'd be better if people stopped trying to kill me." I meant it as a joke, but it falls flat.

"What the fuck, Vitale?" My brother gets right up into Gabriele's face.

I step up to my brother, pushing at his shoulder. "Back off. It's not his fault."

"Stay out of it, Aria," Marcelo grinds out.

"I will not. This is about my life!" I shout.

Mira gets up off the couch. "She's not wrong."

"Jesus Christ. Can I not have one placating woman in my life?" He groans and pinches the bridge of his nose.

"No," Mira and I answer at the same time.

"What happened?" Marcelo asks.

Gabriele explains how we found nothing in my father's office and describes the car that followed us to the helipad. "They weren't trying to hurt her, but they were making a point—they can if they want. I have no idea how they found us at that hotel."

"Fucking Russians," my brother spits out.

"One thing is for sure, we need to step up our efforts to find what they're looking for," Mira says.

"We're not just going to hand over what they want even if we find it," Gabriele says.

I frown. "We aren't?"

He shakes his head and looks at my brother, who seems to share his thoughts. "We're going to use it to draw them out, then we're going to take them out."

Marcelo gives a quick nod.

Gabriele looks at me. "You give in once, and they'll come back for more. Always."

"Makes sense," Mira mutters.

"What do you have in mind?" Marcelo asks him.

"Going to try the easy route first. I'll have a little chat with Andy in security, see if he'll spill who he's working with. If that doesn't work, then it's the hard route—I'm going to bug the rooms of all the heads and next in line of the Russian Bratvas."

My brother stiffens and looks around his room.

"Relax. I have no interest in listening to you and Mira bang," Gabriele says.

My face screws up. "Gross."

"I'm going with you," Marcelo says.

"No way." Gabriele shakes his head.

Marcelo steps forward, which Gabriele meets. "This is my father's mess, and Aria is my sister. What exactly is she to you?" He arches an eyebrow.

I'm eager for Gabriele's answer, and all the eyes in the room seem to be on him. But he says, "You need to stay out of it. If I get found out and kicked off campus, someone needs to be here to protect Aria."

Reluctantly, my brother nods.

The thought of being stuck here on campus without Gabriele is crushing. I'd probably want to leave with him, but I don't say that. I honestly don't know how he'd feel about it.

"You want to tell me what it is they have over you now?" Marcelo asks, looking between Gabriele and me.

"I already told you that isn't happening." Gabriele's voice makes me think that he's trying to hold himself back from showing how agitated he is by my brother's question.

I try not to look embarrassed, though just thinking about my brother seeing that picture makes my face heat. Mira catches my eye, and I can tell she has some idea of what she thinks the blackmail material might be.

Marcelo crosses his arms. "All right then, explain to me exactly why you were holding my little sister's hand when I opened the door."

"None of your business," I snipe, although I kind of want the same answer.

"As the head of the family, it is my business. He's basically made a public declaration where you're concerned—*without* my blessing." He says the last three words with barely restrained fury.

Gabriele shrugs. "People are bound to be talking already anyway.

This is better for you. Makes it seem like you've sanctioned things between us and not like we've got one over on you."

My head whips in my brother's direction, because that comment is going to really piss him off. The vein in his neck throbs at the reminder that we did indeed sneak around behind his back.

Jesus, I hope I'm not pregnant. My brother probably really would kill Gabriele.

Gabriele and I haven't spoken about it, both knowing that it wasn't safe to stop—even after we'd landed, since I'd already been shot at not far from campus. It's up to fate now.

But it isn't like he finished inside me or anything. The odds are in our favor.

"That's a good point," Mira says, giving her fiancé a look that says he needs to think about his next words before speaking them.

Marcelo turns to me. "Are you happy?" It sounds as though it physically pains him to get the words out.

"I am."

He blows out a breath. "All right then." He swings his attention back to Gabriele. "But if you do anything to hurt her, ruin her good name, anything . . . there will be hell to pay." It's obvious he means his words and that he'll follow through on them regardless of the consequences to himself and the family.

I wrap my arms around Marcelo's waist. "Thank you."

His arms come around me slowly at first, but his embrace grows tighter.

I can't remember the last time I hugged my brother—probably not since we were young.

When I pull away, Marcelo looks at Gabriele. "Keep me in the loop, and if you need me for anything, let me know."

Gabriele nods and takes my hand—whether because he wants to hold my hand right then or because he wants to make a point to my brother, I don't know. Maybe both.

When we get to the hallway, Gabriele leads me to the elevator. "Let's head to my room. I want to hack into the scheduling software the school uses and see when Andy is working next."

I agree, and once we're in his room, he pulls me in for a kiss.

"I'm not going to tell you not to go to Dom's room tonight, but understand that you still need to watch out. It's not likely one of the Russians will get into the Roma House, but who knows? I'll walk you there, and you text me when you want to leave, and I'll come get you."

I place a hand on his cheek. I know that what he just said is at war with every instinct in his body. "Thank you."

Maybe there is a future for us after all.

CHAPTER THIRTY-ONE

GABRIELE

"Do you really think by now I'm just going to accept your answer and walk away?" I circle the chair Andy or Andrei is tied to. Blood trickles from his eyebrow, and one side of his face is already swollen from my fists.

Because I have eyes and ears everywhere in this school, I know that the guards who are normally in the basement of the Roma House, keeping an eye on the cameras and administering the Sunday phone calls home, leave at eleven o'clock and turn over their guard duties to the main security office. And since I can hack into their system, I just ran a loop on their cameras so they have no idea that Sandro and I surprised Andy with a visit right after he got on shift tonight and are having a little sit-down.

We've set up shop in one of the rooms the students make their private calls from. It's perfect because it's concrete with just a metal table and chair in it, and there's a built-in drain in the floor. It's as though the founders of the school were thinking ahead—I'm sure they were.

"Spoiler alert!" Sandro says, making a big show of crouching down in front of him. "He's not going to stop until you tell him the truth." He straightens and punches Andy in the stomach, who grunts in pain and slouches further in his seat.

I filled Sandro in on everything so that he could help me with this little endeavor, since it involved me needing to wipe the cameras not only here but from where Andy was abducted. So Sandro got him here, and once I'd done what I needed to do on my computer four floors up from here, I joined them.

I tsk and shake my head, pacing in front of Andy. He watches me warily through his one eye that isn't swollen shut.

"You should know that I can be very stubborn, Andy. Especially when it involves something of mine, something I value and hold dear. And you see, these people who put that money in that account you tried to hide offshore . . ."

His eye flares open a little wider.

"Yes, I know all about that account," I say. "Well, they want to take something from me that I hold in the highest regard, so I'm not going to quit until you talk. So tell me who paid you to intercept that package that was meant for me?"

"I don't know, I swear!" There's an edge of fear in his voice that wasn't there an hour ago. Good. Maybe he gets that I'm serious when I say he's not going anywhere until I get what I want.

Let's be honest, though, he's not going anywhere ever again. Maybe he knows that. He helped the Russians who are trying to hurt Aria, and no one fucks with what's mine. If he does realize that he's not leaving here alive, then the only way to get him to talk is to put him in enough pain that ending him would be a mercy. And we will if he tells us what we want to know.

"Try again." My voice is cutting.

"I swear, I don't kn—ugh."

I punch him across the face before he can finish his sentence. "Try again."

It goes on like this for a while until it's hard to even make out what Andy used to look like—his face is so swollen and distorted and caked with blood, some dry, some fresh.

"I think we're going to have to resort to other measures. What do you think, Sandro?"

"I think so. What do you want to start with, the box cutter or the pliers?" He stands near the table where the toolbox we stole from a caretaker's closet sits.

"I'm always partial to the box cutter. Getting right to the stabbing part . . ." I cluck my tongue. "But sometimes they bleed out before you want them to."

He nods. "Pliers it is." He picks up a pair and tests their weight in his hand before walking over to where Andy's arms are tied to the arm of the chair.

"Let's start with the thumbnail first. I swear those always seem to hurt more than the fingers do, though I can't say for sure." I turn to Andy, who has tears leaking down his face. "You'll have to let us know if that's the case. Unless you want to avoid all this by telling us the truth."

"Go to hell!" he shouts.

"I will. But not before you." I nod at Sandro, who gets started.

By the time three of his fingernails have been pried off slowly, he tells us that a burner phone showed up out of the blue and began texting him. He claims he never had any direct dealings with whoever it was who wanted him to monitor the mail coming into the Roma House.

I'm not one hundred percent sure I believe him, but in the end, it doesn't matter because Andy has an asthma attack and dies before we're finished with him.

"Fuck!" I shout, pushing a hand through my hair.

"Do you believe him?" Sandro asks.

"I think so, but I wanted more time with him." I rest my hands on my hips and stare at his limp body tied to the chair.

Sandro nods at the body. "What do you want me to do with him?"

"Bury him in the woods, I guess." I glance down. "It'll still be dark out. I'll cover the cameras so that you can do it without being seen. Make sure it's far and that it's deep so no wildlife goes digging him up anytime soon."

He nods, then his eyebrows draw down. "Gonna be hard to lug him all the way out there by myself. Want me to ask one of the other guys in the family to help me?"

"No. Antonio La Rosa owes me one more favor. He can help you." I chuckle, thinking how much Antonio's going to hate this. "That way, if any shit goes down with this, he's tied to it, too, and it will be in his best interests to clean up any problems that might arise. Not to mention he's Mira's brother, which will then force the Costas to step in as well."

Sandro shakes his head and chuckles. "Always thinking ten steps ahead."

"Someone has to." I make my way to the door. "Wait here. I'll have Antonio down here to help you in the next fifteen minutes, and I'll text you when I've taken care of the cameras and you're good to go."

* * *

AFTER SANDRO AND Antonio are well away from the range of cameras, I close my laptop and have a shower. My one fist is cut up from the number of times I pummeled that liar Andy's face, but if anyone asks, I'll say I was hitting the bags a little too hard and not wearing gloves at the school gym.

I pull up the cameras in Aria's room again and see her sleeping soundly, which is how I should leave her, but I can't. There's a burning need inside me that won't be sated until I see her for myself and hold her in my arms.

So I slip into the stairwell and use the spare key she gave me days ago to enter her room. She doesn't so much as move when I'm inside. She must be more worn out than I thought.

Pulling up the covers, I slide under them and cuddle into her back, wrapping my arms around her. She makes a noise of protest and stiffens for a fraction of a second before she sighs and relaxes.

"How did you know it was me?"

"Your scent," she says as if it's that obvious.

I'm not sure why, but that makes me squeeze her tighter.

"How did it go?" There's a note of gravity to her voice, so she must be fully awake now.

I sigh. "Not as well as I'd hoped. He didn't give us anything. Said that he was contacted anonymously by burner phone. All he knows is that it was one of the Bratva families. He says he helped them because he was hoping to become a member and thought this might be a good way to prove his worth."

She knows better than to ask what has become of Andy. She is a Mafia king's sister after all.

"So we're back where we were." She rolls over to face me, eyes wide with concern.

"We're on to the next part of our plan. I don't have any bugs here, but I texted my dad when we were in New York to bring some with him when he comes for family day this weekend. I'll have to explain to him what's going on."

She blinks rapidly. "I totally forgot about family day. My mom is returning from her vacation for parents' weekend. Said she wouldn't miss it now that she's our only parent alive."

"Is that a problem?" My forehead creases.

"No . . . I just . . . what do I say to her about us? Do I say anything at all?"

I kiss her forehead. "Do you want to say anything?"

She looks so young and shy that it reminds me that unlike me, she wasn't raised to deal with all the shit she is currently facing. Sure, she knew about some of it, but she was never in the mix. "Do *you* want me to say anything?"

"Cara, I guarantee it's already all over this campus that we're an item, which means they'll all be telling their parents when they're here. No point in keeping it a secret from your mom. Unless you want to try."

She shakes her head. "No, I want her to know. Will you tell your parents?"

There must be something on my face because a line forms between her eyebrows.

"I will." Though I'm not looking forward to it. It's sure to be a fight between my father and me. He'll see my relationship with Aria as a violation of a direct order he gave me, and he won't be wrong. Still, I wouldn't change it for anything. And I'm hoping to soften the blow when I show him the project I've been working on and the success I've had with it. Money always puts him in a better mood.

She doesn't seem comforted by my words. "Gabriele . . . what . . . what exactly is going on between us?"

It hurts that she even has to ask, though I understand it. We haven't had a conversation about the future, even if I'd made it clear to her that I consider her to be mine. I need to have a conversation with my father before I go making promises to Aria.

So rather than tell her I've already fallen in love with her, I kiss the top of her head. "Let's save that conversation for when we're through dealing with all this bullshit."

I hate the way she stiffens in my arms, but there's nothing to be done about it. Not yet anyway.

CHAPTER THIRTY-TWO

ARIA

A couple of days have passed since Gabriele showed up in the middle of the night in my bed, and I still don't feel any better about our conversation. It was clear he was avoiding talking about our future, and though I wanted answers, I didn't want to press him like some needy girl. He said we'd talk about it once we're clear of this whole mess, and that much I believed.

Maybe he doesn't know what he wants us to be, or maybe he really does just have a lot on his mind and wants to focus on the threat to me. Whatever the reason, I've tried to push my need for answers and my insecurities about why he might not want to give them to me to the back of my mind.

Because of what happened, Gabriele and my brother decided that I shouldn't be walking around campus on my own anymore. So if I'm not with one of them, someone from either the Costa or the Vitale families is always skulking around at a distance. It's somewhat annoying to feel like I need a babysitter watching me all the time, but because I'm so on edge, I don't complain.

"Are you okay? You look tired," Bianca asks while we're working on a group project in our racketeering class.

"I haven't been sleeping that well, that's all," I lie.

She grins. "Gabriele keeping you up all night?" She waggles her eyebrows.

We haven't discussed what's going on with Gabriele and me, so the rumors have obviously reached her. I guess by bringing him up, this is her way of asking.

"Sometimes." I give her a little grin and shrug.

"Oh my God, girl, tell me what it's like with him. No one really knows, but he has this intense thing about him, you know? I bet that translates into him being a god in the bedroom."

She looks at me eagerly, and I glance around to make sure no one is listening. Talking about him like this doesn't feel right, and I'm certainly not going to share any of his proclivities with her, but girlfriends talk about this kind of thing, right? I feel as though I have to give her something.

"I'll just say that it's better than I even imagined."

She rests her chin on her hand and sighs. "That's what I want, but man, is it hard to find."

"You'll find it. You're young." I smile at her, and as I do, I get a sensation down *there*.

Shit, I think I need to use the restroom.

"I'll be right back." I push back from the table we're working at and walk up to the professor's desk. "Can I use the restroom?"

He looks at the clock above the door. There's still a half hour of class left. "Yes."

I make my way toward the door and spot my chaperone for the day, one of our family's guys, start to get up from his desk. I wave at him to sit back down and mouth, "Bathroom."

He's a new soldier, and his dad has been one for decades. I don't need him listening to me pee. Besides, the bathroom is literally the next room over.

Once I'm in the stall, I pull down my pants and check my underwear. Just as I thought, there's a trace amount of blood there. I sigh with relief, thankful my period is starting. Under different circumstances, I'd love to be pregnant with Gabriele's baby, but I

THE MAFIA KING'S SISTER

don't even know what we are yet and whether there's a future for us, and there's a very real possibility that someone will try to kill me if I don't find the damn USB that they want.

I pull my pants back up and leave the stall, heading over to the wall where the free feminine products are kept since I don't have my bag with me. Deciding on a panty liner for now, I turn the handle so that one will drop down into the dispensary section, but it gets stuck halfway in and out. I bend at the waist and reach up to grab it.

I straighten and spin around to go back to the stall—right into a firm chest. My eyes dart up to see a man wearing a balaclava. The panty liner drops from my hand.

I try to scream, but he shoves a hand over my mouth and backs me up into the dispensing machine. The handle digs into my back and a muffled cry sounds against the leather glove over my mouth.

I struggle against his hold, but he's stronger than me. My heartbeat and my breathing are so loud in my head that I can't hear anything else. I have no idea if our struggle is making enough noise to alert anyone in the classroom beside us of what's going on.

He moves his hand up to cover my nose, too, and I struggle to breathe. Panic fires in my blood, and on instinct, I lift my knee. I can't get good leverage to really make it count, but I slam into his balls hard enough that he cries out, and his grip loosens on me enough that I'm able to wiggle free.

Dodging around him, I'm only a couple steps away when he yanks me by my hair, pulling me back. I stomp down on his foot, my only option since he's behind me, and he releases my hair. One step away, and I cry out when he snags my leg, and I go down face-first on the floor, hitting my head. It takes me a moment to gather myself and crawl toward the door, but the wind has been knocked out of me, so I can't scream for help.

I look over my shoulder when he deeply chuckles. He's walking slowly toward me, and I know this is it. I have to gather what little strength I have left and make it count, otherwise I'm dead.

When he's close enough, I lift my leg and ram my foot into his kneecap. He cries out in pain and falls. Raising my leg one more time, I hoof him in the face and use the door to stagger to my feet. I open the door and head toward the classroom. There's shock on everyone's face when I open the door, then everything goes black.

CHAPTER THIRTY-THREE

GABRIELE

"Where the fuck is she?"

I ignore everyone gawking at me in the waiting room of the school's medical office and push through them to the hallway, checking every room until I find Aria in one of the hospital beds, asleep. My shoulders sag in relief, but the rage simmering through me doesn't go away. Not even an ocean could douse it.

When I step into the room, Marcelo is pacing on the far side, and Mira sits in the chair in the corner, face clearly etched in concern.

"What the fuck happened?"

Marcelo whips around and faces me. "Best we can tell, someone attacked her in the bathroom. She's banged up. They think she fell during the altercation and hit her head. She needed stitches on her temple."

"Your fucking guy was supposed to be watching her!" I step up to him, ready to take out everything I'm feeling on him, regardless if he's her brother or not.

"He will be dealt with." From the tone of his voice, I don't have to ask how.

"Is she going to be okay?" I turn to look at her in bed again.

"Doctor said she might have a slight concussion, but they have to wait until she wakes up to be sure."

I push both hands through my hair and pull. There's so much coursing through me I feel like a firework on the brink of exploding.

"This is your fault." I step forward and push Marcelo, looking for a fight, *hoping* for one.

"You need to back the fuck off, Vitale." Marcelo's rage is barely concealed.

Mirabella gets up from her chair. "Guys, stop it. This isn't helping anything."

"You let her get hurt on your watch!" I shout.

"What the fuck happened when you were in New York, huh?"

"Guys!" Mira shouts as we stand chest to chest, just waiting for the other one to throw the first punch.

"Stop." Aria's voice is almost a whisper, but it stops us in our tracks, and all our heads whip in her direction. "Stop, please."

I rush to her bedside and take her hand, needing to feel her warm skin on mine. "Are you okay?" I reach to brush a hand over her face but pull back, not wanting to hurt her. She attempts to sit up straighter in bed, and I place a hand on her shoulder. "Just relax. Go get the doctor and tell them she's awake."

I don't care if it's Mira or Marcelo who does it, as long as one of them does. It must be Mira, though, because Marcelo walks to the opposite side of the bed.

"Mi hair fatto paura." I take her hand and squeeze it.

"I was scared, too," she whispers.

"What happened? Who did this?" Marcelo asks, promising retribution with his tone.

But before she can answer, the doctor arrives, wanting to examine her. He asks us all to leave, but I refuse, so I watch as he asks her a bunch of questions and examines her.

When he's done, he turns to me. "She has a slight concussion and needs to stay in bed for a few days. Wake her up every few hours. No screens, keep the lights off when you can. Very little stimulation."

"I'll make sure of it." And I will. I'm not leaving her side until

I've sliced the throat of each and every fucking Russian who played a role in this.

When Marcelo returns, I fill him in on what the doctor said and tell him that I'll be staying with her until she's able to be up and out of bed again. He looks as if he wants to argue but wisely doesn't.

"I want to get you back to your room, Aria, but we have to know . . . do you know who did this to you?" I ask.

"No." She looks as though she might cry. "He had a mask on, and I couldn't see him."

"By the time someone checked the bathroom, whoever it was had already gotten away," Marcelo says.

"I'll hack into the security feed and see if I can tell who it is." And I will. But first I need to get Aria settled. I turn to Marcelo. "I'm going to grab some things from my room before I head to Aria's. Can you escort her back to her room, and then I'll meet you there?"

Once again, Marcelo looks as though he wants to argue, but he looks between the two of us and gives me a sharp nod.

I step up to the bed. "I'll be at your place as soon as I can, bella." I place a chaste kiss on her lips.

As I pull away, she looks up at me with her big doe eyes full of fear and sadness.

"Don't worry, they will pay. I promise you." I kiss her one last time before I leave.

* * *

A FEW DAYS pass, and I spend every second with Aria in her room, either Mira or Marcelo bringing us food every day. When I checked the security cameras in the school the day Aria was attacked, the entire day had been wiped clean, leaving no trace.

Today is the first time I'm going to leave her in days, and I don't feel good about it. It's hard not to feel as though the minute she's out of my sight, something bad will happen. I can't keep her caged like an animal, as much as my control issues demand that I do.

Today is the day parents will be visiting, though, and I need to have a conversation with my father about my intentions toward Aria, as well as get the bugs he's delivering to me, courtesy of my friend in the security department.

Aria is feeling better today—not as sore or tired, no lingering headache—so I take some relief from that knowledge. She's looking forward to seeing her mom today, though I tried to encourage her to stay in her room and let her mother come visit her. But she's feeling cooped up and in need of a change of scenery. Besides, Marcelo will be with her.

As an extra precaution, I texted Sandro to keep a close eye on Aria from a distance. I feel confident that I have her safety covered, but I prefer to be the one who's making sure she's okay. Today, it's not an option. I can't be sure how my father will react when I talk to him about Aria, so I won't be having that conversation around mixed company. We need privacy.

"You stay with your brother, okay?" I say.

She nods, and I kiss her forehead. Her long hair is in a braid she has pulled in front of one shoulder, and she looks up at me, somehow still maintaining the innocence on her face even after all she's been through.

"Are both your parents coming?" she asks.

"Yeah, they always do."

"That's nice." I can tell by the look on her face that she's thinking about how her father can't come visit her. "Maybe you could meet my mom after I talk to her . . ." She lets her question hang there like an empty noose.

I give her a wan smile. "Maybe. I'll come find you when I'm done with my parents. See where you're at."

She doesn't look convinced. "Okay."

"Let's go. I'm taking you up to your brother's room. You can go with him to meet your mom."

After I've dropped Aria off with Marcelo, I text Sandro to make sure he's good to keep an eye on Aria. He texts back immediately that he's on it. He's already told his parents he'll have to keep his visit short.

With that taken care of, I head out of the Roma House toward the main entrance of the school. There are staggered arrivals so that the circular drive doesn't have a traffic jam.

I don't have to wait long for my parents' car to pull up. Angelo and Mia Vitale exit the back of the black SUV looking every bit the part of a Mafia don and his wife. My dad's tailored suit sans tie, slicked-back hair, and thick gold chain around his neck with a cross dangling off the end make him look as if he's come from central casting. My mom's curled dark hair hangs over her shoulders, and she's wearing her usual modest designer label dress.

The moment she sees me, my mother rushes over and gives me a big hug. I'm her only child, and she's always held me in high esteem. While I'm worried about my father's reaction to my news about Aria, I also worry about my mother's. There's a good chance she'll never think any woman is good enough for me.

After my mom releases me, my dad and I shake hands.

"Let's walk over to Café Ambrosia. We can get a cappuccino and catch up," I say.

"That sounds wonderful," my mom says.

I lead them there, and after I've gotten each of them their requested beverages, we sit and catch up. My mom doesn't have much to say except rumors about who's seeing who and who she predicts will be engaged soon or start their family. She's a typical Mafia wife without much exposure to the outside world.

Once we've visited for a while, I give my father a look, and he takes the hint, turning to my mother. "Mia, I see Valentina Albis over there. Why don't you go say hello while I talk business with our son."

Knowing she has no choice, she gives him a small smile and gets up from the table without a word, heading in Valentina's direction like the dutiful little wife. Until this moment, I never realized how much I don't want that for myself. I like the fact that Aria has a backbone. She acquiesces, yes, but when she thinks it counts, she says her piece.

"Let's go for a walk," I say, and we stand from the table.

I lead my father out of the building and into one of the courtyards. The flowers have all died and the gardens aren't as lush, but it's empty, which serves my purpose.

"Did you bring the bugs I requested?" I ask my dad, turning to face him once we're in the middle of the courtyard.

He nods. "I did, but before I hand anything over to you, you need to explain to me what's going on. I've heard things."

That has me arching my brow. "What things have you heard?"

"That you've been mooning over the Costa girl, making it known there's something going on between you." He steps toward me. "That you left campus with her to go to New York and do God knows what."

I blow out a breath and push a hand through my hair. "Both are true."

I meet his gaze, ready for his wrath, knowing it's coming. But hopefully once we're on the other side of it, he'll understand that I won't back down from this.

"Did I or did I not tell you that I want you having nothing to do with Aria Costa?"

I nod. "You did."

"Then why are you risking your life because of some mess she's gotten herself into when, as far as I can tell, it has nothing to do with you?" There's venom in his words and the cruel glint I've grown accustomed to in his eyes.

"Because I love her."

There. The words are out. I hate that he's the first one to hear them and not Aria, but I can't say them to her without being sure that we have a clear path to being together. Today is the first step in that.

"Love." He practically spits out the word. "What about duty? What about putting the family and your oath to us first? What do you think everyone under you in the family will think when they see her leading you around by your cock, not to mention the other families? They'll think you're weak, that's what. They'll think *I'm* weak, and they'll try to take what's ours. Especially her brother."

"Marcelo has no interest in trying to take over our sector of the country."

"Oh, are you two buddies now? This is exactly what I'm talking about. He already has too much power! We can't hand him even more!" His face is beet-red now, voice raised, and as I watch his hand clench at his side, I'm sure he's holding himself back from hitting me.

"The Costas only have as much power as we hand them, and it goes both ways. Me being with Aria gives us stronger ties to the northeast. Think of what we could do with that access. You're being shortsighted."

"I will not back down on this, Gabriele."

I can tell from his tone that he means it. I've known the man my entire life, and he is the most stubborn motherfucker in the world. He never liked Marcelo's father—said he always thought he was better than everyone else because he held New York. I heard rumors once that Marcelo's mother was being considered as an arranged match for my father, but she chose Sam Costa instead. I'm smart enough not to ask about that.

Quickly, I try a tactic change. "If you've heard I've fallen hard for her, then I've done my job well. Let me continue to work my magic. I practically have her eating out of the palm of my hand. Give me more time to solidify our relationship, then we can make it official."

He cocks his head, studying me. "Are you telling me this was all a ploy on your part?"

"Of course it was."

"If that's the case, why didn't you tell me about it?" My dad crosses his arms.

I shrug, feigning nonchalance. "I wasn't sure I'd be able to get close to her, get Marcelo to trust me enough, and I didn't want to disappoint you. But I'm there. Once this bullshit with the Russians is out of the way, I'll ask her to marry me. Then I'll be on the inside, and we can systematically undo what the Costas have built, feed mistrust from the inside, and have a line into what's going on in the northeast." Nausea bubbles up in my gut from spewing these words at him.

I have no intention of doing any of that, minus asking Aria to marry me, but if I can get him to greenlight us being together, I can tell him down the road that I've actually fallen for her, that I won't try to destroy her brother's inner workings.

Buying time is all I'm doing, but that's all I need. Time for him to get used to the idea of Aria and me, to see how it will benefit him.

A slow, satisfied grin spreads across his face. "That's the son I raised." He steps forward with a smile and clamps me on the shoulder, squeezing.

Relief washes through me like a tsunami.

It's not ideal, but sometimes dealing with my dad is all about taking baby steps. At least we're moving forward.

CHAPTER THIRTY-FOUR

ARIA

I catch a glimpse of Gabriele walking into the courtyard and smile.

My visit with my mom has been good. It's been nice to see her, especially after everything that's happened to me recently. Sometimes you just need your mom.

I hadn't expected to see Gabriele so soon today, but when Mira dragged my brother over to speak with her parents, I excused myself to use the restroom inside the school.

As soon as I entered the bathroom, I realized what a bad idea it was. I hadn't been in one of the school restrooms since the incident, and my chest felt tight. I used the facilities as fast as humanly possible and felt an immense sense of relief when I left the bathroom unscathed.

That was when I spotted Gabriele way down the hall, pushing through the door to the courtyard. I couldn't see anyone with him and decided to head down to see if he wanted to meet my mom now.

I make my way down the hallway and silently push open the door to the courtyard, not wanting to interrupt if Gabriele is indeed in here with someone. As I stand there holding the door, he comes into view. His back is to me, and it looks as though he and his father are having an intense conversation, from the pissed-off expression on his dad's face.

That's when Gabriele's words float over to me, and my cheeks sting as though they've been slapped.

"If you've heard I've fallen hard for her, then I've done my job well. Let me continue to work my magic. I practically have her eating out of the palm of my hand. Give me more time to solidify our relationship, then we can make it official."

My stomach lurches. I have to swallow back the bile in my throat.

His dad shifts his head. "Are you telling me this was all a ploy on your part?"

"Of course it was."

Tears well in my eyes as my heart shrivels up.

"If that's the case, why didn't you tell me about it?" His dad crosses his arms.

Gabriele's shoulder lifts in a shrug. "I wasn't sure I'd be able to get close to her, get Marcelo to trust me enough, and I didn't want to disappoint you. But I'm there. Once this bullshit with the Russians is out of the way, I'll ask her to marry me. Then I'll be on the inside, and we can systematically undo what the Costas have built, feed mistrust from the inside, and have a line into what's going on in the northeast."

I rush out of there, not wanting either of them to see me.

Tears streak down my face as I run, not paying any attention to where I'm going. I don't care, I just want to get out of here. I don't want to see anyone, too ashamed and embarrassed that I let myself believe Gabriele actually had feelings for me.

Was I really that desperate and naïve?

I've always been inconsequential in everyone's lives. What I did never mattered because I was just the daughter. Well, daughters matter, too. I want to matter in someone's life. And I thought I mattered in Gabriele's.

A thought strikes me then, and I stop where I am—shaken. Is it possible that he orchestrated this whole thing—the delivery of the invitation to the sex club in Miami, the picture, and everything that came after—as a way to get close to me? Play the hero and earn my trust?

I bend over and vomit, thankful I'm outside.

Jesus, I've been so stupid. I've been around made men my entire life and know they have a duty to their family first and foremost. Did I really think that just because I've seen how much my brother has changed as a result of his relationship with Mira, Gabriele would, too? Marcelo was the exception, not the rule.

I spit the last of the vomit from my mouth and straighten, attempting to take a deep, cleansing breath. But before I finish one inhalation, something is pulled down over my face, and only darkness consumes me.

My attempt to scream is thwarted when a hand clamps over my face, and I'm wrenched back into someone's chest. I struggle, but vise-like arms wrap around my midsection and lift me, carrying me away.

Away to where, I have no idea. Blind panic courses through me. I struggle and struggle, wearing myself out to no avail. Nothing I do makes any difference to the iron grip around me.

My breath comes faster and faster, and my head grows fuzzy. I try to slow my breathing so I don't hyperventilate, but when two guys speak Russian in the background, I panic even more, and it all goes black.

* * *

WHEN I WAKE, the first thing I realize is that my shoulders and my wrists burn. My head is slouched forward, and I lift it slowly, blinking a few times and taking in the concrete room around me. A room that looks exactly like the one I make my Sunday phone calls home to my mom in.

But when I see the two Russians in front of me, I know I'm not in Roma House. I must be in the Moskva House—enemy territory.

"Glad to see you've decided to join us," the taller of the two says.

I know who he is. Everyone on campus does.

Feliks Aminoff.

Feliks is the head of the Aminoff Bratva. He's Gabriele's age and became the head of the organization last year when the previous leader, one with no heirs, was murdered. Feliks stepped in after hunting down who did it and torturing them to death.

At least that's what the rumors say.

As his cold eyes pin me, I realize I'm tied with my hands behind my back—hence the pain in my shoulders—and I know this man has no intentions of letting me leave here alive.

"It's wonderful to finally meet you face-to-face rather than just through text." He smiles, but it doesn't reach his eyes. His Russian accent is present but not super thick, a testament to his time in America.

"What do you want?" I narrow my eyes at him. Maybe if I buy time, it will be enough for someone to realize I'm missing.

I picture my brother and Gabriele in my mind.

Gabriele.

Just the thought of him feels like the lash of a whip. At least Gabriele wasn't making up the Russian thing for his own benefit.

Feliks tsks and steps forward, trailing a fingertip down my cheek slowly. I notice that his other hand is holding a gun. How the hell did he get that in here? "You know exactly what I want, radnaja."

I pull my head away from his touch. "I don't know where the USB you're looking for is. If I did, I would have already handed it over."

"You're lying." He stares at me.

I shake my head. "I'm not lying."

A split second after the words leave my mouth, he backhands me across the cheek.

My head whips, and my ears ring. It takes me a moment to get my bearings again. When I do, I scowl at him. "What's on this USB that's so important anyway?"

He leans in and smirks, but it's cruel. "We got intelligence that he had something on us, something we don't want anyone to know. He was no doubt saving it for the perfect time. That's what I would do. Now, I want it back."

"I already told you I don't know where it is. I looked everywhere."

"Then you're useless to me."

I stiffen.

"Igor, take care of her." Feliks walks to the door.

Panic hits me fast and swift. I need to do something. Anything. "No! Wait!"

Feliks stops with his back to me.

"I can keep looking or ask my brother if he knows anything."

They don't know that I've already pulled Marcelo into this. I just need to keep stalling until someone realizes I'm missing. Gabriele doesn't know that I know about his plan for me. Maybe he'll come, too.

"Don't worry, we'll ask your brother next. With you dead, we think he'll be extra motivated for his fiancée not to end up with the same fate."

"Please, you don't have to do this!" Tears run down my cheeks.

Feliks's face transforms from icy cruelness into rage as if someone flicked a switch, and he stalks back toward me, bending down so we're face-to-face. "You have no one to blame but yourself!"

He reaches forward, and I flinch, thinking he's going to hit me again, but instead he rips my necklace from around my neck and tosses it sideways. I hear it hit the wall. I'm trembling, my chest racked with sobs that these will be my last moments.

Feliks looks as if he's deciding how exactly he's going to make me suffer when Igor says from behind him, "Pakhan."

Feliks looks over his shoulder at him, and I chance a look, too. Igor is pointing at the floor. I follow the direction of his finger to see that he's pointing at my necklace that's bounced off the wall and landed a couple of feet from us.

When I realize what he's pointing at, my eyes widen.

Feliks's head turns back to me, and I meet his gaze as a slow, sadistic smile forms on his face.

CHAPTER THIRTY-FIVE
GABRIELE

I leave my courtyard chat with my father, aggravated that things didn't go how I wanted. Though at least he'll think nothing of me spending time with Aria now, even if I had to lie to him to make it happen.

The bugs my father gave me are in my pocket, which makes me feel a little better. Now I can move on to the next part of the plan.

I need to go find Aria so I can be formally introduced to her mother as Aria's boyfriend. I grin, thinking of how much Marcelo will hate this as I push out the doors to where Aria had told me she'd be hanging out with her mother and brother.

I haven't taken more than two steps out of the building when Marcelo is stalking toward me, fury and panic evident on his face. My stomach bottoms out.

"What's wrong?"

"Where the fuck is she?" He pushes my shoulders, and I step back.

I feel the blood drain from my face. "What do you mean? She was with you."

"I went to say hello to Mira's parents, and when I got back, my mom said she'd gone to the bathroom. My mom doesn't know what's going on. She didn't know to stop her."

This time, I push him. "You mean you lost her?"

"Guys, guys." Mira slides between us as everyone else around looks on with wide eyes. "This isn't going to help her, and you're just drawing attention to yourselves. Be pissed off with each other later. Right now we have to find her."

She's right. I know she is. Still, the burning desire to wrestle her brother to the ground and pound his face for not keeping tabs on Aria is overwhelming.

"Did you call her phone?" I ask.

"Of course I fucking did," Marcelo snarls.

"It's a good thing I don't completely trust you then." I pull my phone from my pocket.

"What the fuck does that mean?"

"I had Sandro keeping an eye on her, too. Let's not panic, he should know where she is." I dial my cousin's number, and he answers in half a ring.

"I was just about to call you." Before he confirms my worst nightmares, I know what he's going to tell me. "I don't know where Aria went."

"You were supposed to be watching her!"

"I had to take a piss. She went to the bathroom, and I figured I'd be good to go, too, but by the time I came out, she'd vanished."

I curse in Italian.

"He lost her?" Marcelo accurately guesses, and I nod.

"Where's the last place you saw her?" When Sandro tells me, I move the phone away from my ear and tell Marcelo. "Go search there. I'm going to go to my room and see if I can find anything on camera that will show us what happened." I'm already walking away from him. "Sandro, you search the grounds while Marcelo looks inside the school. You see anything, you call me."

"Got it." He pauses. "I'm really sorry, Gabriele. More than I can say."

There's real regret in his voice, but I'll deal with him later.

"Just find her," I say and hang up.

I run to the Roma House and don't bother to wait for the elevator, racing up the four stories' worth of stairs two at a time. My legs and lungs burn by the time I push the door of my dorm room open, but I don't stop to rest, opening my laptop to hack into the security feed. It will hold the answers I seek.

After the bathroom incident when the cameras were wiped, I put up some precautions. Obviously, whoever tried to abduct her then has someone who knows computers—probably almost as well as I do. But not well enough, I realize, because when I go through the videos, they're all still there, thanks to the virus I installed. The one that will infect and render useless the computer that's trying to erase the camera feeds. I'm the only one who knows how to get around it.

I flick through video after video around the time I think she must have gone missing, and I see her standing at the doors to the courtyard. My muscles seize, and the breath rushes from my lungs. Aria was there when I was talking to my father?

I don't have to wonder if she overheard what I said because she races away from the area, and I change to another camera farther down the hall. I can see tears streaming down her face.

"Fuck!"

She can't think that what I said was true, can she? After everything . . .

Maybe she's safe then. Maybe she just took off and is hiding because she's upset. Because I broke her heart. My chest squeezes, making it hard to breathe.

I say a silent prayer that that's all it is. That no one has taken her, and she's fine, just upset.

I switch cameras over and over, finding her running through the hallways until she gets outside, where she throws up. My fist slams down on my desk.

And then everything around me fades away. Feliks and one of his goons shove a bag over Aria's head and drag her away.

I pull my phone from my pocket, knowing I'm going to need help with this one. I fire off a text to Sandro, Marcelo, Antonio La Rosa, and Dante Accardi to meet me in my room ASAP.

I watch as they take her in through the back door of the Moskva House, the dorm where all the Russians live—right into the heart of enemy territory.

Getting in there and retrieving her won't be easy, but I'll die trying if I have to. I know Marcelo and Sandro will have my back. Thankfully, Dante owes me a favor, and Antonio will likely help since it's his sister's future sister-in-law who is in peril.

I feel sick. But when I spot the figure standing off to the side of the footage, I want to throw up.

CHAPTER THIRTY-SIX
GABRIELE

Once everyone is assembled in my room, I tell them what's happened to Aria.

"Fucking Russians," Dante growls.

"They're dead men. Every one of them." Marcelo paces the room.

"You're here because I need your help to get Aria back." I fix each of them with a stare.

"Try and stop me," Marcelo says.

"I don't want to get involved in any bullshit," Dante says.

My hands squeeze at my sides rather than around his neck. "Too fucking bad. You owe me a favor, and this will clear your debt."

He pins me with a stare because he knows I'm right—he can't refuse.

"What are you thinking?" Antonio asks.

"Marcelo, Sandro, Dante, and I will go inside Moskva House. There's no time for me to try to get a key for the back door from my contact in security, so we're going to have to go in through the front door."

Sandro blows out a breath. "That's a death wish."

I ignore him. "Dante, you stay outside whatever room we find her in and make sure no one tries to surprise us. Antonio, if you're willing, you stay here at the doors to Roma House to make sure no other Russians show up here to cause trouble in retribution."

Antonio's the only one here who technically doesn't have a reason to help, but he nods anyway.

"We can't go in there unarmed," Marcelo says.

"We're not. I'm going to break into the weaponry room and take what we need." Sandro opens his mouth to say something—protest probably—but I cut him off. "I don't care what the consequences are. Aria's safety is the only thing we're concerned about. Besides, I can wipe the tape afterward anyway. But we don't have any time to spare."

"Well, since I'm in this, let me just say that I fucking hope it comes to bloodshed. I can't wait to take out one of those Russian fuckers." Dante rubs his hands together.

Sometimes I question whether there's something truly unhinged about him.

"Meet me downstairs in twenty minutes," I say, looking between the three men who will be accompanying me to Moskva House. "Antonio, you spread the word to everyone in the Roma House to stay here or to get back here if they're not already, but no details about why." I glance at my watch. "All the families should be gone by now."

He nods.

"See you soon . . . and thank you. I know the odds are against us."

I don't wait for any of them to respond, racing out of there toward the weaponry classroom. The room where the only guns and ammo on campus are locked up.

As suspected, the door to the room is locked when I arrive. There's no chance of kicking down the thick metal door. But that's okay. I knew exactly how I was getting in here before I arrived because I am nothing if not prepared. And I prepared the day I arrived on campus years ago so that if I was ever desperate enough, I could acquire a weapon.

The classroom is located in a corner of a hallway, and in the other corner behind it is the women's bathroom. I'm not worried about anyone being in there since classes aren't going on today.

Sure enough, when I enter the bathroom, it's empty. I go to the last stall and take one step up on the toilet seat, then to the top of the toilet itself, using the top of the stall wall for balance until I'm standing straight up, my head damn near touching the ceiling. I push up on the ventilation grate and shove it aside in the direction I won't be going, then I hoist myself up there, using all my strength.

Without wasting any time, I army crawl toward the weaponry classroom. Once I can see a partial section of it below me, I remove the grate, sliding it forward in the cramped space, then awkwardly adjust myself until I can get my feet through the opening, half jumping and half falling to the floor of the classroom below.

"Well, hello there."

I stiffen at the voice behind me and whirl around.

Mr. Smith leans against the case that houses what I need, arms and ankles crossed.

Shit. Am I going to have to take him out to leave here with what I need? I don't want to, but I will.

"Why are you here?" I ask.

He regards me. "Shouldn't I be asking you that question? This is my classroom after all."

There's no sense in lying. It's obvious why I'm here. "I'm here to steal some guns. The Aminoff Bratva has Aria, and I plan to get her back."

He nods slowly and pushes up off the cabinetry. He walks to the other side of the room where a framed poster explains all the rules of his classroom. To my surprise, he swings the frame away from the wall and behind it is a wall safe. He puts in the code and I notice his movements are stiff. The shoulder he was shot in must still be bothering him.

"Two or three?" he asks.

Is he serious? He's not going to call security on me?

"Four." Might as well go for what I really want.

Mr. Smith moves some things around inside the safe and turns around, middle finger on each hand through the trigger guards of two pistols.

I take a tentative step forward. "Why are you giving this to me? You could get fired."

"I could, you're right. But I won't be fired because you're not going to tell anyone, and those guns are going to disappear after you've done what you need to do."

I cock my head. "Still . . ."

"Aria seems like a sweet girl. Besides, I don't like people that shoot at me."

So that's what he's after—revenge. Good enough, I can understand that.

"Thank you." I take the guns one at a time and tuck them into the waistband of my pants, pulling out my shirt to cover them. I notice on one of the pistols that the serial number has been scratched off. These guns are basically untraceable.

"I trust you'll be erasing the feed from in here?" He arches an eyebrow.

Guess he knows more than he lets on. "Of course."

His only response is a nod.

I leave the classroom in a rush, not bothering to look back at him.

I've always suspected there was something up with Mr. Smith, but now I'm sure of it.

CHAPTER THIRTY-SEVEN

ARIA

I stare at the floor where my necklace lies in pieces, the back half of the locket having fallen off when it hit the wall. In the middle of the locket is what appears to be a small computer chip.

My forehead wrinkles. Is it a tracker or something? Was my dad tracking me?

But when I look back at Feliks and Igor and see their satisfied smiles and the cold gleam in their eyes, it's clear that it's what they were looking for.

"Well, would you look at that?" Feliks walks over to pick it up, but before he can, there's a muffled noise outside, and all three of us turn to look at the door.

The noise vanishes as quickly as we heard it.

Feliks looks at Igor and nods toward the door. "Go check it out."

Igor does as he's told, opening the door and taking one step out before a loud gunshot echoes off the concrete, and he falls back, a gaping wound in his chest. My mouth drops open in a silent scream. Then Gabriele, my brother, and Sandro push into the room, guns drawn and pointed at Feliks.

When I whip my head back in Feliks's direction, my eyes widen, feeling the metal of his gun pressed against my temple.

"Three against one, motherfucker," my brother says.

"Take the gun off Aria, and we might let you live," Gabriele says in a voice that is lethal.

I know that's a lie. Feliks knows it's a lie, I'm sure. He's not leaving this room alive. At this point, it's likely just a question of how many people he's taking with him.

Tears spring to my eyes as the four of them remain still, each of them likely assessing the best path forward.

Another glance at Feliks and his gaze is fixed on the three of them.

"Was it worth it? Whatever it is?" Gabriele asks.

Feliks doesn't say anything, pressing the gun deeper into my temple. I squeeze my eyes shut. When I open them, there's rage I've never seen before in Gabriele's eyes.

What about all the things he said to his father?

"You get that fucking gun away from her head, or I swear I will make your death slow and painful in ways you haven't even ever heard of," Gabriele says in a lethally calm voice.

"Aria and I are going to leave now," Feliks says. "And none of you are going to try to stop us, otherwise I'll blow her pretty little head off, understood?"

"Where are you going to go, Feliks? You'll never get off the property alive," Marcelo says.

"You let me worry about that. Now toss your gun on the floor and kick it away, then come untie your sister's hands from behind her back." When Marcelo doesn't move, he pushes the gun harder against my temple. "Do it!"

Marcelo drops the gun to the floor and kicks it across the room, every muscle in his body tense. Then he comes over and hunches down beside me.

Feliks steps back—probably so that my brother can't attack him. The gun is still pointed at my head, but at least it's not pressed to my temple.

My brother works to untie me, and when the pressure of holding my hands behind the chair slackens, my arms move forward.

I wince at the pain from having them wrenched behind me for so long.

Gabriele lets loose what sounds like a growl in the back of his throat. He isn't acting like he's just here to further his plan, he's acting as though he truly cares.

"Get up." Feliks yanks me up by the arm, pulling me in front of him so my back is pressed to his front, gun to my head. "Remember what I said. One move from any of you and she's dead." He shuffles me backward so his back is against the wall. "The three of you go to the opposite corner."

They do as he says, not looking happy about it. Sandro gives Gabriele a sidelong look, and he gives Sandro a small head shake, telling him to stand down.

Feliks slides around the room, closer to the door, keeping his back pressed to the wall.

I just need to give them an opening to take the shot. They will. If I'm clear of being hurt, I know they'll take the shot the first opportunity they get.

Various possibilities race through my brain. Stomping on his foot—I don't think it would do much. Slamming my head back into his—he's too tall, I'd only hit his chest. Trying to get myself free of the iron grip he has on my arm and running for the door—I don't think I could be fast enough.

And so, after a deep breath and a small prayer, I do the only thing I can think of. As he's dragging me toward the door, I will my body to go completely limp so that I'm dead weight.

He's not prepared for it. It's amazing how heavy the body is when you don't use any effort to hold yourself upright. His hand slides up my arm as I slide down, and the moment my head is clear of his gun, both Gabriele and Sandro take the shot.

The sound is deafening in the small room as I hit the ground, my body slack. I curl up, not sure if they hit their target or if all hell is going to break loose. A few moments later, the heavy weight of a body drops onto mine and warm liquid soaks into my dress, spreading out over my back.

I try to suck in air, but it feels nearly impossible with the weight of Feliks's dead body on me and the knowledge that I'm being coated in his blood. My body shakes, and I wheeze as I try to suck air into my lungs.

Get him off me. Get him off me.

I'm vaguely aware of someone cursing, then the weight on my back is lifted from me. Gentle arms lift me from my hunched position, then Gabriele is in front of me. His hands are on my cheeks, and his lips are moving, but I can't hear him at first, all his words are muffled. Then slowly I make out what he's saying.

"Are you okay? Were you hurt?" He glances at the side of my face where Feliks hit me, and I realize it's still burning, and I must have a bruise or something.

"I'm okay." I nod a bit frantically and wrap my arms around his neck. They're still sore, and I cringe but don't back away from him gripping me tightly as I sob into his neck.

"I know you overheard me talking to my dad. You have to know that was all bullshit just to appease him, Aria. You know that right?"

Relief floods my veins from the sincerity in his words and having witnessed his reaction to having a gun pointed at my head. "I thought I'd never see you again." More sobs rack my body, and he holds me, soothing me by running his hand over my bloodstained back.

Once the sobs subside, he gently pulls back to look at me. "You need to go back to the Roma House, okay? I'm going to have Dante escort you out. Go back to your room, shower, get cleaned up, and I'll be there as soon as I can, all right? Antonio is there, and he'll make sure no one bothers you until I get there, okay?"

I nod, pressing my lips together to prevent another sob fest. He helps me up.

Then my brother is there, hugging me. "Thank God, Aria. I'll message Mira to be there."

Gabriele leads me past Sandro toward the door. He swings it open, and I look away from Igor's dead body to my left, over to where Dante wears a concerned expression. I think this is the first time I've ever seen him so serious.

"Take her back to Roma House to clean up. I have to take care of things here before we leave. Use the fire exit that way," Gabriele says and points down the hall.

Dante nods. "C'mon." He gently wraps an arm around my shoulder and leads me down the hallway.

I stop suddenly, turning to Gabriele still watching us with concern. "My necklace. It's still in there."

He nods. "I'll bring it back with me."

I nod and turn back around, ready to wash off the blood coating my skin and try to forget all this ever happened.

CHAPTER THIRTY-EIGHT
GABRIELE

Once Aria is out of sight, I step back into the room, closing the door, equal parts dreading and relishing what has to be done next.

"What do you want to do with the bodies?" Sandro asks.

I step toward him, hand that's not holding the gun outstretched. "Thanks for helping to save her. I don't know what I would have done if she weren't okay."

He takes my hand, we shake once, then I shoot him in the foot.

The gun in his other hand drops to the floor in his shock, and he screams. He's lucky I didn't shoot his foot clean off. But I don't want him to bleed out right away. I want answers, so I only took off a couple of toes.

I quickly kick away the gun, and Sandro crumples to the floor. I turn and look over my shoulder at Marcelo, who arches his eyebrow. He doesn't know what's going on here, but if he did, he probably would have already shot Sandro himself.

I drag Sandro up by the scruff of the neck and force him to sit in the chair Aria was in, then I step away, keeping my gun aimed at him.

"What the fuck, man?" he cries, staring in horror at his foot.

"How'd you get the bruise on your face?" My voice is calm and cutting and does not waver.

I haven't seen Sandro since before the bathroom incident with Aria because I've been holed up taking care of her for days, then it was family day. The bruise on his cheek and temple isn't super obvious, but it's there. Days ago, it would have looked worse.

"I was sparring in the gym, took one to the face."

"Bullshit!" My finger hovers over the trigger, and I'm so close to shooting him, but I need more information first. "Where'd you get the fucking bruise?"

In my peripheral vision, I see Marcelo look between the two of us. I know the moment it clicks because his body straightens.

"It wasn't the Russians who attacked Aria in the bathroom, it was you." I don't pose it as a question.

Sandro says nothing. At least he has the good sense to look contrite and guilty. Whether it's an act or not, I can't be sure.

"What I want to know is why?"

When he doesn't answer me, I shoot off his other pinkie toe. Sandro screams and bends at the waist in agony.

We can't spend forever down here. Dante is no longer guarding the door and who knows how long before the people upstairs get curious and head this way.

"I'll ask again, and next it will be your hand."

His blood seeps from his feet across the floor. "Your father," he wheezes out.

I almost vomit. I had suspected that would be the case but needed confirmation. "He ordered you to take her?"

He nods.

"Speak!" I shout.

"He thought it was the perfect opportunity—you'd think it was the Russians, then she'd be out of the way." He sucks in a lungful of air through the pain. "He wouldn't have any more power"—he nods in Marcelo's direction—"and you wouldn't be so fucking obsessed with her. This shit with the Russians would end for you."

Marcelo steps toward him, but I raise a hand, and I'm surprised he stops.

"How'd you erase the tapes from that day you attacked her in the bathroom?"

He looks at me slowly from under the hair now hanging in his face. "You're not the only one who knows how to work a computer."

His voice holds a bitterness and jealousy I'd never picked up on from him before.

"Why'd you do it?" I'm unable to keep some of the hurt from my voice at his betrayal.

"When the boss gives you an order, you follow it."

My jaw tics. "You know, I wondered how exactly the Russians knew Aria and I were in town that day we were shot at, or that we'd gone to New York. I wasn't sure until I watched the tape from earlier today and saw Feliks and Igor take Aria, and there, way off in the background, was you, watching them, doing nothing. And did you text me to tell me that she was in danger? No. But you texted someone. Who?"

He sighs, defeated. "Your father. He said to let them take her."

Something like ice moves through my veins. All along, there'd been two parties plotting against Aria, and I missed it.

Before I talk myself out of it, before Sandro tries to reason his way out of this, I shoot him between the eyes. He tried to take away what was mine. Direct order or not, I can't stand for it.

The room goes silent for a minute after the gunshot. I stare at my cousin's slouched body, someone I thought would always be on my side. How wrong I was.

"Let's go." Marcelo finally breaks my concentration.

I nod. "We'll take Sandro with us out the back entrance. Let the Russians clean up their own mess."

Marcelo agrees.

I walk over to Aria's necklace and realize why she wanted me to grab it. Inside the broken locket rests a flash memory chip. The kind they use in USBs. It was on her the whole fucking time. Shaking my head, I shove the necklace into my pocket. I want to know what's on this chip that made it worth all of this, but first things first. I need to make sure my girl is okay.

Marcelo helps me pick up Sandro, and we hurry out of the room toward the fire exit.

"I need to see Aria. I'll text Dante and Antonio to come help you with this and erase the videos. I'll just wipe the entire day; it'll be the fastest and cover all our asses."

"When did you know?" Marcelo asks, looking at Sandro's body as we drag him up the stairs.

"When I saw the tape from earlier today. I knew for sure when I saw the healing bruise on his face." I shake my head.

"I'm assuming we're going to tell them he was killed by the Russians?" His eyebrows raise, and I nod.

We don't speak again until we get to a cluster of bushes, where we throw his body to conceal it until the other two guys get here.

"There's something else that needs to be done." I look up from the foliage at Marcelo.

He stands solemnly. "You must be really serious about my sister if you're asking me to do this."

"I plan to marry her." Marcelo would be a fool to think I'd let anything stand between us—him included. "When you take my father out, make it look like the Russians did it. Use their calling card and take his eyes out. Everyone will think it's retribution for what happened here."

I'm a heartless bastard, and I may have just killed my cousin, but I can't take my father out. Not myself.

Marcelo nods slowly. After what he overheard from Sandro, my father would already be on his hit list, but I'll be the one in charge once my dad is gone. By sanctioning his act, it means there will be no bad blood between our two families.

"All this stays between us. I don't want Aria to know why my father or Sandro were killed. Let her think it was the Russians. She'd never forgive herself, and I don't want her bearing that weight all our lives."

He shoves his hands into his pockets. "Agreed."

"I'm going to check on Aria then. I'll find Dante and Antonio and tell them where to meet you." I start to walk away.

"Vitale?"

I slowly turn back.

"I'll admit, I didn't want you with my sister, but I think you two will be good together now that I've seen what lengths you'll go for her."

I smirk. "Don't go getting soft on me, Costa."

I turn away from him and walk toward Roma House, toward my future.

CHAPTER THIRTY-NINE
ARIA

I bolt up off my bed at the soft knock on my door. It has to be Gabriele or Dante. I pray that it's Gabriele because if it's Dante—who last I saw guarding my door—that probably means something went wrong after I left Moskva House.

After I unlock the door, I whip it open. Something in me gives out in that moment, and everything that's happened rushes forward. My knees buckle, but Gabriele grabs me, lifting me in his arms, shutting the door with his foot, and carrying me to the bed.

"You're okay?" I wrap my arms around his neck, refusing to let go when he leans over the bed to deposit me. So he gets in and lies next to me. "Your hair is wet," I whisper, though I don't know why.

If he was anything like me, he probably wanted to get the blood off himself as soon as possible. I scrubbed and scrubbed until my skin was raw.

"I didn't want to come to you covered in blood. And I had to go to my room to erase all the videos." He kisses my forehead, holding his lips there for a moment.

"What happened after I left?" I search his eyes and find sadness.

"Sandro didn't make it. They confronted us when we were leaving."

I gasp and cover my mouth with my hand. "I'm so sorry." I hug him again.

"You have nothing to apologize for." His voice sounds harder than I expect it to.

Gabriele wraps me in his arms and holds me against his chest. I breathe in his scent, feeling more safe and secure than I ever remember. He must be beside himself about Sandro, but he seems almost . . . accepting.

"I thought I was going to lose you, bella. I can't tell you what that felt like."

"I was so scared," I whisper.

He squeezes me tightly and kisses my forehead again.

"Did you get my necklace?" I lift up to look at him.

He nods. "Yes. I can't believe it was on you the entire time."

"I know."

He brings a hand to my cheek. "I'll have to put it into a USB to see what's on it. It's just the memory chip, but I don't care about that."

I frown.

"Right now, I want to make love to the woman I love."

I suck in a breath and fight back tears. "Make love?"

It's so far from anything we've done before. I love the way he takes control and forces me out of my comfort zone sexually, but in this moment, I realize that's not what I need. I need it gentle and slow. I need him to show me with his body how he feels about me.

Gabriele trails his knuckles down my cheek. Not the one where a bruise is forming, but the other. "Yes, Aria, I love you. More than I ever thought it was possible to love anyone. More than anything or anyone else. There is nothing I wouldn't do for you. *Nothing*."

His words come out so fierce, it's as if they're an oath.

"I love you, too." A single tear drips down my face.

"Then show me." He pulls me down to kiss him.

Our tongues meet in a languid way, so opposite of our usual

frantic and chaotic energy. He slowly undresses me while casting kisses all down my body. Once I'm naked below him, he undresses himself and explores my body.

His hands slide over my breasts while he trails his tongue across my stomach. "I came so close to losing you."

When he brings his face between my thighs, he tightens his grip on my nipples, and I arch my back.

"Never losing this," he says before swiping his tongue slowly through my folds.

A keening sound leaves my lips.

"Sei la vita mia." He sucks on my clit then tongues it, and my hand slides down to grip his hair. "You're mine."

He slowly builds my pleasure until I'm panting and so close to release, then he pulls away. I cry out in agony and look at him. He's climbing back up my body and using his knees to spread my legs farther apart. Holding eye contact the entire time he slowly, inch by inch, pushes inside me until I'm full of him. He holds himself there and kisses my forehead, the tip of my nose, then my mouth before he moves again.

The entire time, he whispers to me in Italian how much he loves me, how we're never going to be apart again, how he'd welcome death if I were to ever leave him.

I kiss him as he rocks in and out of me, building and building toward my climax. And when it comes, I pull away enough to stare into the deep depths of his eyes as he delivers me pure bliss.

Moments later, he holds himself inside me and finds his own release.

I'm not on birth control yet. I spotted for a couple of days after I was attacked in the bathroom, but I find I don't even care. I'm not scared of what will happen if I end up pregnant. Growing this man's child inside my body would be an honor.

Gabriele keeps himself inside me and kisses me again. When he ends the kiss, he trails his lips softly along my jaw on the side that isn't hurt.

"You're the only one I can be like this with, Aria. The only one I'll ever gift with my vulnerability."

It's then that I'm assured that whatever happens next, whatever the fallout from today, the two of us will be okay because we have each other.

EPILOGUE
GABRIELE

A month has passed since everything went down with the Russians, and things have been intense. The tension on campus is palpable, and out in the real world, Italian Mafia and Russian Bratva members have been dying in numbers we haven't seen in decades.

Constantly losing members of your organization and profits dropping doesn't make for good business, so it's a good thing the little project I'd been working on is paying off more than even I expected.

I've figured out how to use artificial intelligence to influence stock buying behavior. The AI plants stories written a certain way in the media and on socials, analyzes the effects they have on the stocks, tweaks, and does it over and over until I see the results I want. All I have to do is buy and sell legally at the appropriate times. Genius, if I do say so myself.

With the state of things, I'm nervous about being away from Aria, which is why I insisted she return with me to Seattle on our Thanksgiving break from the Sicuro Academy.

Aria still has no idea it was her own family's organization that took out my father, and that's how it will stay. I've had to play the bereaved son for the past couple of weeks, which isn't that hard since I do regret how things turned out. But they were necessary. He tried to take the one thing that means the most to me in the world.

So far, we've been holed up in my house, but we have plans to go visit my mother this afternoon. Seeing her is the worst part of everything that went down. She's a little lost without my father, but I know she'll get through it.

There's something I plan to do before we go see my mother, though. And if Aria would ever get out of the damn bathroom, I could get started. She never takes this long to get ready.

I walk across my master suite and knock on the en suite door. "Everything okay in there?"

She doesn't answer, and my hand goes to the door handle. I pause when I hear her voice.

"I'm not sure." She sounds full of worry.

I don't bother waiting for her to ask me to come in. I just barge in. She's standing in her white robe, hair and makeup already done, staring at the marble counter. I still when I see what's before her, and when she turns her head and looks at me, I don't have to ask what the pregnancy test revealed—I already know.

She's pregnant.

I suspected she might be, but she never brought it up, so neither did I, figuring she had enough to deal with after what happened.

I step up behind her and wrap my arms around her waist, letting them rest on her lower belly, then I meet her worried gaze in the mirror.

"Un bambino?" I raise my eyebrows.

She nods, looking a little unsure still. But when I smile at her reflection, letting all the joy inside me at this news show, she relaxes into my body.

"You're happy?"

"Of course I'm happy, bella." I kiss her temple. "I've never been happier. We're going to be a family."

Her shoulders sag, and I know what she's thinking. And I know how to fix it. It was part of my plan today anyway.

"Stay here." I remove my hands from her.

She gives me a funny look, but I hold up a finger, telling her to give me a minute.

When I leave the en suite, I head to the walk-in closet that's really more like a small boutique store, and I go into the drawer where I keep all my watches. I pull out the red Cartier ring box. Nestled inside is the five-carat, pear-shaped diamond ring I picked out for her. One that's fit for a queen—my queen. My Aria.

I slide the ring into my pocket and return to the en suite to find her looking nervously at the door. Without a word, I walk over to her and gently lift her up to sit on the counter, then I give her a slow, languid kiss. Ending the kiss, I take her hand and use my other to slip her hair behind her ear.

"Aria, I was such a fool when we first met, and I tried to push you away, thinking you weren't what I wanted or needed. It makes me crazy to think that if you hadn't been so persistent, we might not be here." I bring her hand to my lips and kiss her knuckles.

"Last night after you'd fallen asleep, I looked up what your name meant. Obviously I know that the translation from Italian to English is air. And that's perfect, because you are the air I breathe. You give me life. And yes, it's also a song or a melody, which felt fitting because you're the one who brought music into my heart. Who made it beat with a melody that only you can."

Tears form in her eyes, and she bites her bottom lip to keep herself from crying.

"In Greek, aria means lioness, which also fits because while you look demure and innocent, underneath that exterior is a fighter, a survivor. And I wasn't surprised to find that in Persian, it means noble. Now, you're giving me the greatest gift a woman can give to a man by bearing me a child. The internet also told me that in Greek mythology, Aria is the woman who bore Apollo a son. I doubt that's a coincidence."

Reaching into my pocket, I pull out the ring. She gasps, hands flying up to cover her mouth.

"Mia regina, I can't fathom being separated from you, ever. I would not survive it. Will you do me the honor of becoming my wife and letting me spend the rest of my life proving to you how much I love you?"

"Oh my God, yes! Yes!" She wraps her arms around my neck and drags me in for an embrace.

I chuckle at how forceful she is. When she pulls back, tears topple down her face. I slide the ring on her finger, then cup her cheeks, using my thumbs to wipe away the tears. "This is supposed to be a happy moment."

She laughs. "I'm just so full of happiness, it's leaking out."

I smile and kiss her again. After she has admired the ring for a few minutes and quizzed me on how I got it behind her back, her face turns serious.

I cock my head. "What?"

"I didn't ask how your meeting went earlier . . ."

I had a video call with the heads of the three other Italian families. "Don't look so nervous. It went fine." I bring the hand with her new ring to my mouth and kiss her knuckles.

"Can you talk about what happened?"

I don't discuss much business with Aria—in part because I don't want to taint her with any more bullshit than she's already had to endure, but also because it makes her less of a target—but she'll find out soon enough anyway. Everyone will. Dante included.

"We all met to decide on a way to curb all the killing that's going on between us and the Russians."

"Did you guys figure something out?"

I nod. "We did. Dante doesn't know it yet, but he's going to be marrying Polina Aminoff."

Her mouth drops open. "Feliks's little sister?"

I hate even hearing that stronzo's name from her lips, and I grit my teeth. "Yes."

"But . . . but why? Nothing like this has ever been done."

"Desperate times." Dante won't like it, but he has no choice. And the Russians will agree because of what was on that USB. "Enough of this. I've never had a fiancée before, and I want to shove my cock down her throat for the first time."

Aria's eyelids instantly droop, and she presses her legs together. "Can we use the belt?"

"I'd be disappointed if we didn't." I lean in and kiss her again— my woman, my future wife, my everything.

Can't get enough of Aria and Gabriele?
Turn the page for an exclusive bonus scene
from *The Mafia King's Sister* . . .

GABRIELE

It's been a long couple of weeks. Aria is due any day and her mother flew in two weeks ago for the birth of her first grandchild. She doesn't want to miss it so she arrived early and she's been staying at our house.

Then Marcelo and Mirabella arrived last week.

It's not the end of the world, but I miss our privacy. Used to be if I felt like fucking my wife—we got married in an impromptu ceremony last Thanksgiving before Aria started showing—I could just strip her in the middle of the kitchen, set her up on the counter, and go to town.

Now she's telling me to be quiet in our own master suite just in case someone overhears us when I'm between her legs, even if they're on the other side of our sprawling house.

Luckily, today all three of our houseguests are flying to Portland to do some sightseeing. It's only a half-hour flight and since they're taking my private plane, if anything happens with Aria and the baby, they can easily make it back in time.

I walk into the kitchen to find the four of them settled around the breakfast table in front of a breakfast buffet the staff prepared.

"Morning everyone." I step up behind Aria and bend down to kiss her jawline.

She shivers in response. One of the great things about her pregnancy has been that she's insatiable. She can't get enough sex, and it takes very little to turn her on these days.

When I straighten up, I lean forward and grab a strawberry from the platter, popping it in my mouth.

"You guys looking forward to today?" I ask.

Vittoria, Aria and Marcelo's mom, turns to me with a smile. "Yes, I heard there's a beautiful rose garden that we can tour."

A quick glance at Marcelo and I have to smother my laugh from the lack of excitement on his face.

Vittoria turns to Mira. "Maybe we can find some beautiful, rare roses that we can use at your wedding."

Mira gives her a tight-lipped smile. "That would be good."

I think Mira was a little put out when Aria and I married at Thanksgiving because once again someone else was getting married before her and Marcelo when they were engaged first. And then they put the wedding off this summer because Aria was due.

"My mom is meeting you at the plane?" I sit beside my wife and rest my hand on her knee.

Vittoria nods. "Yes, I'm glad she agreed to come with us."

My mom and Vittoria have become friendly in the weeks that she's been here, bonding over being widows and the impending arrival of their first grandchild.

We finish breakfast and don't talk about anything of consequence and then the three of them get up to leave for the airport.

I lean in to Aria and kiss her temple. "You relax, I'll see them out."

She gives me a grateful smile. Her stomach is so big that it's hard for her to move around these days and she's been complaining about her constantly swollen feet.

They all say their goodbyes, making us promise to call them should anything happen with the baby. Once they're satisfied we will, I see them to the front of the house where one of my men waits to drive them to the private airport.

"Even if you think it's nothing, you call," Vittoria says before sliding into the back of the SUV.

I nod and wave them off, returning to the kitchen to enjoy a day alone with my wife. Knowing our houseguests would be occupied today, I gave all the staff the day off once breakfast was prepared.

When I walk into the kitchen, Aria is loading the dishwasher.

"What are you doing?"

She looks over her shoulder. "You said you gave the staff the day off, so I'm loading the dishwasher."

I step up to her, shaking my head. "You shouldn't be doing this. I'll do that." I take the plate from her hand.

"Do you even know how?"

I arch an eyebrow. "I'm a man of many talents. As you know."

She giggles and sits down at the table.

Once I'm done loading the dishwasher, I turn to her. "What do you want to do today?"

She looks out the window. "It's a lovely day. I was thinking we could hang out by the pool? The water makes my belly feel like it doesn't weigh a thousand pounds."

"All right. You go get changed, and I'll put together some snacks and drinks for us."

She stands and walks over to me. My hands immediately go to the sides of her belly like usual these days.

"You're so domesticated today." She laughs.

"Don't get used to it." I lean forward and place a chaste kiss on her lips. "Meet you at the pool."

By the time I set up everything for us around the pool, Aria comes out of the house wearing a red bikini. It's not the first time I've seen her in it, but I love the fact that she doesn't try to hide her belly. It's sexy as all hell.

I growl as she heads toward me, surveying everything I've laid out under the large umbrella that sits over the double chaise lounge.

"Good job."

"Did you have your doubts?"

She chuckles. "Of course not."

"I'm just going to go change. Be right back."

I race up to our master suite and change into my swim trunks then return to the pool area.

Aria is laying out on the lounger, eyes closed and head tilted back looking like my next meal. I sit beside her, leaning over to rub her belly with my hand.

"I can't wait to fill you up with more babies."

She laughs and opens her eyes. "Let's get this one out first."

I wasn't sure how I was going to feel, watching my wife's body change over the months while she grew our child inside of her. Would I treat her like a porcelain doll to be looked at and not touched?

Short answer—no. She was more fuckable than ever.

Watching her belly swell with life and feeling our baby kick inside her womb only made me want her more in a surprisingly aching and deeper way.

I haven't even met our child, but I know I would do anything to protect them, just like I would his or her mother.

"I guess, but I don't think it will be long until I want us to have another one."

She shakes her head at me. "Now is not the time to have this conversation. I've enjoyed my pregnancy but I'm over it now. I'm ready to meet our son or daughter."

"You know . . ." I get up off my side of the lounger and go to sit at the end of hers. "I heard that one way to bring on labor is orgasms."

Her eyelids droop and she licks her lips. "Really?"

I nod. "Yep. Maybe I can help you out with that." Reaching up, I untie the bows on both her hips that are holding her bikini bottoms together.

When the fabric falls away, I run the knuckle of my middle finger through her fold, applying more pressure on her clit.

She sucks in a breath, and I watch as her nipples pebble under the fabric of her bikini top.

"Is that something you'd be interested in?"

"Very." Her voice comes out breathy and needy all in one word.

"Let me see what I can do." I gently tug her down so she's not sitting as far up and spread her legs, groaning when I see she's already glistening.

When I lean in to take my first taste her hand instantly threads through my hair and pulls.

It only takes two minutes for me to get her there and during the course of the day she climaxes three more times.

If orgasms really do help bring on labor, then we should be meeting our son or daughter today.

* * *

ANOTHER WEEK PASSES before I'm awoken in the middle of the night by Aria.

"What's wrong? Are you okay?" I roll over and turn on the bedside lamp.

She's pale and shaky. "My water broke and I think—argh!" Aria clutches her stomach.

Panic cuts through me like a blade, not because I wasn't expecting this, but because seeing her in pain and not being able to do anything about it is horrendous.

"I'll call the doctor." I reach for my cell phone on the nightstand and hit the doctor's contact.

"It's time," I say when he answers and hang up. He knows what to do.

Aria wanted a home birth, which there was no fucking way I

was doing. She and our child need the best medical care money can provide and I have lots of money, so for the last several weeks I've housed the Pacific Northwest's premier OBGYN and his staff in a rental down the street from us.

I try to make Aria comfortable as we wait for them to arrive, letting her squeeze my hand as hard as she wants and helping her walk to the bedroom that's basically been converted into a hospital room with all the equipment and a hospital bed.

It's only once the doctor and his people have arrived that I head to the other side of the house to wake her family, then dial my mom up to let her know it's time.

Aria and I decided a while ago that it would only be the two of us present for the delivery, but everyone else will come in beforehand to wish us well.

It's torture watching every time a contraction hits her and she's in pain, but I remind myself it's for a greater purpose. My wife is a trooper. Thankfully, it only takes a few hours for her to get to the pushing stage, something the head nurse says is rare for a first-time mother.

Aria squeezes my hand and cries out as she bears down for her final push before we hear the wail of a baby ring throughout the room.

Carmelo Gabriele Vitale is born just as dawn breaks.

There are tears in my eyes as the nurse lays him on Aria's chest. She wraps her arms around him and looks up at me with such joy that my tears fall as I sit beside her on the bed, looking down at my son, la mia famiglia.

Amazing how life works. I have everything I didn't know I wanted. Thank God for the stubborn woman beside me.

ACKNOWLEDGMENTS

We hope you enjoyed your time on campus!

The Mafia King's Sister *started out slow while writing as we tweaked the characters' motivations and figured out the suspense part of the plot, but by about a third of the way through, we were racing toward the finish.*

Gabriele ended up being a different character than originally conceived when the series began. A lot was lurking under that exterior! We wanted him to be the one who at first glance maybe didn't seem as dangerous as the rest, but if you threatened someone he cared about, he could be a complete savage.

We'd like to think that Aria matured throughout the book. She started out a bit of a naïve, starry-eyed girl who always acted impulsively and, as a result of everything that happened, began to find her place in their world and settle in.

Together these two just couldn't keep their hands off each other! LOL. We think they had more fooling around on the page than any of our previous characters. But who is going to complain about that? We think nobody.

The more we write in this world, the more spin-off possibilities we see for some of the characters attending the Sicuro Academy (ahem, Mr. Smith, anyone?). If there's someone whose story you hope to see, please let us know!

A big thank-you to everyone who helped get this book into your hands . . .

Nina and the entire Valentine PR team.

Cassie from Joy Editing for the original line edits.

My Brother's Editor for the original proofreading.

All the bloggers who have read, reviewed, shared, and/or promoted us and this new pen name!

Every reader who got this far in the book! We hope you were entertained!

Big thanks to May Chen, for loving this series enough to bring it in under the Avon publishing umbrella. Many thanks to the rest of the team who got this one to the finish line! Such a pleasure to work with everyone!

And, of course, Kimberly Brower, our agent, for championing the Mafia Academy series so it made it to the bookstore shelves.

Dante Accardi is up next! How do you think he's going to react when he finds out he has to marry a Bratva princess? We can't wait either! Craving My Rival coming soon!

Ciao,
Piper & Rayne

ABOUT THE AUTHOR

P. RAYNE is the pen name for *USA Today* bestselling author duo Piper Rayne. Under P. Rayne, they write dark, dangerous, and forbidden romance.

DELVE INTO P. RAYNE'S
MAFIA ACADEMY
SERIES

A dark romance series set at a boarding school for the sons and daughters of the most powerful Mafia lords, now with new bonus content exclusive to the print editions.

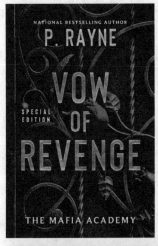

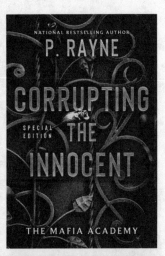

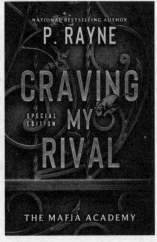